Praise for *Message in the Sand*

"A sweet story about a small town, and the one summer that changes everything for its inhabitants. Right now, more than ever, we need stories about resilience, strength, and how the people we see every day have the power to change our lives—the latest novel by Hannah McKinnon delivers."

—Brenda Janowitz, author of *The Grace Kelly Dress*

"Loyal readers of Catherine Ryan Hyde and Mary Alice Monroe will appreciate the web of relationships spun over decades and the strength of unlikely allies. Blending young love, rekindled romance, and the power of potential, McKinnon's latest is heartwarming to its core."

—*Booklist*

"A gripping, heart-wrenching novel of domestic fiction by Hannah McKinnon . . . In this gripping, emotional story, a shattering tragedy upends the lives of two young girls and those in their orbit."

—*Shelf Awareness*

Praise for *The View from Here*

"A warmhearted yet clear-eyed look into what brings people together and what tears them apart, this makes a delightful case for shaking off childhood roles."

—*Booklist*

"Warmhearted and a perfect beach read."

—9to5Toys, "Best New Summer Books"

Praise for *Sailing Lessons*

"If you are a fan of sisterhood-themed beach reads by Nancy Thayer and Elin Hilderbrand, then McKinnon's latest engaging stand-alone needs to go on your summer to-be-read list."

—*RT Book Reviews*

"McKinnon writes with such imagery that you can almost smell the salt in the air."

—Booked

Praise for *The Summer House*

"Sure to appeal to fans of Elin Hilderbrand and Dorothea Benton Frank, *The Summer House* is an intriguing glimpse into a complicated yet still loving family."

—*Shelf Awareness*

"Charming and warmhearted."

—*PopSugar*

"McKinnon bottles summer escapist beach reading in her latest, full of sunscreen-slathered days and bonfire nights. Fans of Elin Hilderbrand and Mary Alice Monroe will appreciate the Merrill family's loving dysfunction, with sibling rivalries and long-held grudges never far from the surface. This sweet-tart novel is as refreshing as homemade lemonade."

—*Booklist*

Praise for *Mystic Summer*

"When two roads diverge . . . take the one that leads to the beach! Hannah McKinnon delivers a charming gem of a novel in *Mystic Summer*. I adored this book."

—Elin Hilderbrand, #1 *New York Times* bestselling author of *The Identicals*

"Hannah McKinnon's *Mystic Summer* is a heartwarming story of lost love and the against-all-odds chance of finding it again. . . . *Mystic Summer* is a lovely summer beach read that will keep readers turning the page until the very end!"

—Nan Rossiter, *New York Times* bestselling author of *Summer Dance*

Praise for *The Lake Season*

"Seasons of change take us home to the places and the people who shelter us. Well told, and in turns sweet and bare, *The Lake Season* offers a compelling tale of family secrets, letting go, and the unbreakable bonds of sisterhood."

—Lisa Wingate, nationally bestselling author of *Before We Were Yours*

"Hannah McKinnon's lyrical debut tells the story of a pair of very different sisters, both at a crossroads in life. McKinnon's great strength lies in her ability to reveal the many ways the two women wound—and ultimately heal—each other as only sisters can."

—Sarah Pekkanen, *New York Times* bestselling author of *The Wife Between Us*

"Charming and heartfelt! Hannah McKinnon's *The Lake Season* proves that you can go home again; you just can't control what you find when you get there."

—Wendy Wax, *New York Times* bestselling author of the Ten Beach Road series and *The House on Mermaid Point*

The Darlings

◆ *A Novel* ◆

Hannah McKinnon

EMILY BESTLER BOOKS
—
ATRIA

NEW YORK   LONDON   TORONTO   SYDNEY   NEW DELHI

EMILY
BESTLER
BOOKS

ATRIA

An Imprint of Simon & Schuster, Inc.
1230 Avenue of the Americas
New York, NY 10020

This book is a work of fiction. Any references to historical events, real people, or real places are used fictitiously. Other names, characters, places, and events are products of the author's imagination, and any resemblance to actual events or places or persons, living or dead, is entirely coincidental.

First Emily Bestler Books/Atria Paperback edition May 2023

EMILY BESTLER BOOKS/ATRIA PAPERBACK and colophon
are trademarks of Simon & Schuster, Inc.

For information about special discounts for bulk purchases, please contact Simon & Schuster Special Sales at 1-866-506-1949 or business@simonandschuster.com.

The Simon & Schuster Speakers Bureau can bring authors to your live event. For more information or to book an event, contact the Simon & Schuster Speakers Bureau at 1-866-248-3049 or visit our website at www.simonspeakers.com.

Manufactured in the United States of America

1 3 5 7 9 10 8 6 4 2

Library of Congress Cataloging-in-Publication Data has been applied for.

ISBN 978-1-9821-9553-3
ISBN 978-1-9821-9554-0 (ebook)

To Grace & Finley, my reasons for everything.
Who fill my heart and my pages with all the raw,
beautiful, love-worn wonders of life. Keep writing
your story; I'll never stop reading.

The Darlings

Andi

That was the trouble with family; you could put miles and miles between you, but they always knew your favorite hiding places. No sooner had Andi pulled up to Clem's Clam Shack at the base of the Mid-Cape Highway, the last stop before crossing the Sagamore Bridge that would officially land her "on Cape," did her phone ring. It was Hugh. Leave it to her nosy brother, who hadn't returned her calls in weeks, to buzz her the moment she was about to shove a much-needed buttery bite of lobster roll into her mouth. Andi groaned and let the call go to voicemail. Hugh's message was impatient. "Where *are* you?"

To be fair, Andi wasn't exactly *hiding* out at the Clam Shack. She just needed a minute. A minute to herself, with her teenage daughter, Molly, who did not care one bit for seafood and was, in fact, still sound asleep in the passenger seat. No matter. Andi would give herself this final family-free moment to savor her hot lobster roll. It was like a skydiver's last deep breath before jumping out of the plane. Each year Andi pulled over at Clem's Clam Shack, just as each year the entire family reunited at Riptide, her grandmother's Cape Cod summer house. Everyone showed up. Her parents, Charley and Cora; her twin brother,

Hugh, and his partner, Martin. And their little sister, Sydney, who would be getting married there in just a few short weeks to her fiancé, James, a bright New York commercial Realtor.

The annual Darling gathering wasn't a standing invitation so much as a requirement. There were no excuses. Exceptions were not granted. Knowing that, each summer the Darling family members shrugged off their usual responsibilities in the various states in which they lived, packed their beach bags, and put on their game faces. You could beg off Thanksgiving; you could even miss an occasional Christmas dinner without raising too many hairs on their mother's perfectly coiffed head. But no one missed the family vacation at Riptide. It was simply unheard of.

Andi polished off her lobster roll and licked the butter hungrily from her fingertips. Six months after her divorce, she was finally getting her appetite back. But facing the whole family—for a wedding, of all things—was still unnerving. She reached over and tucked a stray wisp of hair behind her still-sleeping daughter's ear. Molly had inherited that gold-spun head of hair from her father, George. George, who'd promised Andi a family and a future, but had not stuck around to deliver on the last part. Who, after only six months of divorce, was already five months deep in another relationship with a new woman.

When Andi broke the news of her divorce the previous Christmas, her mother had stared wordlessly out the living room window at the snowy yard, fiddling with the bulbous ruby ring Charley had proposed to her with. It was a familiar tic signifying her distress. Andi had held her breath, watching as her mother twisted it back and forth on her slender finger. "The twist of disapproval," Hugh had deemed it, when they were little.

"Living alone will be hard," Cora had said, finally.

How would *she* know? Andi had wondered. Her mother had been happily married to her father, Charley, a man of great patience and affection, for over forty-five years.

"Mom, living together is harder. This wasn't a decision made in haste."

Cora's gaze had remained fixed on the snow. "Still."

"She will be fine," Charley Darling said, stepping forward to lay a hand on Andi's shoulder. "Andi always finds her way."

Thankfully, that had been the same Christmas that Sydney and James announced the news of their engagement, giving the family something else to sink their teeth into. It left Andi with some breathing room as everyone rearranged their stricken expressions into smiles and turned their attention to the happy couple.

"You owe Syd," Hugh had mused, holding out a tall snifter of Bailey's by the fire while the rest huddled around the dining room table talking reception sites. "Gives you a chance to step out of the spotlight and lick your wounds."

"I don't have wounds to lick," she'd insisted, snatching the snifter glass and taking a deep sip.

But she had. Even though the decision to divorce had been mutual, it was still heartbreaking. In the span of one year Andi lost her marriage, her home, and her bearings. George had insisted they sell the house, which was yet another blow. Sure, Andi knew she couldn't afford to hang on to it alone, and friends suggested a fresh start might be best. But it was her home, and if ever Andi needed a refuge to heal it was now. Their house was the place Molly had come home to from the hospital. The house where Andi had learned to get her hands dirty and design outdoor living spaces and, after thirteen years, finally established a thriving perennial garden teeming with butterfly bushes and Shasta daisies and hydrangeas. Where she'd painstakingly selected and then painted the soothing earth tones of every room herself and still had the paint-splattered cutoff shorts to prove it. The idea of leaving all of that, of boxing up all the memories of Molly's childhood and taking them somewhere else, was almost more gut-wrenching than leaving her marriage. Another loss to grieve.

It took her months to find their new place: a little two-bedroom cottage in the center of town with a large maple tree in the front yard. They moved in during winter break, when Andi had a week off from teaching at the middle school and Molly was home from high school. The house was modest and historic, which meant it needed a whole lot of work, but it was theirs. And it was where they would start over. For the last six months she'd pulled out her paint rollers again. Hung her favorite artwork from the old house on the new walls. Purchased shiny new appliances during the Memorial Day sales. Andi knew it would be years before the new place felt like home. But little by little it was starting to.

Since then, she'd avoided traveling to family gatherings for holidays and, instead, holed up at the cottage under the guise of moving, unpacking, and settling in. Skipping Sydney's engagement party in February, then Easter Sunday, and her parents' anniversary dinner in May. By then she was as moved into the new cottage as possible, but still she used it as an excuse for staying away. She was too raw. Too tired. She was *reinventing herself*, according to her girlfriends, whatever that meant. Despite her happiness for Sydney's upcoming nuptials, Andi just didn't have the stomach to pour over bridesmaid dress designs or feign joy over reception color themes.

Still, she felt guilty. Her father called weekly to check in. Her mother sent texts asking why her voicemail box was full. She knew she wasn't being a good daughter or a good sister, but the only thing she had energy to muster for was being a good mother to Molly. And she'd make no apologies for that.

Despite her best efforts, she had not entirely escaped the bustle of the upcoming wedding, even from the safe distance of her Connecticut cottage. From the champagne-infused announcement by Sydney and James that past Christmas (which everyone had made it to that year), right up to this morning when Cora called with a blustery smattering of directives: don't forget to bring your bridesmaid gown; make sure Molly has her dress shoes; do you recall the last place you saw my antique French hand linens? Cora had to find them for the bridal breakfast!

Andi hadn't even known her mother possessed antique French hand linens. No one had thought to mention them when *she* got married.

As she pointed her car toward the Sagamore Bridge, she glanced at the sleeping figure of her fourteen-year-old daughter in the passenger seat. Molly's expression was especially sweet in slumber, and Andi resisted the urge to reach over.

Her phone buzzed again, and this time Andi picked it up. "What is it, Hugh?"

There was a dramatic pause. "Well, that's no way to greet your favorite brother."

"Only brother."

"Don't forget Martin."

Andi smiled wryly. "Martin is my brother-in-law and why he puts up with you, I'll never know."

Hugh chuckled. "Uh-huh. So . . . where the hell are you?"

She glanced at the first exit sign off the bridge: Sandwich. Still a solid hour from the family house in Chatham. "Almost there," Andi lied. "What's wrong?"

"What's wrong? Shall I start with the look on our mother's face? Or the ten thousand wedding deliveries piled to the ceiling in each room? The damn wedding is still three weeks away and it's already unadulterated chaos here. I need you."

As much as she dreaded the sympathetic looks and tiptoeing she was sure she'd get as the recent divorcée at her little sister's wedding, Andi had to admit it—she had missed her family. She pictured her father in his fishing hat and smiled. Her mother's clam chowder simmering on the stove for the traditional first night supper. "It all sounds nice, actually."

"Well, it's not. But none of that is why I called." Hugh paused. "You may want to adjust your seat belt."

"Why?" Hugh was a rabid complainer and dramatist. But this sounded concerningly different. "Did something happen?"

"Oh, it's about to. Tish is coming."

Tish, their paternal grandmother. Who pretty much never made an appearance unless someone died or was born. Who owned the summer house, but hated vacations. And the beach. And often, it seemed, her own family.

"No way!" Then, "How's Mom?"

Hugh let out his breath. "Three gin and tonics in."

"Oh, God." Their mother did not drink.

"So we'll see you soon?"

Andi groaned. The call ended. She merged into the fast lane.

Hugh wasn't wrong. This was big news.

Their father's mother, Tish, was no *grandmother* beyond her calligraphed branch on the Darling family tree. For a short time she had permitted the children to call her "Grand-Mère," with the appropriate French accent, but even that could not stick. Standing at all of four foot eleven and weighing no more than ninety pounds (as Hugh liked to say, including all her diamonds), Tish was a life force. Despite the scarcity of her involvement in her grandchildren's lives, she maintained a chilling air of import and ability to inflict trepidation, especially when it came to their otherwise unflappable mother, Cora. The two women had never warmed to each other. It was just how it was.

As such, the Darling grandchildren had rather untraditional memories of their grandmother. She drank dirty martinis. She did not bake cookies, nor did she wipe noses. According to her, birthday parties were savage events best reserved for those under the requisite height to ride a roller coaster, and come Christmas her only nod to family festivities was a card from faraway places like St. Barts or the Maldives. In their father's own words, Tish was an accomplished and cultured woman who'd provided everything her only son could ever need. Except hugs.

In that vein, Tish had not been to the beach house in decades. Though she'd been invited to the wedding, the family wasn't holding out much hope. At best, those who welcomed the idea, notwithstanding Cora, expected a brief appearance followed by a lavish gift and swift departure. What she was doing there, three weeks in advance of the big day, was an outright mystery.

As she tried to pass cars on the narrow two-lane highway,

Andi glanced down. She was not dressed for Tish. Though no one in the family ever really was, except maybe Hugh and Martin. A quick look at the passenger seat confirmed that Molly was still sleeping. Should she rouse her? Molly had only met Tish twice in her life, but had somehow been left with a rather favorable opinion of her great-grandmother. And the feeling seemed mutual. While Tish had never approved of her ex-husband, George ("a simpleton"), she had looked favorably upon infant Molly at her first meeting. When Andi had carried Molly into the living room, Tish had inspected the baby from the safe distance of a wingback chair. Then, after tossing a withering look at their mother, Cora, she remarked, "See that glint in her eye? Finally, some hope."

Andi groaned. She hadn't even told Tish about her divorce.

Indeed, the divorce had not been decided upon in haste. If anything, Andi and George had clung to the frayed edges of their marriage too long. They'd tried therapy; for two years they went. They'd committed to weekly date nights, even though the sitter cost a fortune and it was hard to muster forced smiles and small talk over linguine at La Fortuna. At her best friend's suggestion, Andi tried going back to church. She'd always been what her mother called a Christmas Catholic. But even though she found some comfort in those Sunday mornings, George had not, and Andi felt like impostors standing among the other seemingly united families at coffee hour. As a final attempt to reconnect, they'd left Molly with friends one long autumn weekend and driven the winding leafy roads to Lake Champlain, Vermont. The foliage had given its all that year; the mountains were resplendent in bright shades of coral and red and yellow. But after three days in the most picturesque inn, even the perfect weather and pumpkin-laden streets of Burlington couldn't save them. Outside of Molly, there was nothing to talk about. They'd decided on the drive home to call it quits. Despite knowing they'd tried, it still felt as endings do: sad and uncertain. Andi was still trying to figure out a new beginning.

But that was for another day. Today she was going to the summer house to celebrate her sister, Sydney. With one hundred and fifty guests heading up the Mid-Cape Highway in the next few weeks, Sydney's new beginning was just about to unfold. Whether Andi was ready for it or not.

By the time Andi swung her old Volvo into the driveway, everyone had arrived and taken the good spots. She was hot and tired from the traffic-filled drive. And she could really use a shower. As she unfolded herself from the front seat the front door flew open.

"Here they are!" Her father stepped out on the front porch looking at them like they were the best things he'd seen all day. He threw open his arms just as Molly hurried into them. "Who is this beautiful young lady?" Charley Darling was a people person and, while it was a line any other person might use, Andi knew he meant it. He held Molly at arm's length as she bashfully allowed herself to be looked at. Andi made a happy mental note of this fact: at the perilous age of fourteen, Molly didn't like anyone looking at her. She didn't even like Andi to breathe in her presence.

Now Andi watched in awe as Molly allowed herself to be pulled in for a second hug. "So glad you're here, sweetheart! Now the real fun can begin." He beamed as Andi walked up to him.

"Hey, Dad." Andi inhaled her father's familiar and comforting scent and a wave of nostalgia washed over her. She was five years old again and he was soothing a skinned knee. If only it were true, that her father could make it all better.

"How are we doing?" he asked, looking over his glasses at her in earnest. Since the divorce he'd worried about her, she knew. It was another fallout of divorce; feeling like those you loved also shared the burden.

"I'm fine, Dad."

"Good. There's a whole lot of wedding hoopla going on in there," he said, nodding toward the front door. "I was thinking it might be a good time to head down to the pier."

Andi laughed. "Fishing? Is that the new cure-all for single divorcées at family weddings? Or is that the cure for a son avoiding the arrival of his mother?"

Her father shrugged. "Tomato, to-mah-to." He forced a smile but Andi felt bad for him; he'd had too many years of trying to balance the force field between his mother and his wife. The man was tired. "Come inside and say hi to your mother! Let's get you girls settled."

The second she opened the door, almost four decades of memories swept over her. Riptide had the scent of her childhood: the not-unpleasant smell of a closed-up cottage about to be aired out for another summer, the scent of sunscreens spilled, and the faint whiff of salt air that had worked its way through every crack in every wooden surface, couch cushion, and old book contained within the walls. Simply put, Riptide smelled like summer. Andi dropped her bags and looked around. Nothing changed here. The chintz curtains in the kitchen. The sun-bleached chestnut floorboards. The bookcases lined with dog-eared paperbacks and dotted with driftwood and sea glass.

"You're here!" Her mother, Cora, hurried from the kitchen and pulled them both into deep hugs. As always, she smelled like a mix of the French lavender soap she favored and whatever delicious buttery confection she was cooking. Cora was an incredible cook, and despite the lobster roll she'd just had, Andi found her mouth was watering.

"Is that . . . ?"

Cora glanced over her shoulder at the red Dutch oven simmering on the stove. "Yes. Your favorite."

It was the traditional first meal of every family vacation at Riptide, where steaming bowls of chowder would be passed, wine would be uncorked, and the dinner table conversations would run long into the night as everyone talked over top of one another, giddy with arrival energy and promise of three weeks at the shore.

"Molly, why don't you bring our bags upstairs and I'll help Grandma." She turned to her mother whose smile went tight.

"You heard. She's coming."

Andi felt for Cora. Her grandmother, Tish, reserved a special brand of ire for her mother. "What can I do to help?"

"Nothing! There's nothing anyone can do. That woman is impossible. And now I have to host her as well as help your sister host a wedding."

"Vacation is ruined." Hugh dashed down the stairs and hopped off the last step, throwing his arms up in a dramatic imitation of their mother. "Ruined!" Then, he closed the space between them and picked up his twin sister and spun her around. Martin and Sydney were right behind.

That was one good thing about arriving last: the greeting was a big one.

"You're here!" Sydney squealed. "How was the trip? Did you remember Molly's bridesmaid dress? And yours?" Sydney put her hands to her flushed cheeks and exhaled. Her enormous solitaire diamond ring caught the light, firing off a million tiny sparkles in the air between them.

"Good, yes, and yes!" Andi assured her.

"I'm sorry," Sydney gushed. "This wedding has sort of taken over, but I promise it won't take over the family vacation."

"It better not," Hugh said. "It's not all about you." Despite the smile, Andi knew that he more than halfway meant it. And despite the fact that they were twins, Andi had long felt like the middle child of the three of them, since Hugh and Sydney had a bit of a long-established rivalry for their parents' attentions. Adulthood hadn't improved it.

"She's overwhelmed with wedding plans. Hasn't slept in weeks," Martin reported, with far more empathy.

"It's true. I'm going to look like a zombie bride."

Andi shook her head. "Stop. You look great, and whatever needs doing we'll get it done together." That was the thing about Sydney; no matter what was going down, she always looked dewy and beautiful. Unlike her sister's and brother's dark hair and fair, freckled skin that blotched easily or looked downright sallow in the wrong light, Sydney had been born the perfect color of a peach: tawny skin and blonde hair. Now she flashed Andi her signature smile. "Really? Oh, I'm *so* glad you're here. Let me go find my wedding folder, and I'll show you what's left."

Before Andi could reply, Sydney was dashing back up the stairs to find the folder.

Andi and Martin exchanged looks. "And I thought *I* needed a glass of wine."

Martin wagged his finger. "In the last hour I think your mother has taken first place in that department."

"Yeah, keep the gin away."

"I can hear you!" Cora sang out from the kitchen. She'd returned to her post at the stovetop.

Andi went to the kitchen in search of wine. "Did we not know she was coming?" she asked, referring to Tish.

Cora grimaced. "She wasn't due to arrive until the evening before the wedding. She's three weeks early! It's high season here. The only place she'll stay is Chatham Bars Inn, but God knows if they'll have an opening this last minute."

It was unlike Tish. Riptide was hers only in name. On the rare occasion she came to the Cape, she always reserved her own room at the Bars. They dressed up and met her there in the Star dining room for a formal dinner. And that would be the beginning and end of the visit. Never did she come to Riptide. In fact, Andi couldn't recall a time she'd ever seen her grandmother set foot in its living room.

"Did she say why she's coming early?"

Cora pressed her fingers to her forehead. "You know your father. He doesn't ask questions. God forbid we offend the queen."

Andi felt genuinely bad for her mother. Tish's visits were trying for her.

There was a bottle of chilled Riesling in the fridge and Andi made quick work of opening it.

Hugh joined them. "Is there no vodka?" He rummaged through the fridge.

Andi poured herself a glass and took a long swallow. She'd just arrived and was already drained. But there would be no relaxing yet. She could feel Cora eyeing her. "Yes?"

Her mother made a face. "I need some more littlenecks. Would you make a run to the fish market?"

"Right now?"

Hugh slammed the fridge. "The fish market it is." He winked at his twin. "After the liquor store."

Andi groaned inwardly. The last thing she wanted to do was get back in the car right away. "Isn't this supposed to be the start of my vacation?"

Hugh was already in the driveway starting his Jeep. Sydney trotted down the stairs and held out a bright pink binder, the word "Wedding" written across its burgeoning cover in silvery script. "Found it!" she announced.

Outside in the driveway came the honk of a horn.

"I need those clams," her mother said again.

Only Martin eyed her with sympathy.

Andi tipped her glass back and grabbed her purse. Who was she kidding? This *was* family vacation.

The Chatham Fish Market was a regular stop for vacation dinners. Now in the passenger seat of Hugh's Jeep, Andi stretched her legs out and tipped her head back, letting the wind whip her hair about. The wine was working its happy magic, settling into her limbs. For once, it was nice to have someone else figure out dinner. Do the driving. Maybe this wasn't so bad.

"So how the hell are you?" Hugh shouted over the wind.

Andi smiled. "Better, now. It's good to see you."

Hugh reached over and smacked her knee as they turned down the main drag into the village center. "You, too. You look good, kid."

The fish market lot was packed, and they had to stand in a long, hot line outside. Every now and then a flush-faced woman wearing an apron and a severe expression swung the screen door ajar to shout "Next!" Andi couldn't wait to be allowed into the air-conditioned recess of the store. They were positively melting on the sidewalk.

"So how have you guys been? Martin looks happy to be back on the Cape. The guy's a saint."

It was hard to read his expression behind his Ray-Bans, but Hugh's mouth tightened. "It's good we have a vacation."

"Everything okay?"

The line started to move, and Hugh didn't answer right away. When they got to the door, he took his time reading the blackboard specials. Andi wondered if he'd heard her question when he finally turned to her. His voice was so low she had to lean in to be sure she'd heard correctly. "Martin wants a baby."

"Oh." Such big news.

For all the endless chatter they engaged in, the Darlings had always been tight-lipped when it came to personal matters. It was one of the reasons Andi had taken so long to tell any of them about her divorce last year. They just weren't good with vulnerability. She studied her brother. "And you don't?"

Hugh shrugged. "I used to think I did. But here I am in my midforties. I like to travel. To entertain. To go to a late show in the city and sleep in. I worry at this age I'm too set in my ways. That I won't be good at it."

"How so?"

"Kids seem so specific. Cut the crust off the sandwich. Peel the skin off the apple. The chicken has to be shaped into dinosaur nuggets. It's exhausting."

Andi raised her eyebrows. "Wow. Have you been babysitting on the side?"

"Friends of ours have kids. It seems like most of them do, lately."

"Ah. So you've had a chance to get a good look."

Hugh narrowed his eyes. "It's not pretty."

She smiled. "Sure as hell isn't." And one thing was certain about Hugh: he liked pretty things.

Hugh and Martin lived well and lived out loud; picturing them with juice boxes strewn about the floor of the Range Rover or their cashmere sweaters covered in spit-up was not easy to do. "It's a big deal," she allowed. "Didn't you guys talk about this before you got married?"

"Sure. It was something we both left up in the air, a maybe someday. Neither of us was dying to open the door. Neither wanted to close it."

"And now Martin wants to open that door."

Hugh looked at his flip-flops. "Wide open."

At that moment the screen door swung ajar. The woman in the apron glared at them. "Hurry up, we're not getting any younger."

Andi tried to hold her laughter in, but could not.

"Yeah, yeah. Serendipity."

Inside they got their clams and got out of there. "C'mon. Cora is going to lose it if Tish beats us to the house."

On the drive back, Andi thought about what Hugh had shared. A baby. She just could not picture her twin as a father. Sarcastic, opinionated Hugh taking care of something besides himself? But as they drew closer to Riptide, other thoughts occurred to her. Hugh begrudgingly playing dolls with Sydney when she was a toddler, to keep her busy while Cora and their father made dinner. Hugh spinning Molly through the waves when she was younger; reading bedtime stories to her upstairs at Riptide. The way he took care of Martin, always pouring him the first cup of coffee and taking it upstairs to their room before he had his own. In spite of his best efforts at being a pain in the ass, Hugh had a profound knack for caring for those he loved. Maybe this fatherhood thing would be something he was very good at, after all.

To their combined relief, there was no sign of their grandmother Tish's town car in the driveway. Hugh grabbed the paper bag of littlenecks and Andi grabbed the bottle of vodka they'd stopped for.

"Wait," she said, handing him the bottle. "Bring these in. I'm going to cut some hydrangeas for the table. Mom will like that." The blue hydrangea bushes were synonymous with Riptide and they grew all around the property, bordering the seashell driveway, the front door, and stretching all the way around the house to the backyard patio that overlooked the water. It was the only decoration Riptide needed in summer.

Andi retrieved shears from the small shed and went to the fence where the shrub was most dense. She was clipping the heavy blue flowers when she heard a noise on the other side. She stood on tiptoe.

The neighbors' house, which she still fondly called the Beckers', was completely changed. Gone was the cute little gray-shingled cottage that had been next door every summer she could remember. In its place was a dark, sleek, modern take on coastal living. Andi scowled. The house had been listed for sale the previous year; it came as little surprise, since the Beckers had retired to Florida and hadn't been back to the Cape in years. But it made Andi sad to see how much the new owner had changed it. She glanced at the Ford Bronco in the driveway: New York plates. Figured.

She was just about to go inside when she saw someone walk out onto the side porch. Even though she was on her own side of the fence, she felt like ducking. But she didn't. The man on the porch made it impossible. Andi lowered her sunglasses. He looked to be about her age, maybe younger. Sandy-brown hair highlighted by the sun. And an athletic physique she couldn't help but notice as he was dressed only in red board shorts.

Andi sucked in her breath. However ugly his house was, he most certainly was not. She'd have to find out if her parents knew him.

"Mom?" She spun around to find Molly on the porch. "What're you doing in the bushes?"

"Shhh!" Andi put a finger to her lips. "I'm not in the bushes."

Molly frowned. "Yes, you are."

Andi looked down. She was completely in the bushes and her sneakers were dirty. "I'm just collecting some flowers." She prayed the guy next door couldn't see them. She prayed he didn't hear her either.

"Grandma wants you to come in. She said a big storm is coming." Molly glanced skyward as Andi untangled herself from the hydrangea bushes.

"Yeah, well, your grandma is quite the forecaster." Andi glanced at her watch. Damn—Tish was on her way and she wasn't changed for dinner. And when in Tish's presence, everyone changed for dinner.

"What's Grandma talking about?" Molly stared up at the bright sky. "There's like zero sign of any storm."

Andi scurried up the porch steps and handed Molly the bunch of hydrangeas. She glanced again at her watch. "Stick around. The worst ones blow in fast."

Tish

Riptide had been her husband Morty's idea. Morty, God rest his beautiful soul and big ideas. They'd been on Nantucket to attend his Columbia roommate's summer wedding and decided to fritter away a few days on the Cape afterward. Why not? They were young and unencumbered and smitten newlyweds themselves. It seemed all their friends were getting married that summer of 1954, and it lent a festive sensibility to the already radiant New England season. Tish had never been to the Cape before. She was a New York native and an urbanite at heart. Summer was the only season she'd ever wished to escape her city, when the heat was oppressive and the streets became rank with odors. As a child, the only summer spots she had any familiarity with whatsoever were Coney Island and Rockaway Beach, both crowded and noisy, barely a stone's throw from the city. Until that weekend, Cape Cod was just a postcard notion.

They'd gotten off the ferry in Hyannis and pointed their hunter green Austin Healey north, up the elbow of the Cape. Tish had liked Hyannis just fine and wondered aloud why they couldn't just stay there. The bustling village streets were lined with colorful convertibles, the boutiques and restaurants teeming with tourists. It seemed like the quintessential hub of summer activity. It was good enough for the Kennedys! But Morty had wanted to explore the more rugged environs of the Cape, and had suggested they head north toward the Cape National Seashore, where the coast was less developed and the waves were legendary. "Don't worry, I've found us a lovely hotel along the way," Morty promised her. "It will be romantic." One thing about her late husband, he understood romance.

Tish herself was a pragmatist. Raised in an Irish-Catholic family of seven children in Yonkers, she'd had to be. A working-class daughter of the Great Depression, she knew a thing or two about rationing food, mending clothes, and stretching a dollar. Her childhood had not been easy or anywhere near the vicinity of comfortable. But somehow her parents had managed to feed their large brood, her mother working on and off as a cleaning lady and church secretary, and her father as a felt hatter, where he stood before the factory cauldrons in the scalding room making ladies' hats. How different Morty's childhood had been, growing up the only child of a successful banker in Manhattan. Even during the throes of the Depression, his family remained comfortably ensconced in the safe netting of family money, escaping the city for his grandparents' looming estate on the Hudson. Morty's education had never been interrupted, his stomach never empty at bedtime. Had they grown up on entirely different planets, their early years could not have been any more dissimilar.

But by the fall of 1951, when they first met at a Columbia Lions football game, from all outward appearances they were simply two ordinary college students attending a homecoming game on a golden October afternoon. Tish and her cousin, Maribeth, both second-year nursing students, were taking a rare break from their studies. Tish hadn't even known there'd be a football game that weekend; sports didn't hold much interest for her. Outside of academics, her college experience consisted of a morning commute to campus, attending classes, and an evening trek home to the crowded family apartment on Devoe Avenue. Tish was the first girl in her family, and the only child besides her brother, John, to go to college. "Marry a nice Irish boy," her mother had urged her when she first expressed interest in school. "Settle down."

But Tish had other designs. A child of the thirties and forties, she was desperate to change her life. And she did just that, gaining acceptance to the Columbia nursing program. "I'll be able to get a job at any hospital in the city," she assured her parents. What she did not say was that she'd finally be free.

Tish had no thought of marriage or men; she'd never really even had a serious boyfriend. Her childhood was spent helping to raise her younger siblings and keep house, balanced with school. The little taste of adulthood she'd had had been devoted wholly to her studies. Now on the cusp of graduation, she could not afford to waver. Finally, her hard-earned fresh start was within arm's reach. What she did not realize was that meeting Morty Darling at the Columbia Lions game that fall day would also be a fresh start.

As she stood in the stands shivering in her wool sweater, she did not notice the handsome young man seated on the bleachers beside her. When he offered her his coat, she barely glanced at him before declining. Tish hoped the game would end soon; she had to get back to the library. Not once did she sense anything special was about to happen. But as soon as he'd laid his gentle brown eyes on her, Morty Darling had other plans.

Two nights later they went out on their first date. He took her to Keens Steakhouse, a place she'd only dreamed of eating at. But she would not allow herself to be swayed by the fine cut of his suit. Or his genteel manners. As she dug into the decadent plate before her, she told him all about her big family in the small apartment in Yonkers. About the burns on her father's hands when he came home from the hat factory. And the confusion in her mother's eyes when Tish first told them she wanted to go to college. By the time she polished off her prime rib and sautéed spinach, Tish felt laid open. And unable to look away from those gentle brown eyes any longer. "I'm going to be someone," she told Morty Darling. Though it came out sounding like a warning.

Morty had smiled. "Sweetheart, you can be anyone you wish," he said, reaching across his untouched plate to take her hand. "But I hope, someday, you'll also be my wife."

Tish's eyes still well up at the memory. Who did Morty think he was, saying such an outlandish thing to a young woman he'd just met? Well. He knew very well who he was. And as soon as she got out of her own way, Tish eventually did too. Morty was a family man even before he'd started his own. And what he saw in Tish was a future together. Despite all the trappings he'd grown up with and the sparkling prospects his family status assured him, what he wanted was her. A no-nonsense, first-generation Irish-American girl with steel-blue eyes and a stubborn streak.

By the time he took her to the Nantucket wedding that summer weekend, they'd been married six months. Tish was tired from the wedding festivities and a little queasy from the ferry ride. What she wanted was to get to their hotel. They were only a few miles from it when Morty slammed on the brakes.

"What on earth?" she exclaimed, grabbing onto the car door to steady herself.

"Sorry, honey. But you have to see this!" Before she could object, he threw the car in reverse.

Just as he had with her, Morty knew what he needed the moment he laid eyes upon it. "Will you look at that."

Tish slid her sunglasses down the slope of her nose and squinted down the narrow driveway at the house for sale. "It's not much to look at."

She wasn't wrong. The shingled cottage was small and squat, sitting in a yellowed, treeless yard as if it had dropped from the sky.

Morty threw open his car door and walked around to her side. "Come on. Let's check her out."

Reluctantly, she followed her husband down the driveway. "What time are we expected at the hotel?"

But Morty couldn't hear anything over the hum of his excitement. At the front door, he peered through a smudged window. "Looks like it needs a little love and care."

Tish sniffed. "It looks abandoned." Up close, the shutters hung crookedly. The cedar shingles were bleached by sun and sea salt. The only paint the cottage boasted peeled away from the door in faded red curls.

Undeterred, Morty swung around to the back of the house.

He did this sometimes, stumbled across something. Fell in love hard. Like he did with the matted little stray terrier he named Harrison that he'd found cowering behind a restaurant garbage bin one night and brought home with a sheepish smile.

By that day, Harrison had been cleaned and fattened up and awaited their return from the cushioned depths of his dog bed, back in their New York apartment. Morty was acting just as he had when they were on their way home from a play last spring and saw contractors tossing the unwanted contents of someone's apartment into a street dumpster, when something sparkly had caught his eye. Morty had stopped, rolled up the cuffs of his tweed trousers, and climbed right into the dumpster himself. At first Tish was shocked and embarrassed, but a moment later he cried out triumphantly, poked his head over the side of the dumpster, and held up an old chandelier. The light that caught the crystal pendants was no match for the smile on his face. "Reminds me of my grandmother's! We can polish it up and hang it in the dining room." And that's exactly where it hung today; a restored Tiffany chandelier, found for free and brought back to life. It was wholly endearing, Tish's girlfriends said. Morty was a man of means and yet he loved to rescue unwanted things. Tish couldn't agree more. But in private moments, it gave her troubled pause. She couldn't help but wonder: was she included among the unwanted things Morty rescued?

Now as she waited for her husband in someone else's Cape Cod yard, the sun slanted lazily across the sky signaling the late hour. Tish glanced at her watch. "Honey?" she called. "When are we supposed to check in at the hotel?"

There was no answer.

"Morty?" she called, louder this time.

The grass under her open-toed sandals prickled up against her toes. She thought of the plush hotel slippers she'd grown accustomed to in her recent travels with her new husband and wondered idly if their Cape Cod inn had anything like those.

"Tish!" Morty's call came from somewhere around the back. "Hurry."

"Are you all right?" She lurched toward the edge of the house.

But there was no one in the backyard. Her eyes roamed across the overgrown swath of grass: past the picnic table, the clothesline affixed from the back door to a lone pine tree. "Morty?" she cried. "Where are you?"

"Down here!"

She spun around. Behind her the yard gave way to a thin grove of scrubby trees, light flickering through the narrow branches.

Morty appeared at an opening in the trees, a wild look in his eyes. He extended his hand. "You have to see this."

"I didn't know where you were. You scared me." But he was smiling, tugging her breathlessly between the scrubby trees and down a sandy path.

"Wait, my shoes."

He paused only long enough for her to bend and quickly slip out of them. "Leave them," he urged, pulling her hand.

She looked up, her breath catching in her chest. The path ended, spilling them into an open sea of green dune grass. So this is where he'd been. "Wait until you see!" he puffed, squeezing her hand in his.

As they crested the dunes the view unfolded before her like a summer postcard. A movie scene. What she'd imagined heaven to look like. The beach spilled out beneath them, a golden blanket of sand that rolled right into the roiling sea.

Morty turned from the view to face her, sunlight illuminating the joy in his own. "It's heaven, right? Am I right?"

Tish laughed. "Well, yes. This is . . . incredible." She was at a loss for words.

"What do you think?" he asked, wrapping one arm around her and pulling her against him.

What did she think? It was unspeakably beautiful, no doubt. The surf rolled in below, lapping at the sand in frothy waves. "The view is lovely, Morty. I'm so glad you showed me. But it is getting late." She touched his cheek. "Aren't you the least bit hungry?"

Morty's brow creased. "Hungry?" He looked out at the ocean, then back at her. "This place is for sale."

She'd seen the wooden sign out front. But surely he couldn't be serious. "Is that why you brought me here?"

"Tish, it was pure luck! I didn't even know it existed until you did. But now that we're here . . ."

It was completely unlike any of the weekend houses Morty's family had, and they had many. "But it's so rustic. So small. Nothing like your family's place in Sag Harbor. Or the one on the Hudson."

Morty nodded. "Exactly the point."

"I can't even picture your family here."

"Neither can I."

"They'd hate it," she told him.

"Indeed."

So that was part of the appeal. Tish followed his gaze across the beach. It was too late. Morty had already fallen. "You want this place? For us?"

He shrugged. "I don't know. I'm as surprised as you are, but something about it just feels right." Morty laughed and threw his hands up. "It's crazy, I know."

It was crazy. "We live in New York. So far from here."

"It's only five hours."

"Five hours!"

"Well, more like six."

"Morty." Tish shook her head and turned back for the path.

"Honey, don't go." He followed closely behind.

The sand was still hot, so she veered onto the grass, but it prickled her bare feet. "I'm hungry. And tired."

When she reached her shoes at the end of the trail she bent to retrieve them. Morty waited patiently. Saying nothing.

They traipsed across the backyard and still he trailed behind her, despite the fact that they were no longer sharing a narrow beach path. She could feel his discouragement hovering like a cloud. Morty was always so much fun. And she was . . . so practical.

At the edge of the house she halted and turned to face him.

Morty's hands were jammed in his pockets. He offered her a small smile. "Let's get you to the hotel. You're right, it has been a long day."

The sun flickered through the pine trees, splashing them in gold. A swell of salt filled the air between them. Tish closed her eyes.

"We're here," she said.

Morty raised his eyebrows in confusion.

"Don't look at me like that," she said. "You like this place."

"I don't know." He shrugged. "I like what I've seen."

"Don't shrug. You do know. You like it and you'd like to see more of it. In fact, I'm betting you even love it."

He pretended to consider this. "Love is a strong word."

"Morty."

He smiled again. "Like you said, it's getting late and I am

starting to get hungry. If we want to look at it, we can always come back and stop on our way out."

He was saying it and she knew he meant it, because Morty was a good man like that. Unselfish, even when he wanted something badly. Accommodating, even if he wasn't really tired or hungry—like she was. It drove her mad, and it was also why she was mad about him. "Come on." This time she grabbed his hand.

"Where to?"

Wordlessly, she tugged him around to the front of the house and right up the two sagging steps to the door. There wasn't even a proper walkway. Tish stood on her tiptoes and ran her hands over the top of the doorframe.

"Honey, what're you doing?"

Her fingers darted back and forth across the wood. Nothing. "You want to see the place."

"Well, yes. But we can make an appointment with the Realtor. For another day."

She bent and lifted the edge of the threadbare welcome mat. Nothing there either. "We're here now." There were two scraggly hydrangea bushes on either side of the door, the only living things in the yard. The bleached grass didn't count. Tish bent and reached her hand along the base of each bush, feeling around the ground.

"Honey, please. This is silly. You're going to ruin your dress."

It was too late for that; her skirt had already caught on the branches twice. But she wasn't upset. A whiff of rebellion whirled up inside her. Unwilling to give up, as a last resort she tried the door handle. When it gave, she spun around to face her husband, a triumphant grin on her face. "How about that?"

Morty beamed. "Atta girl."

The inside of the cottage was exactly what she'd feared. Dusty. Dark. And positively musty. But it was tidy nonetheless.

The main room held a small wicker couch and coffee table. In one corner stood a round kitchen table and two wooden chairs. The kitchen was situated against the back wall, light filtering through a small window over the sink.

"It's tiny," Tish said.

Morty pushed open a small door off the kitchen. There was one square room, barely large enough to house the double bed in it. "And spartan."

With nowhere else to go, they stood shoulder to shoulder in the center of the house, looking about them. Examining every angle.

"Well?" Tish said, turning to face her husband. "Are you satisfied?"

Morty draped his arms around her waist. "With you as my wife?" His brown eyes twinkled. "Until today, I did not know I was married to a vandal."

"The door was open," she reminded him.

"Still. You're a trespasser."

She smiled back at him. "Which makes you . . . ?"

Morty pressed his lips to hers and a thousand promises passed between them. One thing Tish knew for sure: this man loved her above all else. And would never hurt her. If she did not like this house, which she really did not, he would leave it at that. That's how Morty was.

"You hate it, don't you?" he asked, his voice soft.

Morty knew her too well for her to lie. She lifted one shoulder. "I suppose I do."

He nodded. "All right then."

"Wait." She placed both hands on either side of his face. "But I love you."

By the end of that weekend, the cottage was under contract in their name. Instead of a lazy hotel stay on the Cape shore, they'd spent the better part of their little vacation swathed not in sunshine but in the fluorescent lighting of the Realtor's office, signing papers. And then, back at the cottage, which they'd already begun to clean out. The previous owner had passed away, and the contents were theirs with the house.

Wasting no time, Tish rolled up her sleeves, pulled her hair back in a silk kerchief, and began cleaning and emptying the kitchen cabinets. She was no stranger to hard work. Morty tackled the heavy stuff, dragging the old furniture out into the yard for the garbage men to take away. Straightening the shutters. Coaxing open the old windows that had swollen shut. As they were finishing up and preparing for the long drive home to New York, Morty came back inside. He found Tish scouring out the old kitchen sink.

"She needs a name."

Tish chuckled. "So she's a *she*?"

"It's a coastal New England tradition. The houses have names. Kind of like boats."

"So what have you got in mind?" She knew darn well he'd already thought of something.

"We'll call her Riptide!"

Tish squinted out the freshly polished window. "Because of the ocean?"

"Because of you," he said, planting a kiss on her flushed cheek. "You pulled me in, hard. And never let me go."

Together they spent many heavenly summers at that cottage.

Riptide was cleaned out and fixed up and renovated. And then expanded. Over the years she quadrupled in size and a second story was added to the first. But the original box of the cottage bones remained at its center; as Morty said, the heart of the house. Despite work and travel and family obligations, not one summer did they miss on the Cape, especially once Charley was born. From Memorial Day to Labor Day, and even into October when the falls were mild, they made the trip (six hours!) from New York as often as they could. Morty had been right from the beginning, the day he first laid eyes on it. It was the place they were happiest.

It was nothing like the wild and sprawling Hudson estate of his grandparents in New York, completely unlike the hedged and shorn expanse of his parents' summer house in Sag Harbor. Riptide remained rustic and simple. Warm and welcoming. It was not lost on Tish that not once did her in-laws come to visit them there, despite the many invitations over the years. No matter. It was their own little haven and they loved it as such.

By then, some of Tish's suspicions had proven true. Things she had not realized would be lasting and therefore unchangeable: that Morty's parents did not entirely approve of their son's choice of wife, polite as they behaved around her. That she did not fit into their Protestant white-collar world, despite the wafting sense of postwar relief and relaxation felt by many across the country during the 1950s. Despite the fact that she'd been educated at the same fine institution as their son. Notwithstanding the fact that she'd worked so hard to acclimate, to memorize, and to adopt their societal nuances and behaviors to better fit in. The truth was, in their eyes she never would. They wished her to stay home: to start rearing grandchildren. That sentiment was the only commonality the Darlings shared with Tish's own parents.

Now, as the town car surges north up the Mid-Cape Highway toward Riptide, that long-ago memory and others like it washed over Tish Darling in the backseat. This summer she is ninety years old and lately the past has begun to shadow her, catching her off guard in quiet moments. The white lace veil her mother had set on her head the morning of her wedding, and the way the tissue paper crinkled as she unwrapped it from her hope chest, brought all the way from Dublin. The flushed look of wonder on his face after she and Morty made love for the first time, the night of their wedding. An image of their son, Charley, all blonde curls and rosy cheeks, dressed in his seersucker jumper that first summer they'd brought him to Riptide. How crystalized the colors were on the beach that day: the blue swath of sea and sky, the green-fingered dune grass blowing against Charley's chubby legs as he stared wide-eyed at the surf. All the memories that made up her perfectly happy new life, until Morty died, and there were to be no more.

Since then, Tish had had no choice but to reach back and dig deep. She'd reverted to her old Irish-American Yonkers self, perhaps her *real* self, and done what she'd had to. Just as she is doing today. Heading to Riptide for the first time in over five decades. She glances at the manila envelope resting on the buttery leather seat beside her. At the name written across it in black ink: "Sydney." Her beautiful, starry-eyed granddaughter, soon to be married. The third and youngest of her son Charley's brood. And the only true heir.

Tish stares out the town car window at the blue ribbon of sky. In another half hour she'll be at Riptide. The house of memories. The house she has stayed away from all these years. Until today. Because the whole family is there, and there was something she has to do before it was too late.

Despite her ninety years, Tish's mind remains as sharp as a tack. Neither age nor romanticism will have their way with her; she knows the task at hand will not be well received by the rest of them. But Tish Darling is used to doing things others found unpleasant. Pragmatism. It is the only gift her childhood has afforded her.

couldn't possibly understand. To be sure, they barely knew her themselves.

For Charley's sake, who was nothing like his mother, thank God, and for the sake of their children, Cora had made diligent efforts to shield the children from the truth of their grand-mother over the years. And Tish had made it very easy for her by staying away. The woman was no doting grandma figure, no! Far be it from her to help with the children in any way over the years, to make herself available, or even knowable, to her grandkids. No, Tish kept everyone at arm's length, as was her M.O. She did not ingratiate herself to anyone within the family or out, nor did she allow anyone to attempt to do so to her.

When it came down to it, Tish Darling showed up for only three occasions: baptisms, funerals, and the occasional wed-ding. Yes, she occasionally dropped in at their Connecticut home for the odd holiday, though she "dropped in" in the most literal sense. There was the Christmas three years ago when she landed at JFK airport that morning, took a limo to their family home in Connecticut, and knocked on the door just as piping-hot Hollandaise sauce was being spooned over eggs Benedict. She'd called ahead to warn them: she was coming for brunch, alone. And she'd kept her promise. Before the remnants of the Hollandaise sauce had cooled in the pan, her limo had already pulled out of the snow-covered driveway. Tish Darling didn't stick around long enough for a present to be unwrapped.

Cora couldn't lie; over the years she'd been as relieved as she was outraged by her mother-in-law's behavior. Her current outrage was not new. But she had good reason for it! Motherless herself most of her life, she'd long held on to hope that Tish would somehow step in and step up, as some form of maternal figure to

Andi, Hugh, and Sydney. But after years of enduring her wither-ing looks and almost inaudible sniffs (almost), Cora had come to understand that those wishes would never come to fruition. In the end, when it came to Tish Darling, it was best to keep both the visits, and thereby Cora's suffering, to a minimum.

As for her own children, Cora wanted them to have a re-lationship with their only grandparent. What kind of mother would she be to deny them that? But the truth was, even though they thought they knew her, none of them did. She never stuck around long enough for them to.

But one thing was for sure: Tish was memorable if not avail-able. She swept in draped in fur coats (appalling!) and doled out large sums of money with reckless abandon. "Yes! I can get my own car!" Sydney had shrieked the year Tish again "dropped in" for her sixteenth birthday, depositing a lipstick-stained peck on the cheek and a five-thousand-dollar check.

"No!" Charley and Cora had cried in unison, at the same moment Tish proclaimed "Why not?" just before the door swished shut behind her.

To that end, Tish seemed to view Cora's attempts to cor-ral her rare but concentrated influence as both a wicked and laughable challenge. Though Tish was rarely present, when she was the house veritably vibrated. No gift was too big. No rule of propriety applied. Martinis were shaken and exotic stories of her travels spilled in the time it took Cora to carry in a cheese platter. Only Tish never stayed for the cheese. Nor did she eat. She swooped in and out with a flicker of her gemstone baubles and an echo of her throaty laugh, the prints of her trademark Dior 999 lipstick on the empty martini rim the only proof she'd been there at all. Of course the children liked her!

"I'm sure she won't stay long," Charley said in the doorway now, as if reading his wife's mind. He came to place his hands gently on her shoulders, which had already begun to stiffen and complain. Cora leaned back into her husband's steady embrace.

"I'm sure you're right," she said.

But why? Why was Tish coming *now*? The wedding was three weeks away. And they'd not even been sure she'd come for that. If she were coming now, something was amiss. Or about to be.

Cora turned and forced a smile, and Charley's gentle eyes softened gratefully. He knew this was hard for her. And Cora felt bad for him always being in the middle. She loved her husband, in spite of his awful mother and her glaring looks and down-turned mouth. And she had never fully grasped just what it was about her that Tish so obviously loathed. Cora had never been anything but a faithful and loving companion to Charley. A good mother, at least a mother who tried every day to be mostly good. She'd stayed home to raise the children when they were very young, then gone back to work as an elementary school librarian when they were school age. Dinners were homemade. The house neatly kept. Like all the other invested parents, she'd done her time carpooling to soccer and dance class and softball. As far as she was concerned, Cora had always kept a happy home; a home where all the kids' friends felt comfortable to stop by, wander in, join the family for dinner. Whatever she had done to deserve the bottomless ire Tish Darling held out for her, and her alone, was beyond her.

"Relax, Mom," Hugh had once told her as a teenager. "You take everything so personally. Tish can be a little sarcastic."

But it was more than that. Tish was strategic. Always asking Cora when she was going to get her hair done (the very day she'd had it cut and colored, at no small expense!), why she'd felt compelled to purchase a sofa in *that* color (a perfectly harmless hunter green that Charley had, in fact, picked out), or where on earth was the copper dragon sculpture she'd sent them from Tibet that one Easter? (It was in the basement, where the garish thing damn well belonged!) The thing was, Cora knew that Tish already had the answers to all these questions (and also that Tish probably hated that copper dragon even more than Cora did). That was the point.

Now she caught herself twisting the ruby ring that Charley had given her the day he proposed and made herself stop. The ring was a whole other problem. It was a family heirloom, belonging at one time to Charley's grandmother. Instead of being handed down to Tish, which had apparently been expected, the ring had been gifted to Charley for safekeeping until he met the person he wanted to marry. How Cora loved that story; that his grandmother had faith Charley would find someone. And that Charley had saved it until he found her. But it was no secret that Tish had wanted that ring for herself. Over time, she might have gotten over the fact that she did not receive it; but what she could not get over was who *did*.

Cora had overheard the ugly conversation with her own ears. Charley had recently proposed and then brought Cora home to share the good news with his parents. Before he could tell them, Tish, suspecting something was going on, had pulled her son into her parlor room and shut the French doors, leaving Cora alone in the hall. There was a scuffle of chair legs on hardwood floors. Hushed whispers, followed by a gasp. And then the hiss of words she would never forget: "Anyone but her."

Now Cora glanced out the window at the empty driveway

and forced a smile. "Let's go downstairs and make the place presentable." Which would be impossible, even if they had a cleaning service, valet parking, and a private chef. Tish hated sharing any space occupied by Cora. Nonetheless, she went downstairs, Charley on her heels.

The family was already gathered, as if on high alert, and busy helping with dinner, which was wholly unlike them. Cora wondered if this was Charley's doing. Molly stood at the kitchen island, dragging chips through a bowl of the heirloom tomato salsa Cora had made earlier. It was a delicious recipe, straight from the backyard garden, but Cora was too nervous to eat. Instead, she planted a kiss on her granddaughter's head and went to inspect the stovetop, where Martin was seasoning the clam chowder. All winter she looked forward to gathering her children and grandchild around the table at Riptide and sitting down to their first seafood dish of many to come during their reunion. Cooking, seafood, big family dinners: it's what the week was all about. Only now there would be one more person at the table, and the very thought of the uninvited guest made her stomach turn.

"Here you go, Mom." Martin held out a spoonful for her to taste. Perfection!

"Well. This is above and beyond." How Cora loved that he called her "Mom." And even more that he'd finished the chowder for her.

Hugh motioned for her to follow him out the back kitchen door to the patio. "You don't have to lift a finger. We're already setting the table."

Outside, Sydney and Andi were putting the finishing touches on the picnic table. Cora watched as Sydney filled water glasses. Andi was busy arranging fresh-cut hydrangeas in a silver pitcher.

Clearly, they could read her mood and she appreciated them taking over dinner. Even as adults, they seemed to view their vacation time at Riptide as just that: their vacation. Leaving her to do most of the cooking, cleaning, and general household work.

"Be sure to set an extra plate," she told Sydney.

"Do we know yet where she's staying?" Andi asked.

Cora lifted both hands in surrender. "Lord help us if she plans to stay here. There's no room."

Hugh chuckled. "In the house or your heart?"

"Very funny."

"I can't imagine she's staying until the wedding," Sydney said. "We've still got three weeks to go."

"Tish never stays. She's probably got plans for that date and is canceling on the wedding altogether. I'll bet she drops off a gift and flies away."

"Canceling?" Sydney's blue eyes widened. "But we just finished the head count for the caterer."

Everyone ignored this. Sydney had done nothing but worry out loud since they'd arrived and that likely wouldn't change.

Martin had just poured and handed a glass of cool Riesling to Cora when the sound of a car door slamming in the driveway met their ears. Everyone froze. Even the birds on the patio seemed to still.

"She's here!"

Charley poked his head out the screen door. "Yep. She's here."

Cora raked her hands through her hair and remained right where she was. "Well, someone better let her in." She watched as Hugh followed his father. Then Martin and Sydney.

"You okay?" Andi asked, pausing in their wake.

"Go on," Cora told her. "I'll be right in."

She could hear the exclamations and greetings. "How are you? . . . What a surprise! . . . Tish, you look amazing." Cora took a deep breath and willed her heart to slow. Tish was a battle-ax and she was no shrinking violet. She would serve their annual first-night-of-vacation dinner just as she'd planned, whether Tish Darling stayed or not. The woman would not ruin tradition.

The moment the screen door slammed shut behind her, all heads turned to Cora and the children stepped back. There in their midst stood Tish, in a sweeping red-and-gold caftan. Looking every bit as glamorous and foreign among the rest of them as always. Cora would kill her with kindness.

"Hello, Tish."

Her mother-in-law took a step toward her. "Hello, Cora."

"What a surprise."

Tish cocked her head. "Am I interrupting?"

"Never. You're *always* welcome here."

Charley intervened. "Mother, may I take your shawl?" They watched as Charley lifted the rich shawl from her narrow shoulders.

"Let me help you with your purse," Cora offered, extending her hand.

Tish clutched it as though Cora were an armed robber.

"I guess you'd like to keep it." Cora clasped her hands, the ruby ring spinning beneath her fingertips.

"Well." Tish turned her attention to the house, her eyes traveling over the deep goose-down recesses of the blue couches, the seagrass rug, the stone fireplace. The mantelpiece filled with collected shells and bits of sea glass. The farmhouse kitchen they'd expanded ten years earlier and redone in a palate of creamy white cupboards and butcher block countertops, where the chowder still bubbled on the stove. Cora could tell she hated every inch of it.

"Well. I see you've done a lot with the place." She sniffed and crossed her arms. "If my Morty could see it now . . ."

Hugh clapped his hands. "Who would like wine before dinner?"

Dinner was served on the patio. Just as Cora wished. They took their seats, Tish draping her purse over the back of her own. The chowder was a pot of summer perfection, a thick, creamy concoction teeming with fresh clams and potatoes that melted on the tongue. Cora watched as everyone at the table spooned generous ladlefuls into their bowls. From his end of the table, Charley smiled at her over his steaming bowl. "Honey, you've outdone yourself."

"Thank you," she said, noting that Tish's bowl remained untouched. Her salad plate held a few sprigs of undressed greens.

"Tish, would you like some salad dressing?" She held up the bottle of homemade dressing she'd shaken that morning.

"It's really good!" Andi rushed to fill in. "Mom makes her own with olive oil and herbs from the garden."

They all watched as their grandmother cast a baleful glance in the direction of the garden. "Is that what we're calling it?" She turned to Charley and lay a hand on her son's arm. "Silly me. I was going to tell you that your landscaper missed a patch of weeds."

"Now, Mother."

Cora set the dressing bottle down and shoved a spoonful of chowder into her mouth. She would not comment. She would not watch as her mother-in-law inspected her plate as if it were poison. If Tish starved that was not her problem.

"So how are you, Tish?" Hugh was always to be counted on for steering conversations and lightening the mood. "Any interesting travels of late?"

"Well!" Tish sat back in her chair and held out both hands. "I had the most divine time in Marrakesh." How she loved to be the center of attention. The table listened enthusiastically as Tish regaled them.

"Did you ride any camels?" Andi asked when she finally concluded.

"Camels?" Tish blinked. "I did not travel all that way for a circus ride." Then, smiling tightly, she said, "My dear, you need to travel more. Like Sydney! Now tell us where you and Jeff are going on your honeymoon!" She turned dramatically to her youngest grandchild.

"James," Sydney corrected shyly.

Andi shot her mother a look and shrugged as Sydney launched into her honeymoon itinerary.

Tish had always been harder on Andi and Hugh and easiest on Sydney. Even though they were all adults, it caused a wave of maternal protectiveness to rise up inside Cora each time Tish demonstrated favoritism.

Cora reached for the bottle of Riesling. She never had more than one glass. Ever. And there was the matter of the previous gin and tonics . . . but she could not sit still another moment waiting for Tish to drop her bomb. How long was she staying? Was she staying with them? She was up to something.

But Tish did not say. Bowls and plates were cleared. Coffee was brewed, a blueberry pie brought to the table. And all the while Tish sat with her empty stomach and smug expression, eyes trained on her son and grandchildren, pointedly fixed away from Cora. That was just fine with her.

When the last drop of coffee had been drained from its cup, Charley sat back in his chair and rescued them all. "So, Mother. To what do we owe this surprise visit?"

Tish removed her napkin from her lap and reached around her seat for her purse. "I come bearing a gift. For the bride-to-be."

They all watched as she unzipped the purse and retrieved an envelope. "I know the wedding is still a few weeks away, but I want you to have this now." She held the envelope out.

Sydney accepted it and looked around, her cheeks flushing with wine and cheer. "Wow. Thank you, Tish."

Tish's eyes crinkled. "You don't even know what it is."

"Still." Sydney glanced at the envelope in her hands, smiling. "It's very kind of you to come all this way to deliver it."

"Why don't you open it?"

Sydney glanced around. "But James isn't here yet."

"So?"

"Isn't it considered bad luck to open a gift without the groom?" Sydney worried.

"And before the wedding?" Hugh added.

"Nonsense," Tish insisted. "It's not for James."

Everyone shifted in their chairs. Cora stole a glance at Charley; he too looked confused.

"Well, Mother, I think if Sydney wants to wait for her fiancé that would be all right, wouldn't it?"

"It would not. I am here now. I'd like you to open it." Tish was smiling, her red lipstick perfectly in place. Probably because she had not eaten one bite of Cora's dinner. But still, she had a remarkable mouth for a woman of a certain age. And her smile, though rarely directed at her daughter-in-law, was striking. "Please," she added. It came out as a directive.

Hugh chuckled. "Go on then, Syd. If Tish says so . . ."

Sydney looked to her mother, searchingly. What could Cora say? Everyone at the table was both perplexed and intrigued. But Cora could tell Sydney really wanted to wait for her fiancé and she did not appreciate Tish railroading her. "Should I?" Sydney asked.

"Only if you want to," she told her youngest daughter, ignoring the heat of Tish's glare from the opposite end of the table.

"Okay. I guess I can always share it with James later." Sydney was such a people pleaser. Cora sighed and sat back. At least the mystery would be over and then maybe Tish would go away and leave them alone.

Sydney opened the envelope and carefully withdrew a piece of paper. The whole table held its breath as she unfolded it and began reading. Her brow furrowed. "I don't understand."

"What does it say?" Hugh could never help himself.

Sydney glanced down at the paper. "Something about Riptide."

"Our summer house?" Andi asked.

"This house?" Hugh echoed.

"Yes, this house," Sydney said. "I think?" She looked at her grandmother and held up the paper. "Is this the deed to Riptide?"

Silence fell across the patio.

Tish stood up. "It has been many years since I have been back here and I know that during that time you have all had ample opportunity to enjoy this house. This house, that my husband Morty bought, many years ago. For me. And for our son, Charley." She turned and smiled lovingly at Charley, but he looked as wary as the rest of them.

"Mom, what is this about?"

Tish went on. "My husband, Morty, God rest his soul, loved this house. When we first happened upon it, I could not understand what he saw in it. Why he would want it. We lived in New York! We had other weekend houses in the family. And this"—she pointed her finger—"this house was in shambles." She paused. "But Morty always saw in some things what others could not."

Cora's breath caught in her chest. Was Tish tearing up?

"And because this house was rebuilt and enjoyed by the Darling family—for the family . . ."

Here she paused and turned to looked at Cora. Cora's blood ran cold.

". . . It is my duty to make sure it stays in the Darling family."

"Mother," Charley interrupted.

"We *are* family," Hugh said.

Tish raised her voice, undeterred. "The real Darling family."

Cora felt the wind rush from her lungs. She gripped the edge of the table.

Charley leapt up, his chair scraping roughly across the patio stone. "Mother, I would like to speak with you. Right now."

"What's happening?" Andi asked, looking up and down the table. She put a hand on Molly's back protectively. Cora could understand why. How she wanted to put a hand on each one of her children, right now. But Cora could not speak. Her voice was gone with her breath.

Tish cleared her throat and like a bad storm, a March wind, a madman, went on, "Which is why, after all these years, it has unfortunately been left to me to clear the air."

"What air?" Hugh asked, glancing between his parents.

"Mother!" Charley snapped.

"My dear child," Tish said, eyes on Sydney, as if she were the only person at the table. "I wish you a long and happy marriage. The first of which I did not have, but the latter I certainly did. And my gift to you is this house."

Sydney's mouth fell open. She shook her head. "For me?"

"For you. The true heir to the Darling family."

Hugh grabbed Cora's hand. "Mom? What is she talking about?"

In slow motion Cora lifted her face. To Charley, whose own was red, his expression ragged. To Molly and Andi, who were staring back at her in confusion. Then to Hugh, whose eyes were already filling.

"Mom," he hissed almost inaudibly. "What does she mean, true Darling heir?"

From the corner of her eye, Cora saw Tish pull her purse over her shoulder and blow a kiss to Sydney. She caught the rush of bright red, the flurry of the caftan's silk as she passed. Charley was right behind her.

Cora closed her eyes as the table before her tumbled into chaos. Her table, of her people.

Tish Darling had finally gone and done it. After all these years.

Cora would not wait for Charley to come back outside. Poor

Charley, who'd stood beside her all these years. Faithful in his silence. This was hers to bear.

Steadying herself, Cora rose. "Children, there's something I need to tell you."

Andi

A ndi took the stairs to her bedroom two at a time on tiptoe, so no one else would hear her. At the landing she stopped, holding on to the railing as she caught her breath. She still could not believe it. She needed a minute to herself.

"Mom?" Molly called down the hallway. "C'mere." Andi couldn't help but smile; Molly could always sense her presence.

"Are you okay?" Molly called out.

Andi stopped at the door and forced a smile. "I'm fine, honey."

From the look on her face, Molly knew better. "Mom. This is all so screwed up."

Andi leaned against the doorframe. "I know."

"So Grampa isn't really my grandfather?"

This was exactly what Andi had not wanted Molly to take away from it. The kid was still reeling from her family's divorce. Now she had to question her grandparents too?

"No, no. Don't think of it like that. Please." She went to sit on the edge of Molly's bed. The look on Molly's face spelled out everything her head was swarming with: confusion, wariness, fear. "Grampa is still your Grampa. Just like he's still my dad."

"But not by blood."

Hearing the words come out of her daughter's mouth drove it straight into her chest.

"It's okay, Mom." Molly leaned forward and wrapped her arms around her and Andi caved to the tears.

"I'm sorry, honey. This is just so . . ."

"Fucked up."

Andi choked out a laugh. "Language."

"Mom."

"All right. Yes. It's completely fucked up." Which made them both laugh, a little.

"So now what?"

Andi shrugged. "I don't know. I guess we give each other some time to let the dust settle. Talk about it."

Molly nodded. "You adults. All this talking. Don't you want to, like, punch something?"

It was a fair question. How many times had Andi felt like punching something when it came to George's new girlfriend, Camilla? She smiled sadly. "No, I think I just need to lie down."

Molly scooted closer to her and folded into the curve of her side. It was something they used to do when she was little and they took an afternoon nap together. Or in elementary school, when they'd curl up and watch a movie. But then came middle school and puberty, and the look Molly gave her mother when she picked her up at school and dared to call out her name and, God forbid, wave hello. Now Andi closed her eyes and pressed her nose to Molly's hair and inhaled: she could not remember the last time Molly had allowed this.

"It'll be okay, whatever happens next. We're all still a family, even if the details are a bit muddy at the moment. Got it?" She tucked a stray strand of hair behind Molly's ear.

Molly nodded uncertainly. "But doesn't this mean that somewhere out there I have another Grampa?"

"Yes, I suppose it does." Andi would not allow her thoughts to go to that faceless stranger, at least not yet. "But we can figure all that out later."

"Okay." She rolled onto her back and stared up at the ceiling. "I bet this is hard for Grandma and Grampa too."

Leave it to a kid. Kids always got to the heart of the matter, sniffed out the hard truths. "I'm sure it is, honey. And for Uncle Hugh and Aunt Sydney too. For all of us."

"Are they mad?"

Andi considered this. "I think they're in shock, honey. Like I am." She turned. "But this changes nothing for us, you know that, right? Even if everyone is bent out of shape right now." She looked deeply into Molly's brown eyes, wishing to press the words into her consciousness. As if doing so might do the same for her. If only it were that simple.

Back in her own room, she flopped on the bed and let her gaze fall on the blue of the ocean, just beyond the dunes outside her window. It was all too much. Coming to Riptide was supposed to be cause for celebration. Here she was not even one night in and the whole family was coming undone.

She was too worked up to lie in bed. But she didn't want to go back downstairs and face her parents just yet either. Outside her window the sky was giving way to dusk; streaks of lavender and pink dusted the horizon. She glanced down; her room afforded her a view of the patio and, beneath it, the trail that rolled down to the beach. Hugh and Martin were gone.

Without thinking, Andi dumped her travel bag onto the bed. She found what she was looking for right away. Before she could change her mind, she undressed and grabbed the faded red swimsuit from the pile of wrinkled clothes she'd hastily packed. As she did, she caught sight of her naked figure in the old dresser mirror. Being back at Riptide always reminded her of her younger years—the summers spent as teens when they hung out with other summer kids and locals, staying out late on the beach having bonfires. Swimming after dark as the tide came in, despite Cora's warnings of undercurrents and riptides. Now the woman looking back at her in the mirror had a few lines around her big, brown eyes. A soft belly where she'd carried a child. Her long, dark curls hung about her face, still pretty enough, she supposed. And her limbs were still lean and strong. But gone was the brave, wild spark in her eye: the teenage girl who'd climbed out this very window countless summer nights. Who was confident in her own skin, as assured of her wit and humor to attract friends as she was in her ability to attract the attention of summer boys. Andi tugged her suit up over her legs and slipped her arms through the holes. She was divorced, in her forties, and now apparently without a biological father. She laughed aloud at the suggestion her friend had offered before she left Connecticut: maybe you'll meet a hot guy on vacation! Who would take on the mess of her life now?

Downstairs, she slipped through the kitchen. Her parents were still in the living room, staring blankly at the television. What must they be feeling? Now was not the time to ask.

Out the back screen door, the patio stones were cold against her bare feet. As she trotted across the yard and down to the beach trail, Andi let her thoughts unravel. Back to the dinner table, to Tish's announcement as the sun was just beginning its lazy pink descent across the sky. To the look on her father's face as the words spilled out. To her mother, holding on to the table as she stood at its head afterward and telling them that she and their father loved them all. "Deeply and dearly," she'd said. And something else—what had she said? "Equally."

That's when Andi knew something was really wrong. Never before had there been any reason to assign quantity to their mother's and father's love.

What came next was nothing Andi could have ever predicted. Not even after the upending past year of her divorce. Not even after selling her beloved family home and moving out. Not after starting over again—*all over*—alone, but for Molly. In all the wild upset of the past year, none of it could compare to what came out of their mother's mouth next.

"Your father and I have raised you together and loved you together, along with your little sister."

The twins had exchanged odd looks. What was she saying?

"But I loved you first."

Hugh understood before Andi did. A sound escaped him that Andi did not recognize; a horrible letting go of breath. And something else. Martin had instinctively wrapped his arm around his spouse.

Hugh cleared his throat. "Are you saying that Andi and I are yours, but not Dad's?"

"What? Don't be crazy," Andi interrupted. But, to her horror, tears were already spilling down their mother's cheeks.

"And Sydney?"

Cora swallowed and smiled sadly at her youngest. "Syd, sweetheart, you are the biological daughter of your father and me." Cora's gaze traveled back to Andi and Hugh. "But you two are all mine."

"Jesus." Hugh had leapt up, his chair tipping back with a clatter against the stone patio.

"Wait," Cora cried. "Please, let me finish!"

Like a child, Hugh had covered both ears. "I can't hear any more. Not now. I need a minute."

Andi watched as her twin stalked away from all of them to the far corner of the patio, nearest the beach path. For a moment she was afraid he was going to run down it, leaving her here to deal with this without him. But he stopped and turned, the sunset casting him in an eerie, fiery glow.

He stared at Andi. As it had always been with them as twins, a thousand words passed silently between them.

Andi started to cry. "I know," she told him.

And in reply Hugh started to cry too.

"Mom?" Molly had asked and Andi remembered with a start that she was still there.

She'd sent Molly inside, gently but firmly. Assuring her all was okay, when of course it was not. And might never be again. When Molly was safely through the screen door, Andi turned to Sydney, who'd remained dutifully in her seat, her knees drawn up to her chin like a child. Always the little sister. "I didn't know," Sydney cried. "I swear, I didn't know."

Andi shook her head. "It's okay, Syd. Please don't cry."

"You are *all* our children." Their father's voice rang out as he returned through the screen door, and all three heads snapped in his direction, just as they had since childhood. "Do you hear me? You have always been my kids. This changes nothing!"

Hugh stood his ground at the edge of the patio, his arms

crossed and back turned. But even he was listening, Andi could tell.

Charley went on. "What happened tonight is . . . god-awful. And confusing, I know. I feel it too. This wasn't how we wanted to tell you."

"But why *didn't* you tell us?" Andi asked. "After all these years. We're not little kids anymore."

Charley draped his arm around Cora, who still could not look up. "We planned to tell you. A thousand times we tried and thought we would, but each time we couldn't."

"Why not?" Hugh demanded.

"Because it was complicated, my love." Cora lifted her eyes to her firstborn, just eleven minutes in front of his sister. "I was so young. And all alone when I became pregnant with you and Andi. From the very beginning, I knew that your biological father wouldn't be in the picture, and he proved me right." She paused. "And then there was your dad. He loved me. And when you two were born he fell in love all over again, with both of you." Here she looked between them and Andi felt her heart give just a little. "And thank God, we made our own little family. You see? By the time Sydney came along, years later, he was already your dad. Had always been, from the first day."

"But that's not the whole truth," Hugh said. "Didn't you think we had a right to know all of it?" He looked at Andi. "We had a right to know."

Andi nodded. Hugh was saying all the things she wanted to, but couldn't find the words for.

"You're right," Charley said. "But we also didn't want to hurt you. Because you were both just as much my children as Sydney was, and we didn't see the point in telling you something that could divide the family. We weren't trying to hide it. We were trying to protect you. You have to believe that."

"I don't know what to believe." Hugh raked his hand through his hair. "If you're not our real father, then who is? I want to know his name."

Charley's shoulders sunk and he turned to his wife. This was her question to answer. "Robert Townsend. Your biological father was a man I dated in college," she said.

"Does he know about us?" Andi's voice cracked as it began to sink in that there was a person out there carrying her DNA, to whom she was closely related, and yet a complete stranger to.

Cora nodded. "I told him I was planning to have you. He knew, and he also knew he was welcome to be a part of our lives." She looked between the two of them, weighing her words. "You have to remember, he was young too. We were just college kids."

"Did he ever meet us?" Hugh asked.

The look on Cora's face was answer enough.

"But you told him about us . . . ?" Hugh pressed.

"Hugh, honey. He knew. He knew you were coming and he knew when you were born." She looked at Charley. "We both made sure of it. I'm sorry he chose not to be involved. The loss is his."

"So you knew him too?" Andi asked.

Charley nodded. "He was my college roommate."

"Jesus." Hugh began pacing again. "This is like some awful soap opera." Then, coming to stand beside Andi's chair, he said, "Maybe he's changed his mind. Maybe he's been waiting for us to reach out to him, all these years. Did you ever think of that, Mom?"

Cora's lip trembled. "I have thought of a lot of things over the years, Hugh. I promise you that."

"What if we want to meet him?"

Andi shook her head. Hugh was asking things she wasn't ready for yet.

But Cora met his gaze. "Then I'll help you find him."

"Okay," Andi said. "Okay, I think I need a break now." Their parents' honesty was painful to witness. Even though she was confused and, like Hugh, hurting deeply, Andi didn't feel the same level of anger as her twin did. She reached up to touch his hand, but he yanked it away.

"You know what?" Hugh was throwing mud and he wasn't done yet. "All of this is nuts, completely and totally fucking nuts. But what I can't get past is the lying. To all three of us." He turned to Sydney. "Aren't you upset by this at all? Don't you have anything to say? You're not even our sister, it seems."

"Hey!" Andi warned him. Hugh was out of control.

Sydney's face flushed with raw emotion. "That's not fair. We're still sister and brother."

"Half," Hugh muttered. "If that's even true."

"Enough!" Andi slapped the table and, outside of the surf on the beach below, the patio fell silent.

Cora was watching them all like she would a pack of wounded animals, like she desperately wanted to reach out to touch but was too afraid of being bitten. "Children, please. I will answer any questions you have. Tell you anything you want to know. But please know, I am so sorry you're finding out like this. I'm just so—" Her voice broke.

"Time for a break," Charley told them with certainty, though nothing was certain among them anymore. "Your mother and I are going inside. Whatever you need to say or ask, please come to us. We will wait. However long it takes." His sad gaze traveled from one face to the next as he said it and Andi's heart broke just a little bit more. This hurt them too.

Charley held the screen door open for Cora and she walked inside, looking smaller and frailer than Andi had ever seen her mother.

Then the screen door creaked shut behind them, leaving the three almost-siblings alone on the patio with Martin.

Sydney stood and tossed the envelope Tish had given her into the center of the table. "Take it," she told them. "I don't even want it."

"Forget the house," Hugh said. "Do you really think that's what this is about? This is about our parents."

A horrible thought occurred to Andi: *can we even call them that anymore?*

Sydney hiccupped through fresh tears. "I can't believe this. It's supposed to be the happiest time of my life, and now this . . ." She stalked across the patio and to the edge of the yard where the grass grew taller and the soil turned to sand. Andi watched as she headed down the beach path for the dunes. How she wanted to run down there herself.

Only Hugh, Martin, and Andi remained at the table. Andi surveyed the scene: half-eaten plates of blueberry pie abandoned at their place settings; wineglasses still full. The first night of their annual family vacation, blasted to bits.

Finally, Martin spoke. "Listen, you two. What just happened is shocking. And I'm so sorry for all of you. But I think you need to be careful. I think you need to let this sink in a bit before you say or do anything else."

Hugh regarded his partner sadly. "Our family, as we thought we knew it, was a lie. Our childhood. Our home. This summer house . . ." His voice trailed off.

For a while they sat in silence, hostage to their own thoughts, listening to the roar of the ocean down on the beach. Andi tried to time her breathing to the rhythm of the waves. To smell the salt air. Anything to make herself feel grounded in the moment.

Riptide had always been their summer haven, their safe place. The place their family came to be together again each year. To reunite, to laugh, to air grievances and fall into old arguments. To play board games by the fireplace and read books on the beach and body surf in the waves. How would it ever feel like that again, after tonight?

She turned her face to the remnants of the sunset. "I used to think that old Thomas Wolfe saying was so stupid, until now."

"What saying?" Martin asked.

"You know the one: you can't go home again?"

Martin nodded slowly. "It's sad. And somewhat true, I suppose."

Hugh sniffed. "Not for Sydney."

"What do you mean?" Andi asked her twin.

"Syd can always go home. Riptide is all hers now."

Andi replayed it all in her head as she trotted along the beach path. She was halfway down the trail moving at full tilt, when she saw someone walking up the path toward her. It was growing dark, but she could tell from his athletic build that it was Hugh. His hoodie was pulled up over his head. The last thing she wanted to do was talk to Hugh—or anyone she was related to, or *not*—anymore that night. So as they pulled up near each other, she kept her head down and picked up her pace.

"Oh, hey . . ." He stopped in the middle of the path, but she was not about to.

As she tried to maneuver around him, her foot slid in a pocket of deep sand and, instead, she crashed right into him and then backward on her butt next to a spray of rugosa bushes. "Dammit!" Andi ignored his extended hand and popped back up, furiously brushing sand from her backside. "Can I just get a minute to myself?"

But it was not Hugh standing across from her on the beach path. It was the guy from next door she'd seen earlier.

"Wow. Okay, I was going to ask if you were all right, but it looks like you are—and like you want to be left alone." He took a step back.

Andi gasped. "Oh God. I'm sorry! I thought you were my brother."

"Nope." He slid his hood down and held up his hands like he was at gunpoint. "Lucky for me. Not sure what he did to you, but I think it's safer if I let you go on your way." He was smiling and Andi couldn't help but notice the cleft in his chin; the unshaven jaw. Up close, he was even more handsome.

"Wait," she said. "I owe you an apology. It's been a tough night and I was rushing down to the beach before dark to try to swim some of it off."

"Oh. Well, you might want to be careful, there are riptides."

"Now you sound like my mother."

He shook his head. "Wow. First your brother, now I'm your mother."

"Look, I'm the one who plowed into you. I was in a hurry. And, well . . . I'm in a pretty foul mood."

"Never would have guessed."

"Very funny." She studied him. His sandy-brown hair was tinted with sun, his eyes crinkling with laughter. "You look very familiar. Do we know each other?"

"Hang on, are you staying in the cottage at the end of this path?" He gestured toward Riptide, his eyes twinkling with recognition.

"That's my family's place."

"No way. You're Andi." His smile was huge now. And so lovely. But she still had no idea who he was.

"And you're . . . ?"

"Nate? Nate Becker."

Andi clapped her hand over her mouth. "Nate? Oh, my God. I thought you guys sold the place. Years ago."

"We did, when my folks retired down in Florida. The next owner had it for about ten years and then last year they relisted it."

"Yes!" Andi said. "The Olsons. They were nice summer neighbors."

Nate cocked his head. "As nice as me? You do remember me, right? I've been told I'm somewhat unforgettable."

She laughed. "Of course I do. But I never expected to see you back! God, wait until Hugh hears. You guys used to be so tight."

"Is he here?"

"Yes. The whole family is, in fact. But . . ." How to explain? No, she decided, there was no reason to sully the reunion with her family's current crisis. "My little sister is getting married, so we're all here for a few weeks until the wedding."

"Sydney's getting married? Wow, that's great. I'll have to come say hi to everyone." He was looking at her differently now. "God, it's been years since I've thought of you."

Andi could feel herself flush. Nate had thought of her? Well, the same could not be said for her of him. The Nate in front of her was nothing like the Nate she remembered.

"So what're you doing these days?"

"I live and work in New York. When the Olsons put the house on the market my mom happened across the listing. And she emailed it to me. Got me thinking."

"So you bought it?"

"Yeah. I was feeling nostalgic, I guess. We had some pretty special times up here as kids." He gestured again up the trail. "I renovated the whole place this past winter. You've got to see it!"

Andi bit her lip and smiled. "That'd be great." So Nate was the one with the modern design taste who'd ruined her memory of his family's place. Though she'd never tell him.

"Andi Darling," he said again, shaking his head. His eyes crinkled and for a beat she could see the little kid from next door again. "It's good to see you."

"You too." Though seeing the man he'd grown up to be was such a surprise. In her memory, Nate had always been the scrawny little boy next door who played with Hugh each summer and cracked dumb jokes. But there was nothing scrawny about him anymore and the boyish charm that had apparently followed him into adulthood now served him well.

"Well, it's getting dark. I should let you get to that swim," he said.

Andi glanced down the trail. Suddenly, she wasn't in such a rush anymore. Their chat had been a nice distraction. A really nice distraction. "Aren't you going to warn me about the sharks? That's something my mother would do."

"Nah, I think they should be more worried about you." There was that boyhood grin again. And before she could think of anything else to say, Nate was already heading back up the trail. "See you around!"

Down on the shore, Andi stood at the water's edge. The tide was creeping in, lapping at the sand in frothy rivulets. She should just dive in. It would be good for her. Instead, she glanced back over her shoulder to the houses on the rise behind her. From down on the beach she could just make out the roofline and second story of Riptide behind the dunes, its cottage windows aglow. To its right, Nate's house was still dark. She wondered if he was sitting outside, listening to the ocean. She wondered if he was here alone.

For over forty years she'd been coming to Riptide to lose herself in the carefree embrace of summer. Only six hours ago she'd arrived hoping to do the same thing again this year. To escape the last painful six months, to heal from her divorce, to rebuild. And instead, in the span of six measly hours, her whole world had imploded.

A gentle wave rolled in. Andi stepped into it and kept going. The night air was balmy, the wind calm. She held her breath and let the saltwater swallow her whole.

Tish

Being back unsettles her, and it isn't just because of her eventful visit to Riptide. Now safely ensconced in her quiet room at the resort across town, even the sparkling harbor view outside cannot alleviate her disquiet.

As soon as the bellboy delivers her bags to the suite, she calls down to the concierge for dinner service. It's not like she ate any of Cora's chowder back at the house; nor would she. Cora has always been a simple woman. Who cooked chowder with such airs and called it a "special" dinner to welcome the family? Has the woman not heard of lobster? They're summering on the New England coast, for Lord's sake.

In truth, her appetite for food these days has waned. Still, Tish's doctor insists she eat, so she orders the lobster bisque from the menu even though she knows she'll just nibble the crackers.

Her work here in Chatham is done, but she wonders if she should stay on. Charley is upset with her, she already knows, and she wonders if she can make her dear son ever understand. She will try. It's not his fault that she and Cora don't get along, in spite of his many efforts to change that. Her son, like his father, is a very good man. But what Charley doesn't realize is that the duty falls on her to maintain the Darling family legacy. Since Morty died, they and Sydney are the last three Darlings. The family foundation may have dwindled to modest remains over the years, but its memory stands large, and it is now left to her to protect it. Morty left her enough to live well on and she's done that. Now all that's really left is Riptide.

Morty's mother had never approved of Tish joining their family, but thankfully Morty was not influenced by his parents' sentiments. He was a remarkable husband and partner to Tish the entirety of their marriage. The darling of the Darlings, she used to tell him. And for his sake and in his memory, Tish has done her best to honor the family foundation work left for her to take up. They were not just any family. Morty's great-grandfather, a young man who'd immigrated to New York from Dunfermline, had seen opportunity. He'd invested early in the steel industry and later in shipping and railroad building, securing a sizable fortune for his family. Morty loved to tell his grandfather's story: how he arrived with few possessions and even less money and had made a name for himself from nothing. Though they didn't achieve the same titanic wealth as the Rockefellers or Vanderbilts, the Darlings skirted the edges of the same societal circles. To Tish, Morty's family resembled the American Dream: a dream beyond what her own family dared to even imagine, and Morty himself was her savior. With his partnership, she had enjoyed a life beyond her wildest dreams.

Then came the horrific day in the place they loved best. The storm off the coast that hurtled unexpectedly up the bent arm of the Cape, landing right on Chatham Harbor. The rain and wind that followed. The capsized boat that washed ashore, empty. And then, silence.

Tish's world screeched to a halt. Her loss was incalculable, her heart broken. If she'd felt lonely in the family before, now she was truly alone. Her own family had distanced themselves from her; they did not understand her lifestyle. And though they remained in touch, it was not the same. Besides, they hadn't the means to help a widowed young mother. Unless she wanted to move back into her parents' apartment, still housing a few of her youngest siblings, she was on her own. Except for the Darlings.

The stark realization hit hard, but there was no time to dwell. Tish had done what she had to do to continue to provide for young Charley in the way he was accustomed to living, just as Morty would want her to. But it meant giving up her autonomy. Living under the Darling family eyes and within the constraints of the family foundation was not at all easy for her, despite the wealth they were surrounded by. None of it was hers. As laid out, in a will Tish had not even known existed, everything had gone to young Charley. Morty's mother was named the trustee and Tish merely Charley's guardian.

"Don't take it personally," Morty's mother had said to her the day after the funeral service when they met in her conservatory room with the family attorney. "It's how it's done within the family." Tish's sad gaze had roamed over the lead glass windows as she listened to the reading of the will. While the sun burned impossibly bright outside, she felt a curtain of darkness settle over her with each provision the attorney listed. The two of them would be cared for, as long as directives were obeyed. The two would have residences on each of the family estates and keep their apartment in the city, all owned and managed by Morty's parents. It was the first time Tish realized her great oversight: she'd not known their apartment was not truly theirs. And an angry plume of shame rose within; why hadn't she asked more questions? She'd known Morty had a trust, that his wealth was familial. But why hadn't he told her that everything she'd thought of as theirs was actually the family's? Why hadn't she insisted on a will?

As Charley's guardian, Tish would be entrusted to make sure he went to the best schools and maintained the family travel schedule with regular trips to Europe, Africa, Asia. As he grew up, she was expected to keep him ever present and prepared, as sole heir to the Darling family. At the best of times she felt cared for; how could she not, with the trappings of car services, well-appointed houses, access to summer cottages and city apartments? But with the wealth that provided for her and her young son came stringent expectations and restrictions that often felt like shackles.

Tish had to keep Charley in the city. Enroll him in the best schools as a child, and later, the finest boarding schools as a teen. Be present always for family holidays and travels—and whatever social events of the season required her presence. She knew it was not about her; she imagined that if anyone had to die, they would have breathed a collective sigh of relief if only it had been her instead. But that had not happened. They were stuck with her, and as such, the arrangements they made for Charley meant that she was stuck too. And though she never gave much thought to finding love again—how could she after Morty?—that was the last condition. Tish would keep the Darling name and remarriage was out of the question. Her life had been full of comforts and opportunities she knew others would give their left arm for; she was not bitter, some would say she was blessed. But the chains of family loyalty hung heavy and ever since the day her husband had died, she was never truly happy again.

Which is why she is doing what she must do now: preserve Riptide for the family. The real family. Sydney was not a son, but times had changed. What she was was the last generation of Darlings. And Riptide was the last place Tish, Morty, and Charley had been a family. The last place they'd all been truly happy. There was no telling how Cora and her children felt about it. As far as Tish knew, if anything happened to Charley, Cora would sell Riptide. And she could not let that happen. Hard as it was, giving the house to Sydney would keep Morty's wish and memory alive.

Besides, she had already done so much for Cora, even if Cora didn't realize it. Against her better judgment, she'd reluctantly kept Cora's secret all these years. But she could do it no longer. Though she had to admit she'd come to feel that Hugh and Andi were like family and, though she did not want to hurt their feelings, she'd always felt they deserved to know the truth. What if something happened medically and knowing their biological father's history would make a difference? What if they simply wanted to know their ancestry? Or the man who fathered them himself? Those were important things. Things that Cora was keeping from them.

Besides, Tish had her own reasons. Over the years, the family foundation had waned under the management of Morty's father. A series of bad investments and a penchant for delegating oversight of his holdings had caused much of it to crumble. By the time his parents passed away, Tish was shocked to learn by how much. Their numerous properties were sold off and accounts settled. In the end, she would be fine: there was enough for Tish to live quite comfortably in the New York apartment. Enough to leave Charley a sound inheritance. And then there was Riptide. The place that had meant more to Morty than any of the rest. If she knew she was the real heir of the Darlings, Sydney would appreciate that fact. She would protect it.

Now Tish glances at the clock. It's seven, and the sun is dipping low over the water outside. She wonders what Charley is thinking back at the cottage. She wonders if he will see the gift in what she did, as it was intended. Despite her devout Catholic upbringing, Tish is not the praying kind, but right now she prays that Charley will forgive her for what she had to do; that he will somehow come to understand. There are some things a family must do to protect their own, and this duty has fallen on Tish, for better or worse.

Despite the heaviness in her heart, Tish smiles to herself; if only her own mother-in-law could see her now. Protecting the Darling family lineage. The "anyone but her" girl their son had tragically fallen in love with, who they'd seen as unworthy of both Morty and the family name. Who'd been an embarrassment to them all, but now held the keys to their once magnificent kingdom. Oh, how her mother-in-law would hate it. She'd spin in her grave!

Tish decides she best unpack as she waits for her dinner. Her suite at Chatham Bars Inn is its own brand of coastal New England luxury. It is not the Ritz or the Savoy, and it does not endeavor to be. Set atop the highest point of Chatham's Shore Road and framed by sapphire sky and emerald dune, the great

Atlantic view is the crown jewel. The resort does not need to try harder.

Tish knows how lucky she is to have gotten a reservation at the high point of the summer season, and she wishes she could sink into the downy recesses of the oversized four-poster and relax. But she can't.

At the dresser she slides her rings down her narrow fingers and deposits them into the small velvet jewelry case Morty gifted her all those years ago. From her wrists, the Cartier watch and her three signature gold bangles, stopping only at the diamond tennis bracelet. That one she never takes off.

She changes into silk pajama pants and stares out the bay window. Such a strange feeling it is being back here. The Cape had always been Morty's place. From the beginning it was his vision for their family, his escape. But not for her. A lifelong urbanite, the flat ocean expanse alarmed her. So bottomless, so endless; and Lord knew what creatures lurked beneath. "All that fresh ocean air," her mother once joked, not very kindly, when Tish returned to Yonkers and told them about the little Massachusetts shack Morty had discovered on their trip. It had been an excessively humid day in the city, the cramped apartment veritably humming with body heat. The family had crowded into the living room upon hearing Tish and her new husband arrive to visit, the younger ones eager to learn about their trip to Nantucket and the Cape. Their family never left the city of Yonkers unless it was to go to the boroughs of New York City.

Her mother had served them iced tea, her smile tight. It was then Tish noticed the silver serving tray. The tray was a family heirloom brought from Ireland. It was also something she never once used in Tish's entire childhood. Not for Christmas or

Thanksgiving. Its place was on the wall in the kitchen, as decoration; "real silver," their mother always told the children. Tish glanced at the kitchen wall where the outline of it was impressed upon the paint, the silhouette a slightly darker pigment of the wall color, and filled with shame. "The tea is delicious!" Morty proclaimed. Tish could not bring herself to take a sip.

Her little sisters crowded them, questions trilling from their mouths like small birds. Tish tried to make conversation, to show her appreciation. But she couldn't focus on anything beyond the oiled edges of Morty's wingtips. The greasy smell of boiling chicken; the basket of wet laundry waiting by the door to be hung. She stared at her hands.

Before she could stop him, Morty told her family about Riptide. With sweeping gestures and wide eyes he regaled them with the romantic details that suddenly sounded foolish. How they'd stumbled across the cottage. How they'd bought it the next day. And how he'd named it Riptide, after her.

Her mother's eyes widened. "You bought a house? Just like that?"

The children were excited, her father listened with a wary expression. When Morty was finished, Tish tried to reel some of his excitement back in from the room. "It's just a little thing," she demurred. "In the middle of nowhere, really." She did not want to seem like she was boasting. Her parents had not raised her like that. But even as the words tumbled from her freshly painted lips, she realized it was not a little thing, this *having a second house* situation she found herself in. She glanced around and her cheeks burned: the tiny cottage she was downplaying was the same size as her family's apartment, where all nine of them had lived.

"It has a great ocean view out the back!" Morty said.

No one said anything. From outside came the sound of a horn over the rumbling of traffic. Finally, her mother had lifted her moist collar away from her throat and gazed at her daughter. "All that fresh ocean air. How ever will you survive?"

Tish realized how she looked to them now and burned with shame. Her mother had always been a practical and busy woman, short on affection, but it seemed whatever ease shared between them had hardened since her marriage to Morty. Tish had mistakenly thought it would make her mother happy. After all, she was doing exactly what her mother had always wanted: marry a nice man! Have a house of your own! She'd even thought her parents would be relieved by what Morty was able to give her. Things they had never had themselves: financial stability, a beautiful home, security. But her marriage had had the opposite effect; instead, it had cast her in an unrecognizable light. They looked upon Tish now as they would a stranger.

"This is so pretty," her sister Amelia said as she reached up to touch Tish's candy straw hat. As Tish caught her hand, she felt her father's eyes on her. He too was staring at the hat.

"Where did you get it?" he asked.

Tish swallowed hard. Her father was a hatter. He recognized it for what it was: an expensive import. Finer than anything produced in his factory. "It was a gift. From Morty's mother."

Morty, not understanding, had smiled broadly. "Why, yes! My parents just returned from abroad. They picked it up in Greece. Doesn't Tish look lovely in it?"

Her father's eyes traveled from the brim of the hat down to her own, then away.

The hat probably cost more than he made in an entire month of wages at the hat factory.

"We should go," Tish said, rising suddenly.

Her mother did not try to stop her. Morty seemed confused, but followed obligingly.

When they left, she stood outside on the landing catching her breath. "Too hot, sweetheart?" Morty retrieved a crisp monogrammed handkerchief from his pocket. He was so polite, so genuine with her family. He would never understand why they did not warm to him. The unbridgeable differences between them were something he couldn't seem to see.

"Yes, too hot," she lied, dabbing her forehead with his handkerchief.

From that visit on, Tish made excuses, or cited headaches or busy schedules whenever Morty asked about her family. They did not visit her parents again together at the apartment.

Now as she looks out the window at the harbor, she laughs sadly to herself. How had she, a girl who didn't even know how to swim, ever shed her urban skin and embraced the wilds of the Cape? For Morty. Because he loved it so.

Having spent his life traversing the starched-collar margins of boarding schools and cityscapes and familial expectations, the barren beaches and scrubby landscape of Cape Cod were where Morty Darling was most himself. To love him was to fall in love with the Cape.

Cora

My family is falling apart right in front of my eyes and I can't do a damn thing about it.

Cora slipped silently from the bed while Charley slept on. She glanced back at her husband, doused in slumber and the dim light of early morning, before she took her bathrobe from the back of the door and tiptoed out into the hall. Unlike her spirits, the hallway was already filled with morning sun. Cora blinked at its audacity. She stood a moment, very still, listening for sounds of anyone else stirring, just like she used to when the kids were young. How many times had she stood outside these very doors over the summers spent here, both night and day, tiptoeing out of bedrooms after the last (and hundredth!) good night kiss? Slinking silently past their doorways to her own, hoping not to wake them. Hugh was always such a light sleeper and Andi too. How she stressed if anyone roused because it would be hours before she could get them back down to sleep. But not Sydney, she remembers. Syd was the heaviest sleeper of them all, even more than her father. Cora used to ascribe it to her being the youngest raised in a noisy house. A fresh plume of sadness bloomed in Cora's chest: maybe it wasn't because

Sydney was the youngest. Maybe it was because Sydney was Charley's *real* daughter.

No one else seemed to be awake yet, so she took the steep staircase gingerly. Her knee ached on humid mornings. Charley teased her about it; called her the barometer. Swore it could predict the weather accordingly.

Before she reached the kitchen, the smell of freshly brewed coffee greeted her. Cora stiffened, wondering who it was that she'd now have to face. To her relief, it was just Martin.

"Morning," he said, looking up from the newspaper at the kitchen table with a smile. Another reason she adored Martin: he still read an actual newspaper in hand, as she preferred. None of that nonsense of squinting and scrolling on a diminutive phone screen.

"Martin. I'm glad to see you."

He waited as she retrieved a cup from the corner cabinet and made her coffee. "Did you get any sleep?" His eyes were full of empathy, which she found sweet and frustrating at the same time. Martin meant well, but she didn't feel like talking just yet.

"A little," she lied.

Relief flooded her when he resumed his reading. Outside the bay window, the sky promised a perfect beach day: the greatest wish of all when they reunited at Riptide. There are always rainy days and that's fine—the Darlings are prepared with board games and cards and books to curl up with. After all, there's nothing like an afternoon nap on a rainy shore day. But not on the first day. The first day was sacred stuff meant for the beach, the beginning of their long-awaited family vacation together. The promise of picnic lunches full of sand and brightly colored plastic pails and shovels and faded beach towels that still smell like sunscreen and salt, despite the many washings. Of digging your toes into warm sand and letting the sound of the surf wash away all the year has brought you, because here you are with your family for one more glorious summer together! It was that last promise that got her through the long New England winters; the thing they looked forward to most of all each year. At least Cora did. She had no idea if her kids did anymore.

Sydney, perhaps, but she was getting married in a couple weeks her reasoning goes beyond family. Hugh, she was pretty sure, comes more and more out of obligation. And of course, Andi. But the last few summers she'd been immersed in the slow, sad unraveling of a marriage and not quite present because of it. Cora sipped her coffee and thought of how she'd had such high hopes that Andi could take proper care of herself this summer; sleep in and laze around the beach with the pressures of the divorce finally behind her. And now this—Tish's malicious behavior and a family's likely undoing. Cora closed her eyes. After all those years of keeping her mouth shut, why now?

"You need to know something," she said, so quietly that at first Martin wasn't sure she'd spoken. He lowered the paper. "I didn't mean to keep the secret."

Martin's big, brown eyes were soft. "Cora, you don't owe me any explanation."

"No, this is important," she went on. She had to. It was like a dress rehearsal, because she knew she'd have to face Andi, Hugh, and Sydney soon. And they wouldn't be calm and rational like Martin about it. Martin was Hugh's husband. And her son-in-law. She owed him this much. "Charley and I swore we would tell the kids when the time was right. But the time never seemed right."

Martin mulled this over. "Life keeps happening."

"Exactly! I kept thinking, when they graduate. When they move out. But there are three of them to juggle. When one finally moves out and gets a good job, another is losing theirs. When someone gets engaged, another is getting divorced. Or having a baby. There was never a right time." Tears pressed at her eyes. She knew she sounded hysterical, but she didn't care. Martin reached for her hand.

"I think if you tell them that, it will help." Martin didn't say that they'd forgive her, but it was a start. This was good.

"How angry is he?" she asked. Hugh held things in the longest but felt the most. She'd long suspected he'd begrudge her the hardest. Another reason she'd kept putting it off.

"I can't speak for Hugh," Martin allowed. "But he's upset, of course. It is pretty big news to find out midlife."

Cora fiddled with her ring, twisting it left and right. "He must feel betrayed. Like I did this on purpose."

And that was exactly what she did, she realized. All those years of saying nothing were, in fact, a choice. She'd once thought her prolonged silence was simply a void of decision, when actually it was a decision in itself. And a selfish one at that.

"I think you guys need to talk," Martin said.

There was the sound of footfalls on the stairs and Sydney appeared in the doorway. Her hair was rumpled from slumber and Cora took comfort in the hope that at least one of them got some rest. "There you are! How're you feeling?"

Sydney regarded them sleepily. "Like crap."

Cora's insides fell. "I'm sorry, honey." She watched her youngest put the kettle on for tea. Unlike the rest of them, caffeine addicts each and every one, Sydney took tea in the mornings. Herbal only, no milk, no sugar. She kept a "clean" diet, she'd told her mother. How people these days deprived themselves of so much joy, Cora didn't understand. Sydney was the picture of health and beauty, sure, but that was youth for you. Like any mother, she wanted her kids to take good care of themselves, but she also wanted them to experience joy. "Eat the cake!" she found herself wanting to shout, when dessert menus were produced at a restaurant and they all shook their heads no-thank-you. "Just wait," she wanted to tell them. "Wait until you see what life throws at you at sixty-five: enjoy the cake while you can!"

Now as Sydney steeped her bland tea, Cora kept her mouth shut.

"Get any sleep, Syd?" Martin asked.

She joined them at the table. "Not really. I kept waking up thinking how crazy this is. That Andi and Hugh aren't my full brother and sister."

The ring spun faster on Cora's finger and she stared at it, unable to look up at her daughter.

"And then I realized that as weird as this whole thing is for me, Hugh and Andi don't even know who their real father is. I do. So how can I complain?" Sydney's voice was earnest, filled with sadness and confusion. What a mess this was.

"It's not a competition," Martin told her. "You all have a right to your hurt."

Cora put a hand over Sydney's. "Martin's right, honey. We kept this from you too."

As if on cue, Hugh filled the kitchen doorway in neon orange running shoes and shorts. Cora's insides ached as she looked at her only son. So handsome, so bright. She stood up. "Honey . . ."

But Hugh wasn't having it, at least not yet. He shook his head and walked past her. "Coffee. I just want a cup of coffee, please."

Cora and Martin exchanged looks and she sat back down. How much longer should she sit and wait? *As long as it takes,* she decided.

The only sound in the kitchen was that of Hugh's spoon clanging against his mug as he stirred in cream. Then the patio screen door slapped shut behind him.

When Andi finally joined them, she was with Molly, which changed her whole plan. Cora didn't want to discuss this in front of her granddaughter. Lord only knew what the child thought at this point. Instead, she leapt up and got to work on her famous pancakes, grateful for a job. At least Molly would eat them.

Molly plunked herself down in Cora's free seat with a cup of coffee and began dumping copious amounts of sugar into it, straight from the bowl. "Excuse me," Andi said, reaching for the mug. "No caffeine, kiddo. It stunts your growth."

But when Molly glared, she let go. "Fine. You'll wish you listened to me when you can't reach the top shelf in the grocery store."

Molly shrugged. "I'll have my groceries delivered. Amazon."

It was the first time anyone smiled since last night.

Cora got busy on her traditional first-morning spread, as the others took seats in locations as far away from one another and from her as they could. Andi on the living room couch. Hugh on the patio. Sydney at the kitchen table. Cora ignored this, and went to work without their help: fresh slices of cantaloupe. Platters of blueberry pancakes, with fresh berries she'd sent

Charley to fetch from the farm up the street, before the kids arrived. A sizzling tray of thick Canadian bacon. "Breakfast!" she hollered when it was done and, to her immense relief, everyone stirred. Even Hugh came in when the smell of bacon wafted out to the patio.

She watched with no small amount of satisfaction as they gathered around the butcher block island and picked up plates. Hugh grumbled at Andi when she cut in front of him. Martin passed out forks. Molly came back for seconds. *All right,* Cora thought. *We will be all right.*

When Molly's phone buzzed and she dashed back upstairs to FaceTime with a friend, Cora seized the opportunity. "Look," she said as her kids sat down to eat, "I know last night was a shock. And we have some talking to do. But today"—she gestured to the bay window—"is our first beach day. Can we at least go sit on the beach and get our toes in the sand? It will be good for us." She glanced longingly out the window once more. It was the perfect beach day and she would not let Tish or her own mistakes rob them of that.

Andi set her fork down on her plate with an audible *clink.* "Mom, I don't know about everyone else, but I'm still in a daze from last night."

"I know," Cora said. "I cannot imagine."

"No. You can't." Hugh said, bitterly. "Andi and I were just told we're only halfway part of this family and you're worried about good beach weather?"

Cora shook her head. "That's not what I meant."

"Then what did you mean? Because I'm wondering if I should pack my things and go back to Boston. Or, I don't know . . . maybe start looking for my real father?"

"What? No!" Sydney cried. "You can't go home. We need to work this out. And what about. . . ?"

"Your wedding?" Hugh shook his head. "You're as bad as Mom."

"That's not what I was going to say!"

Cora held up her hands. "Please, stop. We need to at least talk more about this," she implored. "There are things you don't know."

"Is there more?" Hugh scoffed. "Are you not our mother?"

"Hugh," Martin interjected. "Not helping."

"Yeah," Andi echoed. "Come on."

But Hugh was still as riled as he'd been the night before. "What? Mom needs to hear this. Just because she was silent for forty-plus years doesn't mean we have to be. This is crazy." He stood, set his untouched plate down on the butcher block island with a clatter and headed for the door. "I'm going for a run. I can't think here."

Cora's hands fluttered uselessly at her sides, but she did not try to stop him. At least he wasn't getting in the car to go home.

Martin turned to her. "Let him go. He needs to burn off some stress."

And just like that they all disappeared. Andi upstairs, ostensibly to shower, which made no sense to Cora if they were supposedly headed to the beach, but Cora kept her mouth shut. Sydney to change into her bathing suit, thankfully. Martin, to make a work call.

Finally, Charley came downstairs. He looked around the kitchen at the scattered mugs and half-filled plates. The butcher block island full of pans and trays. "What happened here?"

"You slept late," she said, turning to the coffee maker.

"Sorry, honey. I was up and down all night." She knew; she'd been too. "Where is everyone?"

"Getting ready for the beach," Cora told him, though she had no idea if that were true. It didn't matter. If they packed the picnic and gathered the beach chairs, they would come. *They had to*, she told herself as she began collecting breakfast dishes and setting them in the sink.

"Are you sure?" Charley ran a hand through his graying hair. "They've got to be pretty upset," he said. "Shouldn't we sit tight and try to talk to them, again?"

Cora scowled. She'd tried. While Charley slept. "Give me a hand making sandwiches. We're going to the beach."

By 1:30, with the sun high overhead, her hopes were dashed. Cora and Charley sat on the sand under one of the three umbrellas they'd gone to the difficulty of digging holes for and setting up, the large picnic basket unopened at their feet. "I'm getting kind of hungry," Charley said, reaching for the lid.

She swatted his hand. "Not yet."

It was ridiculous, she knew. A complete charade, this playacting their way through the day like business as usual. As though they could save their beloved family vacation, and thereby, just maybe, themselves. But she was not willing to give it up yet.

"They need time," Charley said, reaching over for her hand and then for the picnic basket lid again. This time she did not swat him away. When he handed her a ham and cheese sandwich she took it. So she'd have the traditional first-day-of-vacation beach picnic without them. They'd come around.

As he tore into his sandwich, and the seagulls circled overhead, Cora studied her husband's profile from under the brim of her straw hat. Charley was everything his overprotective mother, Tish, had always proclaimed him to be. Honorable. Loyal. A kind and decent man who had reached out to Cora and fallen in love with her, despite her swollen belly that cradled another man's babies. Charley, who Cora had bumped into many times as her boyfriend Robert's roommate, but whom she'd barely noticed. A man who'd never have seized her attention in a crowded party, as Robert had.

As she looked out at the ocean, her mind drifted back in time to Robert. She was a junior at Vassar and he a senior when they met; they could not have been more different. Robert, a native Californian to her sleepy Midwestern background, was as magnetic in charm as he was in his movie-star looks. She'd spied him at a few parties her own roommate had dragged her to, always from a distance, always surrounded by pretty girls and boisterous guys. Robert was vocal and funny, the center of any spirited conversation, with firm convictions on everything from politics and the news to free love. Ideas she found fascinating, just as she was fascinated by his confidence in sharing them. Cora was an only child raised in a quiet, religious household where dinner conversations centered around her marks in school or the intricacies of running the shoe store her father owned. Growing up in a small, rural community where church events were the center of town life, she'd been raised to smile politely and listen and to wait her turn in the potluck line. Her future, as her father saw it, was to get married and work in the shoe store, which he would hand down to her husband. A future as bleak, to Cora, as one of her high school art paintings she'd titled *Storm Cloud*: a swirl of gray and dark umber acrylic on canvas. Her "artsy pictures"—as her father called the paintings and charcoal sketches she labored over—were a mere hobby. Nothing practical; nothing with a future. But her mother had other ideas. Quiet ideas that bloomed privately within her and were shared in whispers with Cora when her father was at work. "You have a vision," her mother told her. Cora was never sure if she meant the canvases themselves or the future Cora dared imagine. Regardless, her mother was how Cora had ended up applying to schools in the Northeast: liberal arts schools, where Cora could escape the confines of her dreary childhood town and stretch her legs and her ideas in the wider world.

Getting an art scholarship and going away to college at Vassar had been a personal dream, but meeting a guy like Robert had been a private awakening. In their small pond of Vassar Robert was a whale; he was the popular radio personality of their small college station. Tuned into WVKR, just about every girl on campus went to sleep with Robert's velvety voice in her ear, and many claimed to dream of him. To a reserved late bloomer like Cora, he was the ticket to a slice of life she'd never experienced. One night, as Andy Gibb's "I Just Want to Be Your Everything" rolled across the crowd at a campus dance, Robert crossed the floor and took her hand. "Dance with me." He didn't ask her name, but Cora already knew who he was. Pressed against his chest, hips swaying to Andy's vibrato, Cora fell into a daze. By the end of the dance, he knew her name and her phone number. And Cora knew he liked to French kiss.

Robert took her to plays and protests and parties. On Robert's arm, Cora felt both sexy and smart. No longer a shy small-town girl from Ohio whose parents ran a shoe store. For the whole of her junior year Robert wooed her, and she let him. Why not? There was a line of girls across the quad who'd have jumped at the chance and Cora felt it was her turn. To be not just noticed, but seen.

"You are the sexiest woman I've ever met," Robert whispered to her that first night at the mixer in the college house. "And I'm going to make you feel like it." He had done exactly what he promised, and despite their breathless six-month-long love affair, Robert did what she should have known he'd do all along: he grew bored and left her for a redheaded freshman interning at the radio station. When she found out she was pregnant, a month later, Cora traipsed from the campus infirmary straight to his dormitory door. Robert did not answer, nor did his roommate, Charley. Rather, a girl pulled the door open; not the redheaded freshman, she noted with detached amusement.

"We need to talk," Cora said, looking over the girl's shoulder to where Robert sat at his desk.

As soon as he learned the reason for her visit, Robert sat a long while in silence. And then, in the same velvety tones he used to sign off on the radio station each night, he questioned how she could be sure the pregnancy was his. Cora was floored.

They argued bitterly, but she did not cry. She refused to cry.

In the end, Robert told her it didn't matter: he wasn't interested in becoming a father. Not then and not with her. If she wished to have the child, she was on her own.

Cora had not wished to have the baby, at least not then. She was in a state of shock herself and was desperate for another person to weigh in. Especially hoping that other person would be the father. But it was clear Robert was not who she'd thought he was, nor was he ever going to be.

Afterward, Cora wandered across campus in a daze. She did not notice the storm clouds brewing overhead. Nor did she feel the first pelts of rain against her face. Instead, tentative hand on her belly, she kept walking until she reached a park bench outside the library. It was where Charley found her.

When Charley stopped to ask if she'd like to borrow his umbrella, she looked up at him in confusion; she'd not even noticed it was raining.

Charley held his red umbrella over her head and insisted on walking her back to her dorm, out of the cold, wet weather. Cora did not want to go and face her roommate or the phone in the hall, where she would soon have to call her parents back in Ohio with the news, but there was nowhere else to go. Back in her dorm, she was relieved to see her roommate was out. And suddenly exhausted. Still soaked, she left the door ajar and headed straight for her bed, where she collapsed in a fit of tears, unable to keep them in any longer.

Charley did not shrink away from the outpouring. Nor did he duck out. Instead, with quiet gestures, he draped a blanket across her narrow shoulders and heated the tea kettle on the hot plate in the corner. Moments later, he handed her a cup of hot cocoa.

Cora stopped crying and accepted the cup. She did not know why her ex-boyfriend's roommate was being so kind, but she didn't question it. The hot cocoa was warm and comforting. She sipped it gratefully and managed a smile.

Charley looked relieved "Better?" he asked.

But Cora could not answer. A wave of nausea rolled through her. The hot chocolate rumbled in her stomach. She'd barely had time to run down the hall to the bathroom.

When she returned, running the back of her hand against her lips, Charley looked up at her with startled concern.

"Sorry," she said. "I'm pregnant."

Now sitting on the beach these forty-five years later, she took a bite of the ham and cheese sandwich and let her gaze fall on her husband's hand as he set it upon her own. Charley's hands were capable if not beautiful. The sandwich felt gummy in her mouth, and tasteless. Cora swallowed hard. Her kids would come around. She'd explain herself and they'd come around. They had to.

Andi

There were four empty stools at the Chatham Squire bar, and before Andi could slide onto one Hugh had already signaled the bartender. "Four shots of Patrón and the cocktail menu, please."

"Wait, whoa," Sydney said, sitting down to Andi's right. "I'm not doing a shot in the middle of the morning."

"Then I'll have yours." Hugh took the cocktail menu from the bartender and slid it across the wooden counter in her direction. "But you'd better pick something. This conversation requires booze."

Martin eyed Andi over Hugh's bent head. "Easy, sailor."

The four had barely talked since the night before. After the disastrous dinner followed by Tish's swift exit, Sydney had disappeared. They'd heard her crying into the phone to her fiancé, James, back in New York. Hugh and Martin had gone for a long drive and not returned until after dark, the only evidence being late-night footfalls down the hall and the click of the door handle. Andi, after her run-in with Nate, had been the only family member who'd managed to take the first-night-of-vacation swim. The bracing cold of the saltwater had been a balm to her singed senses, and she'd floated on her back in the shallow water as the sky gave way to purples and grays, and the first sliver of a crescent moon appeared overhead. Floating in the ocean was her favorite thing to do every summer—ever since she was a little girl and their father had taught her how—and it had calmed her then just as it had now. Only when she remembered that the sharks tended to feed at nightfall did she jerk upright from her repose and wade quickly back to shore. She'd gone to bed restless and after a fitful sleep had woken with a headache. Nothing about their first night together at Riptide was how it was supposed to go.

As soon as her parents went down to the beach that morning she'd gone looking for her siblings. Their parents may have wanted "to talk," but the kids needed to first. Now having rounded everyone up, at Hugh's suggestion they'd gotten into his Jeep and gone into town. Apparently, Hugh couldn't talk without first wetting his gullet.

The bartender set the four shots of Patrón down in front of them. It was late morning on a gorgeous beach day, and here were the four of them in a dark Main Street tavern.

Sydney sniffed the tequila and wrinkled her nose. "My wedding is ruined."

"At least you have a partner you love who wants to marry you," Andi countered.

Hugh stared into his shot. "We don't even know who our father is."

Martin turned to all of them and raised his glass. "To missing biological fathers, ruined weddings, and half siblings. Cheers!" All four tossed back their shots without complaint.

Without waiting, Sydney ordered another round. Hugh

looked down the bar at her with fresh admiration. "There you go, sis."

She narrowed her eyes at him. "Don't you mean half sis?"

Hugh winced. "I'm sorry. Look, you guys know I use sarcasm to deal with shit. But that was mean."

"Sure was," Andi agreed. "But let's agree to something right now. Moving forward, however we feel about what Mom and Dad did, we don't take it out on one another. This was their decision to hide the truth from us. Not anyone's here."

"Good point," Martin said. "Not that I think you should gang up on your folks either . . ."

Hugh ran his tongue around the rim of his shot glass. "They kind of have it coming."

"Doesn't matter. They have their reasons, whether you guys like them or not. I think you need to talk."

The next round of shots came and this time without comment they tossed them back.

Sydney wiped her hand across her mouth. "You know what James said last night on the phone?"

Hugh sniffed. "That he wants to pick out paint colors for his new summer house?"

Sydney slumped on her stool. "Never mind. It doesn't matter."

"Hey, I'm sorry." Hugh held up his hands. "Even I think I'm being an asshole. I need another drink."

Andi handed him the cocktail menu, though she wasn't sure that was the best idea.

"What did James say?" she asked Sydney. Even though she really liked the guy, Andi was glad James wasn't there. Sure, he was a perfectly relaxed match for Syd's type A personality and would've calmed her nerves, but James could be outspoken, and

Andi wasn't sure she wanted other people weighing in on her personal hurt just yet. Worse, he had just been gifted Riptide: a family treasure he'd only been to visit once in his life. Suddenly, she didn't want to hear what James had said.

"James said that we shouldn't make any big decisions yet."

"So no new paint colors, for now." At least Hugh was laughing this time.

"Seriously, you guys. He said that when people go through a traumatic experience they should wait to make any big decisions. That they're in fight-or-flight mode. And you can't think as rationally until you've had some time."

Andi agreed. It made perfect sense. After her divorce, her therapist had pretty much told her the same thing: not to make any major life changes until the following year. Which was impossible for her to follow, as it turned out. They had to sell the family home since neither she nor her ex, George, could afford it alone. Then she had to buy a new place and move. All major life changes and during the worst time of her life.

"How does that apply to us?" Hugh asked. "Are you hinting that I should stay put and not go back to Boston, even though I'm furious at Mom and Dad?"

"Pretty much," Sydney said. "That, and maybe James and I should go ahead with the wedding and not cancel. I guess we'll figure out the rest of it after our honeymoon." She welled up as she said the last bit.

Andi wrapped an arm around Sydney and pulled her in. "Hey, none of us think you should cancel the wedding. It's the one good thing going on right now."

"Well, I do. Everyone is fighting. No one is really speaking to Mom and Dad. It's a mess."

Hugh raised his hand and ordered a beer. "Look, Syd. I'm not going anywhere, okay? I'll stay until the wedding. I just need a little time to figure this out."

Sydney wiped her nose. "I know, and I get it. Really. But I also worry that you guys are mad at me too."

"Because of the house?" Andi asked.

Sydney looked away. "I had no idea. You need to know I never wanted it for myself."

"Well, let's talk about that," Hugh said. "Now that you bring it up."

Andi felt the air about them shift.

Sure, Riptide was dear to each of them. But it wasn't like it was being sold to a stranger or torn down. It was still in the family . . . something she wasn't so sure could be said about her and Hugh's relationship with their father. "Listen, we all just agreed we'd get through the wedding. I don't think it makes sense to get into the weeds right now."

"What?" Hugh said. Sydney brought up the house. I have a question about what she said."

Sydney shrugged. "Shoot." But Andi could tell she didn't really mean it. Hugh could be imposing, especially to Sydney. She was ten years his junior, and the two had never been particularly close. "What do you want to know?"

"Riptide. What is your plan for it?"

Sydney blinked. "I don't have a plan. I just told you—I never wanted it for myself."

"Right. But now you have it. And you're about to marry a guy who works in commercial real estate, who I imagine will have all kinds of plans for it. So do we not get to ask about that?"

Martin, who was seated on the other side of Hugh, rested

his hand on his arm. "She said she doesn't know. Let's leave this alone for now."

But Hugh could not. It was eating him up, and now that Sydney had mentioned it he saw it as fair game.

"Hugh, what do you expect her to do?" Andi asked. "She's focused on her wedding. Shouldn't we let her enjoy that?"

"This has nothing to do with the wedding. Let's be honest here, people. Let's talk about the elephant in the room: Syd was just handed the deed to a million-dollar property that belongs to the whole family." He looked pointedly down the bar at his sisters. "If we're still calling ourselves that."

Andi turned to Syd. "You don't have to answer him."

"No, I want to." Sydney leaned around Andi, both elbows planted on the bar. "Since you're burning to know, I'll tell you. James and I did talk about Riptide."

"And?"

"He couldn't believe it."

Hugh laughed sharply. "I bet he couldn't."

"Just as I couldn't," Sydney went on. "At first, he was shocked. The more we talked about it, the more we thought about how unfair it seems."

Hugh nodded. "It is unfair."

"Sure it is," Sydney said. "But then I thought more about it."

She hesitated and, in the moment's pause, Andi tensed. Like Hugh, it worried her that James was in commercial real estate. For her family, Riptide held more emotional value than anything else. To an outsider, it was a gold mine. Sure, James was a sweet guy who adored Syd. But Andi was pretty sure he'd not gotten so successful in his career by being sentimental.

Sydney grew pensive. "I may not have asked for Riptide. Hell, it may not even be fair. But you're all right—I was given it."

Andi didn't like the shift in Sydney's thinking. "What are you saying exactly?"

"Riptide doesn't really belong to our family. Not even to Mom and Dad. It has always been Tish's house."

"But she never went there. Not once in all the years we've grown up. She hates it," Hugh reminded them.

Sydney shrugged. "We don't know that for sure, and it doesn't matter anyway. It's hers. And if Tish wants me to have Riptide, why shouldn't I keep it?" Her eyes were bright with determination, even if her voice wavered.

It was like the air was sucked out of the bar area. "Oh man." Martin ran his hands across his closely cropped hair and looked away.

Hugh sat very still and silent. Too still and silent.

Andi couldn't believe what they were hearing.

"So you are planning to keep the family house?" she asked.

Sydney crossed her arms. "Like I said, I have no definite plans. But I'm considering everything. I'd be a fool not to."

Hugh slammed his beer down. "I knew it. She's going to keep it for herself. Until maybe James arrives and does a quick market analysis."

"This has nothing to do with James!" Sydney insisted.

"Well, it shouldn't! It's the place our grandfather rescued and restored for his family. For *all of us,* no matter how distantly we're related or not. What makes you think you've got a greater stake in it?"

Sydney pushed the shot glass away from her and it clattered

noisily to its side, threatening to fall off the bartop. As she lunged to catch it, Andi caught a glimpse of what Hugh saw: a little girl. Always right underfoot. Always needing something. Perhaps the favorite of their parents. It was an ugly and unfair thing to think; and yet Andi realized it was also mostly true.

Sydney stilled the rolling shot glass and clasped her hands. "You've always treated me like an afterthought. A little joke. Someone to be pushed aside. Well, I'm not a child anymore. I've got one more graduate degree than you, Hugh. And I'm getting married. So your big-brother bullying isn't going to work anymore."

"I never bullied you!" Hugh looked at her with exasperation.

"No? What would you call it?" She made a face. "Sissy Sydney? Princess Cry Baby? You made it pretty clear how you felt about me growing up. Like I was some kind of baby."

"We're ten years apart. You *were* a baby!"

Sydney looked askance at Andi and Hugh. "Do you have any idea how lonely it was growing up in your shadows? You were the big kids with all the big privileges. Always going off and leaving me behind."

It was somewhat true, but Hugh also had a point. "Syd, we didn't mean to leave you out. But you were in fourth grade when we were seniors in high school. Besides, we had our own challenges as twins," he added.

At that Sydney scoffed. "Don't even get me *started* on the twin thing."

This brought Martin to life. "Yes! She's got you there."

"What does that mean?" Andi asked. She and Hugh exchanged a look.

"There! That's it right there!" Martin said, and he and Sydney reached over to high-five across the counter between the twins.

"It was like you two had this secret society," Sydney told them. "Some weird twin-speak thing that none of us could break through. It was always just the two of you in your own little world. And I was never welcome."

Andi almost looked at Hugh again to see what he thought of all this, but caught herself. So maybe there was some validity. "I'm sorry, Syd. It wasn't intentional."

Syd lifted one shoulder. Suddenly, she looked smaller and less angry, as if unloading all of that had worn her out. "Maybe not. But it hurt."

Hugh had been unusually quiet. Now he leaned around Andi toward Syd. "I'm sorry if that hurt you," he said.

Sydney narrowed her eyes. "Not a real apology."

He cleared his throat. "All right. I'm sorry that I hurt you. It wasn't my intent." He looked to Martin. "You and I can talk about this later." Then, to Sydney, "You also need to know how hard it was to grow up with a sister so much younger, from our perspective."

"See? 'Our' perspective. Like it's two against one."

"Fine. I will speak for myself. If we're going to be honest, it seemed like you were the favorite. Mom and Dad doted on you in ways they never did with us. You got away with stuff we never would have."

"That's not true," Sydney said. "Maybe it felt that way because I was younger. I needed more from them at that age than you did as teens. I was a little kid."

"Exactly," Andi interjected. "I don't think that Mom and Dad necessarily did things on purpose, as far as treating us differently. But they had to. Not because they thought we were more capable or that you were more special. But because we needed such different things from them at those ages."

"Yeah?" Hugh said. "Well, then how does that explain Tish?"

It was the biggest question of all. "You're right," Andi said. "Tish has always treated us differently. Now I guess we know why."

It was one thing none of them could argue about. Riptide aside, Tish had always regarded the children differently. Though they didn't see much of her, it was crystal clear on the limited occasions she did visit. The twins were tolerated. Sydney was adored.

For the first time Andi became aware of the bustle and noise behind them in the restaurant section. The bar had begun to fill with the afternoon crowd. Lunch patrons and shoppers who'd grown hungry for fish and chips or lobster rolls. Normally her own stomach would be growling by now, especially with the smells coming from the kitchen. But the conversation had soured her appetite. She looked at her watch. "I've got to get back for Molly. She's been home alone all morning."

Poor Molly, Andi thought as she reached for her wallet. Here on a family vacation to spend quality time with her mom and reunite with her uncles and aunt and grandparents. And now sitting home alone on a glorious beach day. Her chest tightened. When her ex-husband, George, arrived to pick Molly up the following week, he'd probably have all kinds of fun things planned. None that involved family fights over dinner and being left home alone while the adults went to duke it out at the local pub.

"Let's settle up and go," she said. When she tried to get the bartender's attention to hand him her credit card, Martin was faster. "You've all had a rough start. Let me treat." Andi was grateful and relieved. She couldn't remember how much she had left in her checking account. Things were tight these days living on just her teaching salary alone and she was still learning to budget. A simple thing like treating friends or family to drinks—something she used to do all the time without any thought—could tip the whole cart. Another ripple of divorce.

On both sides of her, her sister and brother remained quiet. "So what's next?" Andi asked. "We need a plan before we walk back in the house."

"I'm not ready to talk to Mom and Dad," Hugh said too quickly.

"Well, I think I need to," Andi said. "I have questions."

Sydney sank back on her stool. "This is going to ruin my wedding, isn't it?"

"No!" they all said in unison.

"How about this?" Martin asked. Martin was famous for trying to make peace. "What if we all go about our business as usual, even if we can't really talk openly just yet. So we'll proceed with things like dinner and beach trips as a family. And we'll do what we have to to help Sydney and James get ready for the wedding. But aside from that, we don't get into it until everyone has cooled down. Agreed?"

It was what they had agreed to before and had already failed at. But Andi found herself nodding along with the others. She was numb. Their parents had been forced to reveal a family secret that had implications far beyond their childhoods. Somewhere out there was a father Andi and Hugh had never known existed. And their grandmother had given away the one possession the whole family treasured most.

But Martin was right. They needed to pull together, despite the animosity and fresh wounds, if only for a little while longer. Andi had a daughter to take care of and a little sister's wedding to face. What other choice did any of them have?

Outside of the dark confines of the Squire, the sun on Main Street seemed impossibly bright. They all blinked like vampires. They walked up the sidewalk past the Candy Manor with its bubblegum-pink awning. The area in front of the door smelled like sugar and melting chocolate. Molly loved that place; Andi would bring her back into town after dinner. She glanced in the boutique windows they passed: women's resortwear, canvases of ocean scenes in the gallery window, a line out the door at the ice cream shop. Downtown Chatham was humming with happy tourists and vacation goers, a sea of pastel attire and smiling children. Andi looked at the faces around her: Hugh's scowl. Sydney's downturned mouth. Martin's resigned expression.

They were almost back at Hugh's Jeep when a pale blue Bronco rolled past. The doors were off and the top was down: Tom Petty's "Free Fallin'" floated out of it. The driver was wearing aviator sunglasses and a backwards baseball cap. Andi did a double take.

Hugh waved. "Hey!"

The Bronco braked to a sudden stop.

"Wait, do you know who that . . . ?" Andi started to say.

But Hugh was already jogging over to the driver's side.

Sure enough, it was Nate. Andi stood back, straining to hear the conversation from the sidewalk.

"Wow. He's pretty cute," Sydney said, beside her.

"Do you remember Nate, from when we were kids?"

Sydney grinned. "I do now."

"Your parents mentioned him; something about him being an old family friend," Martin said. "They said he's back here for the summer."

Andi shook her head. "Why does everybody know this except me?" She watched Hugh and Nate talking. She was pretty sure she heard the word "tonight," but it was hard to tell over the bustle on the sidewalk. An impatient line was starting to pile up behind the Bronco. The sun glared down on them on the sidewalk. Somebody beeped.

Just then Nate looked up at Andi. She felt like a schoolgirl, just standing there. Staring.

"Hey, girls!" There was that boyish smile again. And with it that flutter in her stomach.

Beside her, Sydney popped to life and waved hard. "Good to see you again, Nate!"

Andi waved back with what she hoped was far less exuberance.

Someone beeped again, Hugh stepped away, and Nate was off.

"What were you guys talking about?" Andi asked as soon as Nate returned.

"I don't remember him looking like that," Sydney gushed. "Didn't you guys used to describe him as kind of nerdy?"

"Nah, he was always a cool guy," Hugh said. "Just a scrawny kid like the rest of us were. I can't believe he's back after all these years."

They were clogging the sidewalk just as they had the street. Downtown was so busy, Andi thought irritably, as someone bumped against her and kept going. All these tourists. Though as a summer resident, she realized, the locals considered her to be no different.

"So he's the one who renovated his parents' house?" Martin asked as they began moving with the crowd.

"I remember he used to throw me in the waves," Sydney said. "He was my favorite summer friend of Hugh and Andi's because he didn't ignore me like the rest of them did."

"Yeah, Nate and I were pretty tight," Hugh mused. "I can't believe how many years it's been."

"Did you say something to him about tonight?" Andi asked again, trying to keep up and be heard over their chatter.

They were all walking ahead of her, still talking, not one of them replying to her question. Andi raised her voice. "What did you say to him?"

They were back at Hugh's Jeep and they all turned.

"What?" She hadn't meant to yell. "Nobody listens to me."

Hugh was eyeing her. "Why are you so curious?"

Andi pushed past him and climbed into the back of his Jeep. "Oh, shut up."

They were all looking at her now with smug expressions. It was a relief, at least, and a reprieve from all the shared tension. "If you must know," Hugh said, hopping behind the wheel, "I invited Nate over for dinner tonight."

"*Tonight*? Because last night's family dinner went so great? You aren't even talking to Mom and Dad."

"It'll be fine. And will force everyone to behave." Hugh looked at her in the rearview mirror. "Better find something cute to put on."

Andi glared back at him. "Oh, please. I'm a divorced single mother with enough on my plate." The whole way home she mentally ticked through the clothes in her closet back at Riptide. Dammit. She had absolutely nothing cute to wear.

Tish

To her great surprise, she sleeps through the night. And then some. When she puts on her glasses, the small clock on the bedside table tells her it's nine-thirty. Tish gasps.

She cannot remember the last time that happened, but it has been years. Part of getting older, she told herself. It was what all her friends said too. One of life's cruel jokes. Once their kids moved out or they retired from jobs and could finally stay up late and sleep in the next day, none of them could.

But now she wonders if it's because of Morty. She feels him here, on the Cape. He is all around her: in the salt air, in the ebbing sea, in the late daylight over the dunes. And she finds her mind wandering, chasing after his memory.

Gently, she pulls the covers back and swings her legs over the side of the bed. The room is bright with morning sun. She must have forgotten to close the curtains last night. She studies the heavy brocade pattern, the color of seashells. There is no escaping the ocean, even in this room.

After calling down for coffee, she opens the French doors. Her suite is on the shore side of one of the resort's private cottages, situated on a grassy rise overlooking the harbor. As the

French doors swing open a gust of salt air meets her. *Morty,* she thinks, closing her eyes. *I've come back.*

It is brighter and warmer than she expected. These days she is chilled all the time, even on a summer day. But not today. She glances left and right, to the neighboring suites, but sees no other hotel guests, so she steps outside in her pajamas onto her small patio. Just beyond the white picket fence the bay sparkles splendidly and for the first time in a while she finds herself entertaining an appetite. She will order breakfast too, she decides. One of those blueberry scones with whipped honey butter from a local farm. When she'd read it on the menu last night it held as much appeal as cardboard. Today, she wants to eat one. Maybe two. Her stomach growls. She will order the pancetta-wrapped cantaloupe too. And an egg.

While she waits for her breakfast, she calls Charley. She hopes he answers the phone, and not Cora. She has nothing to say to her. But Charley—oh. Her chest aches.

The phone rings several times before he answers. "Charley?" she says, suddenly breathless.

"Mother." Charley's voice is heavy. There is a long pause. "Why did you do it?"

It's the question she's expected since before she did what she did. She knew it was coming as she packed her bags back in New York. As she sat in the backseat of the town car all the way up the Mid-Cape Highway. And yet, despite all that time to prepare, she finds herself with nothing as an answer. "I'm sorry," she says instead. Then, "Not that I did it, because I had to. But I am sorry for the hurt this has caused you."

It is not the answer he sought. "It has caused all of us hurt, Mother. Do you understand that? The kids most of all." He is angry, she realizes with a start. She should have known he would be, but still, it comes as a surprise. Charley is quiet-natured and soft-spoken, especially with her.

She steels herself. "Those kids had a right to know. Why you and Cora did not tell them is beyond me. The hurt they are feeling is not from me but from the truth. A truth Cora talked you into keeping a secret all those years ago . . ."

"Mother, we are not going down that road again." Charley has always insisted it was not Cora's decision or desire; that it was his too. But Tish will never accept that. Cora had manip-ulated him. Just as she did back in college, right before gradu-ation, when he was slated to start medical school in the fall at Yale. Yale!

Cora had always been calculating. It was Tish's fault she'd not raised her son to recognize that in a woman. To be on the lookout for those who might wish to prey upon him. After all, her Charley was a catch. Bright, kind, handsome. And . . . well, let's face it: rich. She'd tried to protect him; oh, it was all she'd spent her whole life doing, it seemed. But despite her endless efforts, she'd failed.

Charley was not finished. Cora must've gotten him worked up, knowing Tish would call. "What you did was wrong. And I can't begin to imagine how we are going to make this right with the kids. Sydney's wedding is in two weeks! Did you give any thought to that before you dropped this bomb on all of us?"

She has never heard him this angry. Well. Maybe she should not stay on, here in Chatham. Maybe she will eat her scone and pack her bags this very morning. But no, she has to make things right with Charley, before she goes. Time is too precious, these days. She feels it, more and more. She will stay, she decides in that moment. She will make it right with her son before she leaves, if only he'll listen. "Charley, this bomb was Cora's, I shall remind you. And I have been holding it in silence for over forty years. As a favor to you. And in deference to your wishes. But you are a Darling, and your father would have wanted you to share the family legacy with your child. And that means—"

"Children," Charley says sadly. "They are all three my children."

Tish sighs. "Well, isn't this the biggest part of the problem."

It's been the division between them since Cora. The true divisor, as Tish has come to call her.

Tish thinks back to the first time she met that woman; the first day of the rest of their ruined lives, she has long thought with ire. A verdant late-May day on the campus of Vassar. The weather was warm and bright, perfect for Charley's graduation ceremony.

She and Morty's parents had driven up from the city the night before. They'd stayed at the same hotel, but at opposite ends. Since Charley had gone off to college there was no longer any reason to maintain the pretense and posture of a functioning family. It was an unspoken arrangement that suited both. Tish stayed in the smaller New York apartment she'd shared with Charley before college, and Morty's parents divided their time in their usual way between the city, the Hamptons, and the Hudson Valley house. They did not talk on the phone. They did not get together for dinner downtown, even when both parties knew the other was in the city. Only when Charley came home from Vassar for the holidays did they gather, feigning lukewarm pleasantries and donning false smiles until

Charley returned to school, leaving them to scuttle to their corners without so much as a word or a wave goodbye. It was how things were.

As such, the day of graduation, the three of them met at the north end of Vassar's campus at an agreed-upon time and place, and, seemingly together, took their seats for the ceremony.

"Beautiful day," remarked Morty's mother.

"If they start on time we can be on the road by dinner," his father said.

Tish turned her body slightly away from them. How could they not be happy to be here celebrating Charley? How proud she was of her son graduating magna cum laude! Pre-med *and* an economics major, with a minor in English literature.

"Well, he's certainly a jack-of-all-trades if a master of none!" his grandparents had joked last Christmas to friends over the punch bowl at their annual holiday party, to Tish's astonishment. "The plan is medical school, but who knows? It may very well be the circus." To which their friends had laughed and laughed.

Burning with fury, Tish had glanced feverishly about the room to determine Charley's whereabouts, praying he'd not heard. After all his hard work! After making dean's list semester after semester. Though they rarely communicated, she'd long assumed his grandparents held the same depth of pride for their grandson that she did.

Morty's parents had clung to Charley since they'd all lost Morty, but not in the same vein Tish had. It was because he was their legacy. Morty had been an only child, as had his father. And now there was just Charley to carry on the Darling name. Tish supposed they loved Charley in their own arm's-length formal way but Tish would argue they did not know him. They did not know his character or his humor or his easygoing nature any more than they knew his ambition; if Charley said he was going to medical school, to medical school he would go.

A woman in a cranberry suit took the seat beside her. "Mother of a graduate?" she asked Tish brightly.

Tish beamed. And, after making sure to ask the woman about her own graduate, she extolled her seatmate with Charley's academic prowess. "My son is going to Yale. For medical school."

"My goodness! Yale. You must be so proud!"

Tish knew to expect the look of admiration and wonder people got when she told them the news, but she never tired of it. It filled her up that morning, just as it had the first time she told someone (the doorman in their apartment building!) that Charley had gotten into an Ivy League school, his first choice. They had been a lonely team of two, she and Charley, all these years without his father. But she'd endured. Having kept her promise to Morty and seeing Charley along the path to his promising future, today was her day too.

"Well," Morty's mother said, as the first graduate's name was called. "You were right. Charley's going to medical school." It was the only thing nearing kindness that Morty's mother had ever said to Tish and, even though she was used to steeling herself against all interactions with the family, Tish felt herself give in and well up just a little.

Later, when Charley's name was called and he walked across

the stage wearing his magna cum laude medal, Tish could not help herself. She leapt to her feet and, ignoring the mortified looks on Morty's parents' faces, placed her index finger and thumb to her lips and whistled with all her might. It was uncouth and over the top and something she knew Morty would have loved. When Charley turned her way and waved, it was all worth it.

After, as joyful graduates searched the grass for their tossed caps and made their way to find their families with arms extended, Tish scanned the crowd eagerly awaiting her turn. She was bursting with pride. So much so that she'd even accepted the invitation by Morty's parents to join them and take Charley out to lunch. Yet another surprise. Anything was possible that day, it felt.

"Where is he?" Morty's mother wondered aloud.

"Don't worry. He'll find us!" And then, emerging from a group of fellow graduates, there he was. His face bright, his cheeks flushed as he hurried toward them. So handsome in his cap and gown! Tish waved her arm excitedly. But Charley did not wave back. His hand was stretched behind him and as he neared someone stepped out from the swirl of his gown, holding it. A tall, blonde, young woman. Who, even with her ducked chin, radiated beauty. When she looked up at them and smiled, Tish's gaze fell straight to her swollen belly.

They did not go to lunch to celebrate. Instead, Tish propped herself up in his dormitory doorway as Charley tried to explain. "I love her, Mom."

"You've never even mentioned her. And she's *pregnant*?"

"I'm going to marry her," he told her.

Charley stood apart from her across the room, calmly zipping his suitcase. Tish wanted to grab it. To hurl it out the window. And herself after it. "Have you lost your mind?"

"I know this seems sudden, and I'm sorry. But it's the right thing to do."

"For who?" she cried. "For that trollop?"

"Mother!" Charley looked so pained for an instant she almost felt bad for him. But what could he be thinking? Brilliant, sensible Charley. And after all those years of hard work. The private schools. The tutors. The isolated whole of her life living in the shadows of the Darlings, giving up any chance of happiness for herself, all for Charley. So he could have it all. So he could be it all. And now . . . *this girl*.

He crossed the room and faced her, his expression full of worry but also something else. Already, he was unrecognizable to her.

"Nothing is going to change. All of our careful plans are still going to unfold. Just as we've always hoped." He pecked her cheek. "I promise."

Everything did change. Charley did not go to Yale that fall. Instead, he deferred and married Cora. They moved into a small apartment in the city, quietly arranged by Morty's parents with hushed tones and urgent whispers. Having been largely disowned from her own family, Cora had no family of her own to count on. Tish remained in her own place on the Upper East Side, alone. On Thanksgiving Cora gave birth to not one but two babies. Morty's parents sent a stuffed giraffe from FAO Schwarz in their place; Charley's shotgun wedding to a pregnant woman had caused quite the scandalous ripple through their circles. As for Tish, it took her two days to visit the hospital.

She arrived empty-handed and unrested, there for one answer only. She got it the moment she looked at her son: Yale was all but forgotten.

Now on the other end of the phone, she hears Charley let out his breath. Her sweet, brilliant Charley who gave up his dreams to raise another man's children. Who has given all of himself to a woman. A woman who had seemed destined to deprive him of a child of his own, until ten years later (blessedly), Charley could call himself a real father. Just as Tish had lived all those years alone without her Morty, raising her son as a single mother in the shadows of the Darlings, so too had Charley. Despite her best efforts and most valiant fights, history repeated itself. She has to make him understand that Riptide is the last piece they have of Morty. That he built it for them and found happiness there, with them. That he would want Charley's child to have the same. Maybe now, finally, Sydney can uphold some part of the dream Tish had all those years ago. "I am going to stay a few days," she tells her son. "I know how angry you are. But someday you will see."

"This can be undone," Charley says. "You can come back to the house and undo all of this."

Tish thinks about this. She is honoring Morty's memory. She may be old-fashioned, but these modern families create all kinds of havoc. Who pays for college? Who inherits? Haven't she and Charley rescued Cora and her twins and provided enough already? As she was raised, family is blood. And Sydney is the only real family.

"Mother, it would help us all if you fixed this."

Cora, Tish thinks. It would only help Cora get out of the fire she has found herself in. A fire of her own making. Tish has kept her secret all these years. Charley has already sacrificed the life he was meant to have, for her.

"No, I'm afraid that's not going to happen," she tells Charley. "What's done is what should have been done years ago. I'm at Chatham Bars Inn, in the Mooncusser Cottage. You're welcome to visit me here."

Cora

When they came up from the beach, it was clear the kids had been out. Hugh's car was parked in a different spot on the seashell driveway. There was a pile of kicked-off flip-flops and sandals strewn across the entryway's sisal rug. A sign that used to bring joy to her heart because it meant everyone was home—under Riptide's roof—together for a few weeks of summer fun. Something that seemed harder and harder to accomplish each year they grew older and further apart, busy with their own lives. But now, here they all were, during what should have been a joyous start to vacation, and there wasn't sight nor sound from any of them.

Charley set the picnic basket on the butcher block island and began emptying its contents. Six uneaten sandwiches, ruined. Three plums, bruised from being toted around. An unopened wedge of cheddar. Cora tore off the cellophane wrapper and broke a piece off. Hell, she may as well enjoy it before it spoiled.

"Any sign of them?" Charley asked, listening overhead for footsteps or sounds of movement. Over the years Riptide had been built up and added on to, but the cottage was still cozy enough and the pine floors creaky enough that it was always easy to tell where people were.

Cora shrugged. "What's the difference? None of them are speaking to us."

"Oh, honey." Charley came around and rested his hands on her shoulders. Cora leaned back against his chest. A solid chest, a chest she had lain her head on for many decades. Charley was so dependable, always. "Give it time. Riptide has a way of washing away the hard stuff. My dad always said so."

Cora had heard this before. She'd never met Morty, but Charley referred to him so often it sometimes felt as if he'd been with them all along. To her, Morty had always sounded almost too good to be true. A privately educated and successful businessman from a powerful family who had fallen in love with a first-generation, working-class Irish-American woman, against his parents' wishes. A man who despite all material wealth preferred the simple life with family over all else, and had gone against the grain of his parents' expectations to live a life that afforded them that. The fact that Cora had not met Morty made her sad. But the fact that he left Charley at such a young age was far sadder. Sometimes Cora wondered if Charley remembered his father through his own boyhood experiences or from the stories told by Tish. Memory was a funny thing; sometimes the things we thought we experienced firsthand were really just stories told or suggestions made to us at a young age by others. In her smaller moments, Cora wondered if that were the case with Morty, who as far as she could tell had achieved near sainthood in his wife's and son's views. He was just a man, after all. As human and flawed as the rest of them.

But then she would reprimand herself for even doubting

her husband's rose-colored memories. Look at the evidence! Charley Darling, salt of the earth despite his affluent upbringing. Gentle and kind and true. He certainly didn't get any of that from his mother.

As she watched him put away the remains of the picnic, there was the sound of footsteps on the stairs and Cora brightened. Molly appeared on the landing. "We're having company," she said. "Mom sent me down to help."

"Company?" Cora asked. She turned to Charley who shrugged. "Who's coming?"

Molly tugged the fridge open and stared at its contents. "Don't know. Some guy, I think. Mom said to pull out the cheeses."

"Some guy." Cora glanced at the wedge of cheddar that certainly did not look appetizing enough for company. "Well, I can't say I had anything planned for dinner. But I suppose we can dig something up."

At that moment the kitchen came to life. "Don't worry, Mom. We've got it under control." Martin pecked her on the cheek as he passed. "Molly, why don't you grab the cutting board from the pantry. The big one."

Hugh followed. He looked about the kitchen, right past his parents. "Someone needs to mix some cocktails."

The front door closed with a slam. It was Sydney and Andi. "That would be you. But don't think mixing a few drinks will get you out of making dinner." Andi sailed past them with overloaded bags of groceries and set them on the island with a *thunk*. Her sister followed suit.

Cora watched her daughters unpack. "My. What've you girls got there?"

Andi kept her eyes on the food, but at least she was speaking to her. "Corn from the farm stand. Clams from the pier. Oh, and two bottles of wine."

Hugh looked up. "That's my girl."

Charley looked between them, a mix of curiosity and frustration. "Is anyone going to tell us what's going on?"

"We're making dinner. Remember Nate from next door? He's coming by."

"Oh." This was certainly news to Cora. Nate was a childhood fixture in their house back in the day. His family would come for the summer, as theirs did, each year. Always sandy-footed and bronzed, his hair would burn bleached blonde with sun by August. She had always liked Nate. She was also dying to get into the renovated cottage and see what he'd done to his parents' place. "Are we invited?" she asked.

All of her kids looked up at that. Well. Let them think a moment of how they'd treated her these last twenty-four hours.

Andi answered for all of them. "Don't be silly. You live here."

There was a collective pause as everyone seemed to remember that it was officially now Sydney's house.

Sydney, for her part, flushed. "Let's have a nice night together. Okay?"

Cora wasn't exactly sure how to take that. Charley squeezed her shoulder. "Sounds like a plan to me."

Hugh hooked his phone up to the little speaker on the counter and Billy Joel crooned across the kitchen. Cora watched as Andi, Molly, and Sydney shucked corn, smiling and talking. Martin was washing littlenecks in the old, dented lobster pot in the kitchen sink. Hugh was busy mixing God only knew what kind of concoction, though it looked good, humming along to "Piano Man." Cora and Charley were not exactly a part of any of it, but still, it was nice to see.

Well, they clearly weren't needed in the kitchen and Cora was still sticky with sunscreen from the beach. So she poured herself a glass of wine from the open bottle on the counter and took it upstairs to shower. Maybe this arrangement would work out just fine.

Upstairs, under the gentle stream of the shower, Cora's mind drifted back in time. To Charley finding her on the bench in the rain that day outside the campus library. The cup of hot cocoa he'd made for her. And to what happened after he walked her back to her dorm.

One thing was clear: Robert was not going to have any part of this and it was time to tell her parents. She waited until the common room area in her dorm was clear and went to the payphone. It was impossible to have any kind of private conversation, but she had no other choice.

Her mother picked up on the second ring. "Oh, hi, honey! I was just thinking about you. Just a few more weeks and you'll be home for the summer."

The excitement in her mother's voice filled her with sadness. Cora was the first person on both sides of her parents' families to go to college and she'd made it through her junior year with almost perfect grades. "Cora is so talented. She's going to be an artist!" her mother had told everyone when she was home for Christmas.

The door to the common room opened and Cora waited for two girls to pass through before she spoke. "Mama, there's something I have to tell you."

"What's wrong?" Even from six hundred miles away in Lima, Ohio, her mother could sense the news was not good.

"You know Robert? The boy I was dating?" Cora swallowed hard.

"Of course. He was all you could talk about over winter break. How is he?"

"Well, he's not my boyfriend anymore."

"Oh, sweetie. I'm sorry to hear that, but these things happen. Isn't he a senior? He's probably got big plans for next year. Things on his mind. Don't worry, you'll find another nice boy in no time."

"That's not it, Mama. I'm afraid something has happened." Cora took a deep breath and laid an involuntary hand across her belly. "I'm pregnant."

There was silence on the other end of the line.

"Mama?"

"Are you sure?" Her mother's voice was strangled.

"Yes. I've been to the infirmary. They gave me two tests."

"Oh, Cora." And with those words she could hear all the hope her mother had held out for her over the years fall away. "What does Robert say? Does he want to get married?"

Cora closed her eyes. "No, Mama. That's not going to happen."

What if we talk to his parents? I'm sure there is something that can be worked out. After all . . ."

"He was very clear. I am on my own with this." Tears pressed at her eyes as Cora cradled the phone to her ear. "I'm so sorry, Mama."

On the other end her mother let her breath out. "What are you going to do?"

"I don't know. I think I want to have the baby."

Her mother's voice was shrill. "Well, of course you're having the baby!" Cora had been raised Catholic and in her parents' minds there was no other way. "You need to come home. Maybe the church can help. These days they have all kinds of places you can go until you have the baby. And find a nice home to adopt it. Your father will not be happy about this, of course. But don't worry, honey; we can figure this out."

"No, Mama, that's the thing. I'm not sure, but I think I want to keep this baby."

"With no job and no husband? Heavens, honey, you have to finish college."

There was a sound in the background and Cora sensed her father had walked in during their call. "Hold on." She could hear her mother cover the phone, the sound of muffled voices. Her stomach turned over. She was not ready to tell him. He would be livid, and he had a horrible temper.

"What in the hell?" Her father's voice boomed through the phone. "Cora Anderson. Tell me this is not true."

Cora started to cry. "Dad, I'm so sorry."

"My God. What kind of mess did you get yourself into out there in New York?" He was furious. Not sympathetic, not even surprised. She should have known better. "I told your mother from the beginning, that art school out there in the East was a bad idea. All those liberal ideas. And look! Look what you went and did!" Cora held the phone away from her ear, tears streaming down her cheeks.

As she listened to her father rage, she thought about her mother, stuck in Lima all her life. Married to a man who did not like her "big ideas" for their daughter. About her steadfast belief in Cora. How her mother had secretly helped her fill out her application and write her college essay, and even walked her to the mailbox at the end of their long dirt driveway to send it off. All without telling Cora's father. "I'll handle him when you get in" was all she'd said.

Her father was still not done on his end of the call. But Cora was. Slowly, she lifted her free hand and let it hover over the switch hook before she made up her mind. The audible *click* signaled the end of that conversation.

As Cora hung up the phone, across campus there was a conversation of a different kind. Charley Darling, who'd never been in a fight in his life, waited with a clenched jaw for his roommate Robert to get back. When Robert eventually sailed through the door, his forehead still beaded with sweat from playing basketball down at the athletic center, Charley confronted him. Asked what his intentions were for Cora. Robert, shaking his head with a smile, had set his basketball down. "Intentions?" he said with a small chuckle. "Look, Charley, I don't know what the girl told you, but she and I are over."

"She's pregnant, Robert. You two were in a relationship."

"I've been in relationships with lots of girls, Charley. You should try it sometime."

"But the baby?"

Robert peeled his sweaty shirt over his head. "Who's to say it's even mine?"

Before he could utter another word, Charley Darling threw the first punch of his life. The sound of his fist smashing Robert square in the nose was a sickening noise. One he would remember all his life. But never regret.

Now, from the looks of things in the living room, Cora could see that Nate Becker was exactly what her family needed. As she made her way downstairs, Cora thought she recognized a male voice. Sure enough, there stood Nate, in the middle of her kitchen, just like he had all those summers as a child. But instead of eating popsicles at the kitchen island, this time he was armed with a bottle of beer.

Had she not known the whole family was up in arms, there was no telling from the postcard scene before her. It was a party. Hugh was decked out in his favorite Nantucket Reds and a white polo, head thrown back in laughter. Sydney was perched on the edge of the slipcovered sofa in a pale blue maxi dress, the picture of youth as she listened ardently and tried to interject, which was hard to do among all the boisterous conversation. Her cheeks were flushed, leaving Cora to wonder how much wine she'd had. Molly and Martin were manning the cheese board at the island and Cora was pleased to see how engaged Molly was. She'd worried so much about her granddaughter that year, what with the divorce and all. But it was Andi who stole her gaze.

For the first time since her arrival, Andi looked herself. Effortless and lovely in a white shirtdress tied at the waist, her dark, curly hair falling about her shoulders. So different than the Andi who'd landed on the doorstep the day before. Chatting away with Nate, it was the most animated Cora had seen her in . . . how long? More than a year, she'd bet. Cora narrowed her eyes from her vantage point on the bottom step. Nate had grown into quite the handsome devil. She wondered how much of Andi's sudden good cheer had to do with that not-so-small detail. Well, good for her.

As if they felt her presence in unison, her children's heads turned.

"Mom. Don't you look nice." It was the most Hugh had said to her all day; when he came over and brushed her cheek with a kiss, Cora felt herself give. There was hope! But when she looked in Hugh's eyes, there it was: the guarded vacancy he affected when angry. He was being polite in front of company. Well, she'd take it.

It was Nate whose welcome was pure warmth. He met her on the bottom step with a big hug. "Mrs. D! Great to see you again." Cora smiled. Nate had always called her Mrs. D and she liked that he still did. Made her feel young again.

"I'm so glad you're here," she told him, squeezing his hands. He had no idea how glad.

All day she'd harbored such skepticism, but the evening was off to an impossibly nice start. Cora kept stealing knowing looks with Charley. On the kitchen island were artfully arranged fruits and tiny, sweet yellow tomatoes and cheeses. And a bushel of oysters from Nate. "Fresh from the pier!" Everyone gathered like spectators as he commandeered the sink, produced his own shucking knife, and served the oysters straight up with lemon.

"Good Lord," Andi said, tipping one back appreciatively. "So fresh and briny."

Their bellies content with libations and snacks, they made their way leisurely out to the patio for dinner. Martin grilled clams and Hugh poached cod with butter and homemade tarragon aioli, the herbs straight from Cora's kitchen garden. There was fresh corn from the farm in Orleans and Sydney arranged a Caprese salad with local mozzarella from the cheese shop in town.

"When did you go into town?" Cora asked, nibbling a piece of the mozzarella. It was what they always did together on the second day of vacation. No one had even asked her.

"Earlier today," Molly said. "It was fun. I love cheese."

So do I, Cora thought to herself. "I wish I'd known you were going," she said, trying to keep the hurt from her voice.

Sydney raised one tanned shoulder as she drizzled balsamic glaze over the salad. "You guys weren't around."

Cora looked at Charley to be sure he'd heard too. "We were down at the beach. For the first-day picnic. *Waiting.*" But no one was listening. Just as no one had come.

"Hey, Uncle Hugh," Molly said. "I tried some of that blue cheese you're always talking about."

"And?"

"And it's as disgusting as I thought it would be." Molly wrinkled her nose comically. "But I did like the Camembert. And the Morbier wasn't so bad."

Hugh grinned appreciatively. "Morbier. There's hope for you yet, kid."

Andi narrowed her eyes at her daughter. "I'm always telling you to try new things and you refuse! Why doesn't Morbier ever happen with me?"

"Because you're boring and don't take me to cool places like Aunt Syd?" Molly flashed a wicked smile. Everyone laughed.

Cora sat back in her chair in disbelief, watching her family members like she were watching actors rehearse a scene. Who were these people? And how were they suddenly so jovial?

Nate gave them a detailed account of his recent master bathroom renovation, next door, from the plumbing to the tile choices, and Cora watched them hang on every word. "Those are some high-end fixtures," Hugh chimed in. A surprising comment from her son, who loathed all things DIY and whom they teased endlessly for once hiring a handyman to change the light bulbs in his apartment.

As Cora listened to her children applaud Nate's bathroom renovation choices, she began to feel more and more like an uninvited guest in her own home. Sure, Nate was charming. And the food was good. But this was too much. Last night they were outraged and bickering. Today they'd come together to boycott her beautiful beach picnic and then went to town without her. Suddenly, a TOTO toilet was captivating dinner conversation?

She looked down at her plate. The bright colors and aromas had seemed enticing, but now with each forkful she lifted to her mouth Cora found it hard to swallow. She looked up at Charley, seated at the head of the table across from her and a familiar dread settled over her. They were right back in their spots from the disastrous night before. It felt like a haunting redo, everyone all gussied up and behaving; passing heaping plates of food, pouring one sparkling glass of wine after another. Suddenly, Cora found herself dizzied by the display. Because that was all it was. A big, fat display.

Even Charley seemed momentarily caught up in it, nodding along and smiling. And it infuriated her. Cora pushed her plate away. They were going on about their vacation without her, leaving her to watch from the sidelines as some kind of punishment. And the more they seemed to enjoy themselves, the angrier she got. She stood up from the table. No one even noticed.

The slap of the screen door behind her did not interrupt their lively conversation. She headed through the kitchen, past the butcher-block island strewn with dirty plates and empty glassware, half-eaten boards of melting cheese, and browning fruit. Into the living room and right through the front door. A tear slipped from her eye and she cursed it. If only her kids knew the sacrifices she'd made for them. The reasons she had kept that secret all those years. If only they had the decency to hear her out or to ask her more about it. But no, they were holding tight to their grievances and uniting in their stubbornness. Well, so could she. Cora walked down the porch steps and down her seashell driveway. *Wait,* she thought. *My mistake!* It was *Sydney's* driveway.

At the mailbox, she took an abrupt left onto Bay Street and kept walking. She'd heard from Charley that Tish was still in town. Cora pictured her holed up at Chatham Bars Inn in a fancy room. Pouring tea for herself. Tapping her bony fingers together as she considered her last line of attack. Behind her, laughter rose up on the balmy evening air. From Riptide? Were they really having that much fun with her gone? They likely hadn't even noticed her empty seat. Well. She hoped they didn't choke on their nice dinner.

At the end of their road was a dead-end lane that branched sharply downhill, leading to a small bayside marina. She took it, out of habit. All through the kids' childhoods, Cora and Charley had walked with them down here. The water was quiet and shallow and it was the perfect place to while away summer hours when they were little. It was the place they'd learned to sea kayak. The place they'd come to fish off the docks and search for fiddler crabs in the seagrass along the tidal pools. Now it was the place Cora walked to on her morning strolls. Where she could sit on the edge of the dock and watch the smaller boats come in through the inlet. Where she could dangle her feet in the water and stare at her reflection. How it had changed, from the days the kids would come with her.

Now as Cora lowered herself onto the weathered boards of the dock and searched for her reflection in the water, she wondered. What did her children see when they looked at her? Was it a woman who had raised them carefully and loved them fiercely, despite the odds? Or, now that the secret was out, did they instead see a woman who had bartered with their truth? Did they have any idea of what she saw when she looked at herself: a woman who gave up on romantic love and instead traded it for another kind: the kind between mother and child. Oh, she had loved her children madly and deeply since the beginning. She sighed inwardly. If only it could have been that way with Charley.

As Cora dangled her feet over the water, a small wave of sadness came over her. The secret was out, but her kids did not know everything. There were more truths than the ones Tish had exposed.

Andi

For the first time since arriving on the Cape, she slept hard. When she finally stirred the next morning, the sheets felt crisp and cool against her bare legs and she stretched her toes to the end of the bed, reveling in the luxuriance of a good night's sleep. Whether it was the little bit of fun they'd finally managed to have the night before, or the wine, she woke with a smile. Instantly, her thoughts turned to Nate.

The night before, her divorce had come up in conversation. Andi realized that Nate hadn't known she was no longer married. "Oh, wow, I'm sorry to hear that."

"Don't be," Andi had said, never quite sure how to respond when people expressed sorrow for her situation. "It was for the best and we're in a good place now."

But there was more. He'd met Molly and he'd been surprisingly good with her, talking about YA fantasy fiction and all their favorite authors.

"You read YA?" Andi had asked him and Molly had glared at her.

"Mom. We're in the middle of a conversation." Andi had left them to it, but the happy sense of surprise over Nate had stayed with her. Which was all new territory for Andi.

Despite her friends' best efforts, she hadn't dated a single guy since her divorce. At first she chalked it up to fatigue. The transition from marriage and sharing a family home to single parenting, sharing custody, and moving into her own place had exhausted her both literally and figuratively. Even when she'd finally moved into the cute little cottage by Molly's school and unpacked the last box of kitchenwares, she was consumed by fatigue. Her therapist had warned her it would take months to feel like herself again. The truth was she was still waiting to. Then, over the spring, friends and co-workers began trying to set her up. It was innocent enough. A neighbor's single brother. A co-worker's cousin. All recommendations by people she knew and trusted. What was scary about that?

Everything, it turned out. Andi may have looked okay on the outside, but on the inside she was a ball of nerves. Most nights she'd awaken wondering if she'd set her alarm clock, turned off the stove, paid the electric bill. Silly things, but things nonetheless that fell squarely and solely on her shoulders now. She simply didn't have the energy or focus that dating would require. Then there was her sense of confidence. Sure, Andi knew she was smart. And accomplished. But was that enough? She thought of a divorced single mom she knew on her old street. Sheila Drake. Sheila had lost thirty pounds, began sporting a year-round tan, and highlighted her once-dark hair to the color of Beach Barbie. Not to mention the boob job Andi knew for sure she'd gotten. You could tell from across the street. When Andi looked in the mirror she saw crow's-feet by her brown eyes and stray gray hairs mixed among the dark. Her jeans didn't fit the way they used to, but worse, she didn't move the way she used to either. Gone was the spring in her step when she entered a room. The direct gaze. The easy laugh. Suddenly, Andi was unsure of everything, from whether she locked the front door at midnight to whether she'd spend the rest of her life alone. All of it left her overwhelmed. No, she was not ready to date.

But seeing Nate Becker made her wonder. Not about dating, because that was just silly. He lived in New York and she in Connecticut. They were both on the Cape for a matter of weeks. Nate was a bachelor with no kids. He had no clue what her life looked like or required of her, let alone what it would require of the man she might partner up with. But still. Nate made her wonder about small things. About what it would be like to kiss those full rhubarb-colored lips. Or to go for a walk on the beach together and slip her hand in his. To stay up all night talking, because suddenly that seemed like such an easy thing to do. Maybe her friends were right and she was finally ready. Or maybe it was all about Nate.

The light outside her curtains was not the gauzy early-morning light she was used to keeping company with; she checked her phone: 9:30! Andi sat up. She and Molly were sup-posed to go with Sydney to the florist to confirm centerpiece designs for the wedding. She hopped out of bed.

Across the hall, Molly was still sound asleep nestled beneath the covers. In sleep, it was the one time Molly still looked like a little girl, and Andi fought the urge to slip beneath the covers and cuddle with her. She pecked her quickly on the cheek, then roused her. "Time to get up, sleepyhead. We've got wedding things to do."

Downstairs the smell of coffee permeated the cottage kitchen, but aside from Sydney, the house was empty.

"Where is everyone?"

Sydney looked up from her phone. "Don't know. Haven't seen anyone yet today."

"That's strange." Andi poured herself coffee and joined her sister at the table. "This whole week is just . . ."

"A mess?"

Andi looked at Sydney. Her eyes were steel blue and her gaze so earnest, that Andi hoped her fiancé, James, saw the beauty on the inside as much as on the outside. "Yeah. But we've got a wedding to take care of that."

Syd smiled, but it wasn't convincing. "Not sure a wedding can rescue the family." She looked at Andi softly. "How're you doing?"

It was the first time the two were alone. Andi wasn't going to sugarcoat it. "Processing things. We've all been gobsmacked. Hugh and me, especially."

Sydney nodded. "I feel so bad for you guys."

Andi wasn't sure if she meant the fact that Charley was her father but not theirs, or the gift she'd been given of Riptide. "Well, you shouldn't feel bad. Hugh and I have to work through the stuff with Dad. We need to talk to him and to Mom, now that we've had a day to cool down. Before it drags on any longer."

"Do you want me to be a part of that conversation?" Sydney asked. "I'll do whatever you guys want. Say the word."

"No, not really. But you can help me with something else."

"Name it."

"I'm curious what your intentions are with Riptide."

And just like that, Andi could see her little sister start to close down. Sydney cleared her throat. "Like I said, I don't really feel comfortable talking about the house until James and I have a chance to. He doesn't get here until next week and even then, we both think it's best to wait until after the wedding."

"All right, I respect that. But that's a good two weeks out and this is sort of hanging over all of us right now like a dangling elephant."

Sydney smiled. "Dangling?"

"You know what I mean. It's in the room. It's huge. And this one is being dangled. Deadly, all around."

"Andi, you're asking me to do what I just said I wasn't comfortable with. I want to wait until after the wedding to even think about it."

Andi sipped her coffee and tried to slow her thoughts. She didn't mean to push. But the prospect of living under the same roof, that supposedly now belonged to Sydney, for the next two weeks while pretending nothing was bothering her seemed impossible. "Just tell me this. Did it occur to you that you should give the house to Mom and Dad?"

"Give it back? It was never theirs. It belonged to Grandma."

"Sure, up until now it did. But isn't that what we expected all along—that Mom and Dad would inherit the place from Tish when the time came? And it seems the most fair."

"I guess. But it's not like I gave it much thought."

"Well, maybe you should. It could solve a lot of problems."

"Problems? What are you thinking? That I'll take the key and lock the doors? That I won't share it with you guys like we always have?" Sydney's eyes flashed.

"No, of course not. But who knows. You might sell it."

"Why would I do that?"

"Let's face it, Syd. You're marrying James. This house will

become half his now. And James doesn't have the same ties to this place that we do."

"It doesn't mean he'd sell it. Or try to make me sell it."

"You don't know that. He may look at this entirely differently. It's a beach house in one of the most coveted spots on the New England coast. The taxes are probably high. It's a lot to manage a second place. He may not want to sell it, but I'm sure he'll at least think about it. He'd be stupid not to."

Sydney stood up. "And here we are talking about Riptide again."

"I'm sorry! But how would you feel if the roles were reversed?"

"Good question." Sydney leaned across the table. "Since you ask, what would you do, Andi? What if Riptide went to you instead of me?"

Andi had considered this, of course. At first, deep with envy, she'd fantasized that it had been her who'd gotten the house. Her own beach house! To enjoy with Molly forevermore. Or turn into an income property. Or both! And, in a less selfish moment, she'd wondered how she'd handle the family dynamics if that were true. "I'd talk to the family instead of acting like nothing happened. I'd ask them how they felt about it and what their wishes were. Not that I'd be bound to honor any of them, because the house would technically be mine, but fostering goodwill and extending some trust would be where I like to think I'd start."

"And I haven't done that?"

"Syd, you haven't done anything. Or said anything. Except about wedding plans."

"Because I'm getting married!" Sydney burst into tears and raced for the stairs.

Andi rested her head on the table and willed the words of

her marriage therapist into her mind. He hadn't been able to save her marriage, but there were a few takeaways she'd hung on to. Like a gratitude exercise she at first loathed, but now liked: "When things get tough, think of all the 'at leasts' you have going for you. Focus on gratitude for the positives." It was something Andi had initially rolled her eyes at, because it seemed so simple and yet was so hard to do. But now she tried.

At least Molly was still asleep and didn't overhear the argument.

At least Hugh hadn't been there. Would likely have been louder. And uglier.

At least George and his insipid girlfriend, Camilla, weren't coming that day for Molly.

At least she'd finally had a little bit of fun last night. Thanks to Nate.

Her mind screeched to a halt there. Nate Becker had given them all a night of reprieve; even though he had no idea what was going on with her family, they'd managed to get through one meal without a battle. Nate had been gracious, bearing oysters and wine. Steering their conversation to the safe harbor of their shared Cape Cod childhood summers. And he'd been funnier than she remembered. Much funnier, in fact. Andi appreciated a sense of humor; it showed intelligence and an ability to not take yourself too seriously. Two things she valued after the last ugly year of her divorce.

Not that her ex, George, was arrogant or dumb. But oh, the stupid things he'd done that year. Leaping into a new relationship straight out of the separation. Dragging all three of them into the craziness of his new "true life partner," Camilla. It was already so hard to navigate their new normal between two houses and shared custody and the growing pains of co-parenting. And here he was, throwing another person—with her own staunch set of ideas and expectations of her place—into the pot.

She looked at the clock: 10:15. There was still time to shower and rouse Molly again before the florist appointment, assuming Syd had calmed down and would still let them come with her. At least she wouldn't say no to Molly. There—another "at least"!

"So how did the roses smell?" It was midday, the florist appointment safely behind them, but from the looks of it Hugh was still nursing a hangover from the night before. He was one with his beach chair, legs akimbo, one arm draped across his forehead. The other held a giant Yeti tumbler of something iced.

Andi bent and sniffed the lid. "That is water, yes?"

"Shut up."

Andi smiled. "Just checking." She plopped her beach chair in the sand between Hugh and Martin. The beach was busy, the flawless weather pulling the tourists from their vacation rentals. "The flowers had no scent. Syd went with hydrangea centerpieces, not roses."

Martin nodded approvingly. "Hydrangeas. Very coastal New England."

Hugh frowned. "Where is the bride-to-be? I'd look, but my head hurts too much to lift."

"Safely ensconced in her room talking to James about the bouquets and arrangements we chose."

"Poor bastard." Hugh lowered his sunglasses. "Though he does have a new beach house to console him."

Martin stood and peeled off his shirt. "You two are awful. I'm going for a swim. Anyone want to come?"

The twins shook their head in unison.

"Martin's right. You're going to have to stop doing that," Andi told Hugh. "I had a conversation with her this morning about it and it did not go well."

Hugh lowered his shades. "Oh? Well, my morning wasn't so swell either. Between packing all my childhood belongings from the family beach house to make room for James's crap and searching the internet for my real father, am I supposed to feel bad for her?"

Andi glared at him. She knew the former was a joke, but she wasn't so sure about the latter. "Are you seriously looking for our birth father?"

"No. Not really. But I think we should. Don't you?"

Andi did not. "No. Dad is our dad, just as he said. He's been there since the beginning. And let's remember, our so-called real father has wanted nothing to do with us. He knows we exist and yet he's never once reached out."

"So you're not even curious?"

"Maybe a little curious, but what's the point?" Andi meant what she said. As curious as she might be about any traits she might share with this mysterious new person in their life, the truth was he was not part of their lives. Never had been. She turned to Hugh. "I think you're just mad at Mom and Dad. And you're allowed to be. But searching for this guy, Robert, right now? Makes no sense to me."

Hugh listened quietly until she was done. "I'm not saying I want to go on a Boy Scout campout with the guy and make up for lost time. In fact, I don't care to meet him, based on how he treated Mom. But that's just it—what little we know is according to what Mom shared. There are two sides to every story."

"Two sides to what story?"

They turned in unison as Sydney lowered her beach bag onto the sand and herself into Martin's beach chair. Instantly, Andi feared what she may have heard, but Syd was smiling, so all appeared safe.

"Hey," Hugh said. "I heard the flowers went well."

"Yeah, they went." She reached for his bottle of water. "I miss James. I wish he was here to help too."

Andi threw up her hands. "Am I chopped liver? I thought we had fun!"

"We did." She gazed out at the water.

"Just an FYI, that's Martin's chair," Hugh warned. "You know how he is about his chair."

"Well, I didn't feel like lugging one down. Do you guys have snacks?"

Hugh looked at Andi.

"We were just talking about what Mom said about our birth father. How he knows about us. And yet . . ."

Sydney bit her lip. "Are you thinking about reaching out to him?"

"Maybe," Hugh allowed. "I'm curious."

"I would be too." Sydney leaned back in the chair and began applying Hugh's sunscreen.

"That stuff is expensive, but help yourself."

"What?"

"Nothing." Hugh shook his head. "You're just a bit empty-handed, is all. What's the point of that giant beach bag if you don't have sunscreen, snacks, or water. You could fit Australia in it." He poked the bag with his sandy foot.

Nonplussed, Sydney reached into her tote and pulled out a

stack of wedding magazines. "It's only natural to wonder about your biological father. You could look him up if you really wanted to."

"Yes, but that has huge implications," Andi reminded them both. "Which is why I'd like to steer clear of this, at least for now. I have no expectations of this person. I'm a grown-up. And I've got enough grown-up problems of my own to deal with right now. I'm busy."

Hugh smirked. "*So busy*. Divorce. Ex-husband. Teenage daughter. Oh, and Camilla the Gorilla. When does her primate majesty arrive?"

This is what Andi loved most about her twin. "In three days," she said, grateful for Hugh's indulgence. "And when she does, we are going to keep our mouths closed and smile politely. For Molly."

"Right. For Molly. But the second they pull out of the driveway . . ."

"Fair game." Actually, Andi was counting on that. Her family had made her laugh through the hard stuff, Hugh especially. Being with them as Molly drove away with George and his crazy new girlfriend was the one thing she hoped would get her through it. Assuming they hadn't all killed one another by then.

If getting through her divorce had been hard, Camilla had brought a second wave of upset to the past year. The first wave had brought the sort of things Andi expected: guilt for the breakup of the family, lying awake at night worrying about making the mortgage payment, consternation when her (married) friends all went out to dinner and she was left out because "we didn't want to make you feel like a third wheel, you know?" No. Andi did not know. She could never have anticipated how difficult it would be to unwrap her identity from that of her marriage. They were no longer George and Andi. She was just Andi.

Until Camilla came on the scene.

Camilla, George's first and only girlfriend since the divorce, had seized upon him with swift force, wedging herself into the family fold with surgical precision. Camilla, who initially presented as professionally coiffed, but has since revealed herself to be personally unhinged. Camilla, who had declared herself George's "true life partner," and insisted everyone else refer to them as such. A term that Andi had plenty of questions about, but did not waste her time asking. It didn't matter, but it did give Hugh lots of material to work with when Camilla the Gorilla came up, which occurred in equal measures of frequency and delight when wine was plentiful and Molly out of earshot. In a matter of days the two would be vacationing with Molly in nearby Martha's Vineyard and Andi had to come to terms with that. But she didn't have to like it.

"I'm not thrilled about Molly going away with George and this woman. I'll need you guys to distract me."

"Speaking of distractions. Can we talk about Mr. Becker?" Hugh turned in his beach chair and leaned in obnoxiously close.

"Careful. Your hangover." She tapped her head for emphasis.

"Worth it. Now talk. Someone was all dressed up and happy last night. And that's not the sister who arrived on the doorstep a couple days ago."

Andi did not want to discuss this right now. She focused instead on Martin jogging up the beach, dripping wet. "How's the water?"

"You should all get in. It's so refreshing. Perfect temperature today." Martin did this every year. Swam while they sat. Cooked while they ate. He embraced vacation while they deigned to survive it. Andi smiled up at him.

"I don't believe you. That water was frigid yesterday," Hugh said. "But there's hot stuff in conversation."

"Oh?" Martin toweled off and gave Sydney a playful tap on the shin with his big toe. "Out of my chair, dear one."

"Okay, okay." She made a face and was slow to get up. But she did eventually. "Does anyone have a towel?"

Andi threw one at her. "We love you, but you're unreal."

"So what's the hot topic?" Martin asked, reclaiming his chair.

"Nate Becker," Sydney sang. "The super-cute one."

"Oh! Says the soon-to-be-married Syd. Does the newly single Miss Andi agree?" Martin winked. Andi stuck out her tongue.

"You guys are insufferable." But she relented. "Yes, I guess it was good to see Nate."

Hugh pursed his lips. "Good to see him or good to gawk at him?"

"Yes, Hugh. He's good-looking. And funny. So I enjoyed myself. Is that not allowed?"

"On the Darling family vacation? No. None of that is allowed." Hugh studied her a moment. "But seriously, you two had a little chemistry. Yes?"

Andi shrugged. The last thing she needed was her nosy family getting involved in what little shred of a private life she might patch together. "Like I said, it was nice to see him."

"Uh-huh. Okay, that's how we're going to be." Hugh leaned back in his beach chair and closed his eyes. "I'll be watching. Just remember, when your ex-husband shows up with Camilla the Gorilla, you could have that too."

"Excuse me?"

"Well, no one's suggesting you go ape." Hugh snickered to himself. "That one Instagram photo you showed me. . . . But that aside, George is dating. He's out there again. And yes, it's too soon. And yes, he's an ass about it. But it wouldn't hurt you to have a little fun yourself."

It was what Andi's friends at home had been telling her all year. And what her therapist echoed. And their mother, last they'd spoken, had also hinted at. Maybe Andi should think about getting back out there. Even if the idea simultaneously electrified her and filled her with dread.

Andi groaned. "Okay, that's enough about my private life. Let's talk more about our biological father. Please."

Hugh threw her a look, which only made her lean back into her beach chair in a fit of giggles. It was the first time the three siblings had actually enjoyed each other in any kind of organic way since they'd arrived. Maybe there was hope for the family vacation. Maybe they'd all make it through the wedding, after all. She was about to say as much when Hugh cleared his throat.

"Just so everyone is clear, do you all know Tish is still in town?"

Andi felt the wind go out of her sails. "Dad mentioned that. They talked on the phone, I think."

"Yeah, well, I'm sure it was unpleasant. Mom wants to end her."

"Can you blame her?" Martin asked. "That was pretty ballsy of your grandmother, even for her."

"I'm wondering if we should go see her."

It had occurred to Andi too. But she was still raw from Tish's revelation. "You think she'll change her mind?" She glanced at Sydney warily as she said it.

"No. But I want to know why. What have we ever done to her?

I mean, was she really that concerned that you and I would take over her family inheritance somehow? It's just all so bizarre."

"And unkind," Sydney allowed.

"Yeah. She's pretty much rejected us."

Andi shook her head. "I don't know that it was spiteful. I think she's getting old, and she's probably thinking more about her estate. Her legacy."

"And pushing us out of it?"

Andi looked at Hugh sympathetically. "Who knows if we were ever really in it."

"Older people do some crazy things as they age," Martin interjected. "Tish has always been extravagant. Maybe she's afraid of losing it."

Hugh scoffed. "Her marbles or her money?" He turned to Andi. "She always treated us differently. Always. Remember?"

Andi thought back. Tish had seemed to favor Sydney, for sure. But she'd assumed it was because she was the baby of the family. "Maybe a bit. But we didn't see her that much. She never really let any of us get close to her."

"A bit?" Hugh said. "She was so obvious about it. Mom used to get visibly upset." It was true. Andi recalled her mother biting her lip or cutting visits short. The strained look on her face when it came time for presents to be given out.

"Syd, do you remember any of that?" Hugh asked.

Sydney had been listening quietly and Andi wondered how it made her feel. "Not really. I thought she was different than other grandmas, compared to my friends. She didn't visit much. Wasn't exactly the hugging kind. But I thought she was generous when she was around."

Hugh kicked at the sand with his toe. "To you, maybe." He looked at Andi. "Remember the split checks? Every Christmas and birthday!"

Andi cringed. She'd forgotten all about that. "Now I do."

"What're you talking about?" Sydney asked.

"Nothing," Hugh quipped. "Just the pattern of imbalance."

It was clear Sydney didn't get it, but Andi empathized. How could she? "When we were little, Tish used to send us checks instead of presents."

"Oh, yeah! All I wanted was a doll. Mom would take the checks to the bank and straight into the college fund they'd go." She rolled over onto her side. "Who gives a little kid a check?"

Hugh shook his head. "No, it wasn't that."

"What, then?"

"It had more to do with the amounts."

Sydney frowned.

"You were little," Andi explained. She looked to Hugh, re-membering.

Each year Tish sent the family a card and inside would be two checks. One check made to Hugh and Andi. And one to Sydney. "They were fifty-dollar checks."

Hugh raised an eyebrow. "You do remember. Only it wasn't really fifty dollars, was it?"

Sydney was looking between them. "How much was it?"

Hugh inhaled, his eyes still fixed on Andi. "You got fifty dollars. Andi and I got fifty to split."

"Seriously? As in, you ended up with just twenty-five each?"

Hugh nodded gravely. "And then your checks got bigger as we all got older. But ours didn't really."

Andi could tell from the look on Sydney's face that this was all news to her. News that made her feel awful. "Syd, this is on Tish. Not you."

"I know, but . . ."

"And then there was the year of the car," Hugh reminded them.

"She didn't exactly get me a car."

"No, but she gave you something like three grand so you could get one. And after pestering Mom and Dad, you did."

"Okay, I think we've covered all the bases," Andi interjected. "Can we switch the subject before everyone starts fighting again? Let's go up to the house for lunch."

No one budged.

"I'd always wondered why she didn't seem to like me as much," Hugh said. "What I might have done wrong. That's pretty crappy to make a kid feel like that." He looked at Andi and shrugged. "Now we know why Tish treated us like we weren't really family."

Sydney heaved herself to her feet. "No, I hate to think of Tish like that. We've got so few memories with her as it is and she's older now. I think I've heard enough."

Hugh watched her grab her bag and collect her things. "It doesn't mean it isn't true."

"I'll tell you what it is. Mean. It implies she favored me."

"She did!" Hugh cried. "Because you were blood."

Sydney snatched a towel and hastily brushed the sand off her legs. "Why do you always have to be so negative, Hugh? She gave us a lot over the years. I recall you getting a car."

"Yeah, from Mom and Dad! Which I shared with Andi."

"You two were twins! Two new cars at the same time is a

bit spoiled, isn't it?" Sydney shook the towel hard one last time, covering them all with a hot layer of sand.

"Hey!" Hugh swiped at his mouth, spitting. "Jesus. Everyone in this family is rainbows and unicorns. No one likes to hear the truth."

But Andi was done too. "Hugh, I think we've dredged up enough."

Hugh turned to her. "Really, Andi? I expect this kind of cluelessness from Syd, but not from you."

She spun around to face him. "Cluelessness?"

"Don't you remember the year I came out to the family? Do you have any idea how hard that was?"

Andi did. It was their senior year of high school. Hugh had been so miserable that year. Quiet. Detached. Brooding. Their parents had been worried he was depressed or drinking or worse, but when they tried to talk to him about it he refused.

"Part of the reason I was so scared to come out was because I knew something was off. I had always felt it. That I was different. That somehow I was less loved."

"Than me?" Andi sputtered.

"Yes, even you. I was gay in a straight neighborhood, a kid hardly sure of himself, let alone his sexuality. All I knew was that I felt different from everyone." He paused. "So finding out now that we weren't really Dad's kids has thrown me back in time to some pretty ugly days. Days I don't care to revisit!" He was starting to shout now and Martin reached for his arm.

"Honey, let's go." He pulled Hugh up to his feet. "It's okay."

But it wasn't okay. Andi felt hollowed out by the things Hugh was throwing at all of them. By the realization of how he'd been made to feel and the horrible fact that, in the vacuum of the truth, he'd blamed himself all those years ago. "Hugh, I'm sorry," she cried.

"You can't tell me you didn't feel it too! I know you did. I felt it. *I was different.*"

Tears pricked the corners of Andi's eyes. Because what Hugh was insinuating was something awful. And because, maybe, buried somewhere deep, she did remember something.

"You don't remember Mom and Dad fighting at times? About how Tish treated us so differently from Sydney? About how small she made Mom and the two of us feel?"

"I don't know," Andi cried. "Maybe some of it?"

"Don't be so naïve, Andi. You of all people should know better. You're my twin."

Andi leapt to her feet. "Screw you, Hugh."

Tears spilling, she spun away from him and across the scorching hot sand to the beach trail. It was one thing to delve into the bomb their grandmother had dropped on them. But to try to connect that to the pain of his coming out all those years ago? To suggest this secret may have caused unnecessary hurt, even back then? Even for Hugh, it was too much. One had nothing to do with the other.

Andi pounded up the beach trail, putting quick distance between herself and the rest of them. Her feet burned with each step, but she barely noticed. She was livid with Hugh. With the ugly questions he was asking.

But most of all, she realized, gasping for breath at the head of the trail, with herself. For not asking them sooner.

Tish

She supposes a late-morning tea service will buoy her spirits. Charley has called asking for a meeting. It will not change her mind, but it will give her a chance to lay eyes on her boy, and for that reason alone she agrees to it.

The front desk has secured a car for her. At first, the young girl at the reception desk (Tish could tell she was young; far too much hope and cheer in that tone) tried to suggest she take the trolley into town. Tish laughed. She has seen those trolley cars—jaunty little reproductions and quite well done, she might add. But they are open air and she imagines quite bumpy, and they are crammed full of other resort guests. Tish does not comingle. What tickles her most is the assumption by this hopeful young girl at the main desk that Tish is young enough to manage the walk up to the trolley car stand. The wait in the sun. The act of riding it about town and waiting for its return. That assumption of her youth is nice and makes her smile momentarily. It then occurs to Tish that maybe some of that girl's chipperness has worn off on her; she'd best be careful.

As her car rolls down Main Street, Tish gazes out the window at all the tourists doing their touristy things. Downtown

Chatham's bustle is what appeals to so many. Not to her. The village boutiques are bright and cheery: window boxes teeming with flowers, shops filled with coastal goods, gaily-colored awnings abundant. It is the Americana summer postcard scene by definition.

"Shall I stop somewhere special for you, ma'am?" the driver asks. His voice is rich and deep, reassuring to Tish.

"Drive on," she tells him. Her destination does not lie in this pastel haven.

They pass Where the Sidewalk Ends Bookstore, which Charley always recommends. Then they pass Tale of the Cod, which opened shortly after she and Morty bought Riptide and where she could always count on finding an elegant hostess gift. Outside Buffy's Ice Cream shop, a line has already formed on the sidewalk. It's far too early in the morning for ice cream. When the driver pauses for pedestrians to cross, which he has to do often—*heavens, these crowds!*—she squints at the window display in a gallery. There is a large painted canvas of a couple walking to the ocean, their little boy running ahead. The couple is holding hands. Tish's heart skips. Before she looks away, she wonders if either of them knows their time together is not guaranteed.

When they finally arrive at the rotary, Tish directs the driver south on Route 28 and on to Yarmouth. The drive will take them about twenty minutes, but to Tish time is of little concern these days. She is glad to be out and about on a sunny summer day. Her suite at Chatham Bars Inn is lovely, the service impeccable. But she is feeling stifled by all the thoughts in her head and all the personal history shadowing her now that she's back on the Cape. It's good to have a diversion.

The Captain Farris House tearoom is where she has chosen to meet Charley. As her driver pulls up to the stately inn, she can see her son is already waiting for her on the porch. The driver opens the backseat door and helps her out, just as Charley swoops up to take her hand.

"Thank you," she tells them both. Tish is a feminist right down to the marrow of her bones, but she will never understand this new brand of thinking that women should insist on opening doors for themselves.

The tearoom is swathed in late-morning light and Tish blinks as she follows the host to their table by a bank of windows. She orders the Windsor tea service: Earl Grey, scones with raspberry jam and clotted cream, cucumber and salmon tea sandwiches. As they wait, Charley sits stoically and bears small talk. She has raised him well. He knows to wait to get to the meat of the matter.

"Have a scone," she tells him. They are still warm and buttery. Once more, Tish is surprised by her appetite. She does not nibble but eats the small pastry in its entirety. Then helps herself to a tea sandwich. The cucumber is crisp. As she sips her tea she contemplates the salmon. To her dismay, Charley has only had a bite of his scone.

"Have I ever told you the story about the first dinner party I was invited to at your paternal grandparents' house?"

Charley perks up a bit. He has always loved stories about his late father.

"Your grandmother did not exactly invite me, your father did. We were newly engaged and terribly in love with the notion of it. Your father wanted me to meet everyone he knew. I felt like I was on tour!" She laughs softly at the memory. "We both went to Columbia, so when he introduced me to his school friends the playing field was what you might call even." She studies his expression to see if he follows. "The same could not be said when your father took me to Sag Harbor."

They had just graduated, and Tish already had two nursing position interviews in the city. She was still living with her parents in the family apartment, but not for long. Soon she would have her own job and income and get her own place with her husband. The wedding was not until that winter, but already Morty was keeping an eye out for the perfect apartment. Tish was on top of the world. Her new life would be so different.

She had first met Morty's parents in the city at a restaurant downtown. And then she'd seen them again at a dinner party at their place near Central Park. Both times Tish had felt overwhelmed. Morty's mother, Matilda, was impeccably dressed. She had a penchant for beautifully tailored suits of nondescript color, further elevated with furs and fine jewelry. What was most imposing was her carriage. Matilda maintained an erect posture and staid expression that Tish found difficult to read and impossible to emulate.

Unlike her own mother, who was expressive and vocal—yelling for children to come to dinner, breaking up sibling squabbles, assigning chores—Matilda spoke softly and addressed Tish minimally. Her greetings were swift and formal; an unnerving sweep of her gaze from Tish's hair down to her sensible shoes, followed by the same tight smile. Then the abrupt dismissal, as Matilda turned her attention, often lavishly, to whomever else was nearby. Their interactions never extended beyond formalities, despite Tish's best efforts to make a connection. In Matilda Darling's presence Tish couldn't help but feel guileless and awkward. Their stately homes and worldly lifestyle did not help. Tish was a fish out of water.

"Your grandparents hosted an annual lawn party at their Sag Harbor house over Memorial Day weekend. Do you remember it?"

"I think so," Charley said, his eyes brightening. "I remember sailing at a club one summer. Didn't Grandpa take us out on his boat?"

Tish nodded. "We only went to that party a couple of times. Once you came along your dad preferred to spend his summers here, on the Cape. Just us." She'd never told Charley why. Perhaps it was time.

"That first summer your father brought me to Sag Harbor, I was fresh out of college and feeling my oats. Remember, I was the first of my family to get my degree. And the only girl to go. It was a pretty big deal."

"Columbia, no less."

Tish shrugged. "It was a nursing program of all-female students. A very different time. But still, I was feeling like an adult in charge of my own future. I was very happy that summer as we headed to Sag Harbor.

"When we arrived, the party was in full swing. Your grandparents' place was right on the water. Very elegant. Fully staffed. I had never been before and I remember being quite taken by the setting, let alone the kind of people who attended."

Sag Harbor was a mere two-hour drive from the city, but it was a world away to Tish. Out in the green expanse of the Hamptons, Tish had never imagined the magnitude of the houses, the scope of the sea. No sooner had Morty parked in the horseshoe-shaped pea-gravel drive did a valet sweep in to take the car.

As they rounded the shingled house to the rear, Tish's breath escaped her. In the center of the emerald lawn loomed a white tent housing linen-covered tables and gold chairs, servers in uniform, twinkling lights. There was a jazz band playing on a stage. And a croquet green where men in straw hats and women in tea dresses laughed and sipped champagne. And everywhere, clusters of guests dressed in summer whites and seersucker. But beyond all of that was what captured Tish's attention.

"Come, there are family friends I want you to meet," Morty said, pulling her by the hand toward the house.

"Wait," Tish said, gently breaking free. She had to see it up close.

Morty watched as she crossed the lawn, stepping around guests as she went. Past the tent where real chandeliers sparkled from its peaks. To the edge of the yard to the seawall. There, atop the stone wall, the wind whipped at the edges of her dress and the surf drowned out the tinkling sound of the jazz band. Tish looked left and right at the endless blue stretch. How could such a heavenly enclave exist so close to the gray streets and wilted buildings she'd grown up among?

Until then, the only summer spot she'd been to had been Coney Island, where her parents brought them on the rare day off work. And once, Rockaway Beach, where she went with her nursing friends. Tish's parents had not taken the family on vacations. They had jobs to work, mouths to feed. The very notion of a vacation was absurd.

Standing in the backyard that day staring out at the Atlantic Ocean, Tish had felt both an overwhelming sense of awe and smallness in the world. She had no idea it would be nothing compared to the smallness she would later feel in the house behind her.

"That weekend changed my life." Among all that beauty and decadence, there had been ugliness.

Whatever Morty had seen in her that fateful day at the Columbia football game, his parents never would. Not when she'd given them a grandson; an heir to the family. And not later, when Morty was unthinkably stolen from them and she and Charley were all that was left. Now she looked at Charley, whose expression was earnest. He wanted to hear more.

Morty had done as he promised that Memorial Day weekend and lovingly presented his bride-to-be to all of his family friends. Never once letting go of Tish's hand, he led her from group to group and table to table of well-heeled guests curious about the young woman Morty Darling had so suddenly proposed to. They had never before heard of her. O'Malley was not a name within their circles.

Tish was unprepared.

"Where is your family from?"

"What does your father do?"

"Where do you usually summer?"

The mouthwatering lobster was difficult to choke down in the midst of such inquiries. The champagne soured in her stomach. Tish could tell by their reactions, however polite, that they were disappointed. And worse, suspicious. But the worst was to come. Sprinkled among the generation of Morty's parents' guests was her own generation, the now young adults Morty had grown up with each summer in the Hamptons. Played tennis with at the club. Raced against in regattas. Been expected to keep company with, when he proposed. And there was one among them, in particular, who his family had not given up on.

It was Matilda who delivered her. Tish and Morty were standing by a table of desserts when they heard his mother approach.

"Look who I found! And she tells me you haven't even said hello to her yet."

"Our dear Rebecca" was the first clue. The elated look on Matilda's face as she escorted Rebecca to them was the other.

Rebecca Whitmore's glowing smile was for Morty alone. Tish stepped back as Rebecca threw her tanned arms around her fiancé's neck and squealed.

"Rebecca is a dear family friend," Matilda said, as if that explained the effusive greeting, though to whom it wasn't clear. What was clear was she represented far more to Matilda.

What made Tish more uncomfortable than the deliberate show of affection was that Morty did not seem to mind. "Rebecca!" he said, his smile almost as wide as hers. "How long has it been?"

Rebecca demurred. "Who can say? You missed the Christmas party last year. And New Year's." Her tone was both chiding and teasing and Tish read right into it. Morty had spent both of those holidays with her.

As if suddenly returning to his senses, Morty turned to her. "You remember me telling you about the Whitmores?"

Tish forced a smile and extended a hand. While she may have recalled the Whitmores being mentioned, she certainly did not recall a young blonde of exquisite attractiveness being in the mix.

"Pleased to meet you. Tish O'Malley." Then added, "Morty's fiancée." Which, to her consternation, Morty had failed to do.

"Hello." Rebecca gave her a quick once-over, then redirected her focus immediately. "Morty, I hear you're staying in the city, now that Columbia is done with you! How I wish I could say the same for Harvard." She sighed. "One more year!"

So she was not just smart, but younger.

"You two used to be thick as thieves!" Matilda said adoringly. "You really ought to catch up. Rebecca, tell Morty about your trip to Spain."

"Spain!" Morty said it as though he'd never heard of the place.

"I just got home yesterday," Rebecca went on. "But you know my mother. Straight to the club for a tennis match!" She paused to take a breath. "Do you still play? You were so good!"

Tish had not even known Morty played tennis.

Morty lifted a bashful shoulder. "Not very much anymore."

At the mention of it, Matilda bubbled like a champagne bottle about to uncork. "Remember when you two were doubles partners? Rebecca, dear, you really should take Morty to the club for a game before he goes back to the city. How about tomorrow?"

"Mother, Tish will be here."

They all turned as if suddenly remembering her.

Matilda feigned surprise. "Oh. You're staying for the whole weekend?"

Morty threw Tish an apologetic look. "I believe I mentioned that, Mother. A few times."

"Do you play?" Rebecca interjected brightly.

Tish shook her head. "I don't."

"Do you sail?"

"Not really."

Rebecca's bright expression dimmed. "Oh." But then she grabbed Morty's hand. "Remember that time we stole the dinghies and took them out into the sound? We got in so much trouble!"

Matilda clapped her hands. "Trouble! I seem to recall your father rescuing both of you. The club was not happy. We thought they'd revoke our memberships."

Tish forced a smile as they all laughed uproariously at the memory.

And then Matilda did something she had never done before. She took Tish's hand in her own. "Let's go get you some of that wonderful lemonade. We wouldn't want to bore you while these two catch up. It will probably take a while."

Tish felt a wave of outrage course through her. It was the only time Matilda Darling had ever addressed her personally, and while she could not refuse the invitation, she knew it had nothing to do with the lemonade.

As Matilda led her away, Tish glanced back. Rebecca was chatting away, that giant, stupid smile still plastered on her glowing face.

"You'll have to forgive Morty," Matilda said. "He and Rebecca go back a long way. You know how first loves never quite leave you." She handed Tish an ice-cold glass of lemonade, her eyes steely as she said it.

So they *had* been a couple. Morty had never mentioned that fact either.

"Morty is a gentleman," Tish concurred.

"You should've seen them! Inseparable, those two." Matilda cocked her head and gazed dreamily past Tish. "So many memories together."

Tish followed her gaze, turning just in time to see Rebecca reach for the sleeve of Morty's linen jacket. She tipped her head back laughing, as though whatever he'd said was the funniest thing she ever did hear. Tish waited for her to remove her hand. Rebecca did not.

"If you'll excuse me, I need to freshen up in the ladies' room."

Matilda barely registered. "Of course. In the main hall, just past the conservatory."

Tish could not escape fast enough. As she climbed the granite steps up to the main patio, she cursed herself for feeling so small. Rebecca Whitmore was just a girl. But that wasn't the whole truth. She was an Ivy girl. With almond-colored skin and perfect white teeth and a golden mane of hair. From a moneyed family who belonged to the same clubs and pedigreed circles. Everything Matilda Darling could dream of in a daughter-in-law.

Tish stumbled through the large French doors. Even in her state, she had the sense to halt and take it all in. The marble floors echoed beneath her square-heeled shoes. Her eyes traveled to the sweeping ceilings, the silk drapery, the imposing oil portraits on the walls. A single jade velvet settee and two gilded armchairs flanked a baby grand piano. Austere in its formality, Tish could feel Matilda's touch on every surface.

Standing in the bathroom, Tish splashed her flushed cheeks with cold water and stared into the blue eyes looking back at her. Her dark hair was pinned back and curled, her eyelet dress perhaps not as striking as the rest of them, but the determination in her gaze was unrivaled. These were not her people and tonight she felt with certainty she was not theirs. But if she wished for a life with Morty, concessions would have to be made. She straightened in the mirror.

"When I came out of that bathroom, your father was waiting for me," she tells Charley now. While she has spoken, Charley has eaten the rest of his scone and three tea sandwiches. She orders another tray.

"What did he say?" Charley asks. "Please tell me he stuck up for you."

Tish is grateful for this remark. Perhaps the beginning of an understanding between them is finally being laid. "It's your father we're talking about. Of course he did."

What Morty did was take Tish's hands in his own and press his lips to hers. "You are the most beautiful woman here. And likely the smartest of all. Don't let anyone make you feel any different, you hear?"

Then he led her outside and down the steps and right to the middle of the dance floor. "Just a moment, my love." An East Coast swing was just wrapping up as Charley approached the stage. He nodded to the band leader, who tipped his ear. A moment later, Charley returned and took Tish's hand again. The band started up, and to Tish's delight the lead singer began crooning Tony Bennett's "Because of You." Morty pulled her in so tight Tish's breath escaped her, but in his arms so too did all the doubt and frustrations she'd been feeling. As they circled the dance floor together, slowly, Tish could feel eyes upon them.

"Let them look," Morty whispered in her ear, as if reading her mind. "Let them see what we have."

Now sitting across the table from Charley at the Captain Farris House tearoom, Tish recalls the elation of that moment. "Your father saw in me what his own family could not."

Charley sits back in his chair, an unreadable expression on his face. She'd thought this story would help him understand. But instead, he looks pained.

"What is it?" she asks.

"Mother, you must realize the irony of what you're saying."

She does not.

"The way Dad's family treated you. Do you not realize it's exactly how you've treated Cora all these years?"

"Ridiculous!" A plume of frustration rises within her. Clearly, Charley has not heard a word of what she's been saying. The sacrifices she's made; the rationale for her gifting the house to Sydney. "You were on a carefully crafted path to an Ivy education. To practicing medicine! To steering clear of all the Darling family expectations and forging your own way. And you gave all of it up because of her *situation*!"

Charley shakes his head. "Mother, that choice was mine. And though I'm sorry it disappointed you, it was the best choice I've made. I enjoyed working for the family foundation and later I loved my career in teaching. But most of all, I love the family Cora and I have made." This last part he emphasizes with a firmness of tone she is not used to.

Tish sets her teacup down. She is not prepared for this rebuttal from her only child. His accusations are simply not true. "Charley, please. Unlike what your grandparents did to me, I have never objected to Cora's background. What I objected to is that Cora took advantage of you. She saw a young man of means. Poised for a bright future. While she was on a path of ruin."

Charley pushes his plate away, his eyes filling with what Tish recognizes as sadness. She had wanted him to understand. But somehow she's made things worse.

She cannot give up now. "You must listen, dear. I have only ever tried to protect you. From your grandparents' rigid expectations. From a life that would have made you dependent on them. That's why I wanted you to go away to Yale. Have a good career. Be your own person and lead your own life, unlike what happened to me." Does he not see all that she did? If she cannot make him understand this, then all of it has been for naught.

To her great relief Charley reaches across the table. "Mother, I hear the sacrifices you had to make back then. But it's not like that now. You don't need to protect Riptide or me from anything or anyone. Certainly not from Cora or Andi and Hugh. They *are* family. And if you'd just let them in, you'd see that."

She does not have the heart to tell him why she cannot let Cora in. Because the truth is, Charley has always loved Cora. Tish knew it from the first time she saw them together at Charley's ill-fated graduation. The problem was, Cora had *not* loved him.

Not in the way her beautiful, wonderful son deserved to be loved. Not in the way Morty had loved her and she him. It was one thing to miss out on Yale and a career in medicine. It was another, entirely, to miss out on requited love.

If he has not figured this out by now, she does not want to break his heart. Instead, she tells him this: "Riptide was the last place your father, you, and I were together. It was our haven. That's why I'm leaving it to Sydney. To preserve a little bit of that. To honor it."

"That doesn't mean it has to go to Sydney, Mom. This could divide our whole family. I know that's not what you want."

Family. It is what binds them and yet it is the one thing they cannot seem to agree on. "Family is blood, Charley." Cora may have lured her son away, may have convinced him to take on her children and care for all of them years ago. But it does not mean Tish has to hand over Riptide to her too. Cora can't possibly appreciate what Riptide meant to her, to Morty. It's all that's left in the Darling trust and, as such, Tish wants it to stay in the Darling family.

With nothing more to say, Tish steers her gaze across the tearoom. She sighs heavily, her breath an audible wheeze. The hard truths of their conversation have exhausted her.

Her son is an intelligent man, a good husband and father. Is it possible they are fighting for the same thing? It's exasperating. She'd hoped today would clear the air between them, but apparently that will take more time. Something she does not have a lot of left.

Cora

"One more week until the wedding!" Sydney bounded down the stairs like she used to as a teenager and they all looked up from their various posts in the kitchen.

"Cool. And my dad arrives tomorrow," Molly echoed. "He's coming to take me to the Vineyard."

Cora noticed Hugh and Andi exchange one of their twin looks, though Cora wasn't sure if it was about the wedding or Andi's ex. "That's wonderful, Syd. When does James arrive?"

Sydney was all smiles, barely able to contain herself. "He's been working on this huge project, but he'll be here two days beforehand to help with final details. And hopefully relax!"

"It'll be good to see him," Hugh said. Cora had to wonder how much her son meant that. They all liked James immensely, always had, but the sudden giving away of Riptide had sent ripples through the family that Cora knew were not finished. In fact, she fully expected a squall to blow through before it was done with them. James's arrival would inspire a slew of questions that she knew Sydney did not want to entertain. Tish had done a number on them. She returned her attention back to the honeydew melon she was slicing to take down to the beach. If only they could all just get through the wedding.

"While he's here I want to wrap up the wedding plans." Sydney looked at her siblings. "Which should relieve you of most of your duties. Be happy."

Andi reached around Cora and popped a piece of melon into her mouth. "Does that mean he'll do my dress fitting for me? Since I've arrived, all I've done is eat. I'm worried it'll need to be let out."

"Very funny," Syd said. "That's still on for three o'clock today. You girls good with that?"

Molly was good with all of it, which Cora adored watching. She perked up at the mention of the bridal boutique. "Ooh, Aunt Syd, can we look at floral headpieces or tiaras while we're there? I saw this picture on Instagram of a bridesmaid's headband. It looked *so* pretty. You *have* to see it."

As she whipped her phone out of her back pocket, Hugh elbowed her. "Aren't you a flower girl?"

Molly screwed up her face. "Junior *bridesmaid*. Oh, my God. I'm not a kid." As Hugh held up his hands, Molly turned her focus right back to her aunt. "So, Aunt Syd, can we look at headpieces? I want to look my best."

Andi smirked. "Because, let's be honest, Aunt Syd's wedding is really your day." Which made everyone chuckle because it clearly wasn't inaccurate.

"What about me?" Hugh complained, leaning over Molly's shoulder to peek at her Instagram account. "Do I get a headpiece?" He turned to Martin. "You want one, right?"

"Definitely."

Undeterred, Molly ignored them all and continued scrolling through pictures. "Anyway, Aunt Syd, here's an example with rhinestones. Oh, and here's one with daisies. Wouldn't that look so good with my dress color?"

Cora laughed. For as much complaining as people did about teenagers, Molly had been nothing but a bright light and comic relief for all of them. Like now. Now they were actually interacting.

"I'm heading to the beach," Cora announced. "It's a beautiful day and there's plenty of time before the dress fitting. Who's coming?"

As she looked from face to face, their eyes slid away from her own. Andi's to Molly. Hugh's to his phone. Even Martin, who busied himself with the fruit bowl. "Martin, put the plum down." That got everyone to look up again. "Did you all hear me? We are going to the beach."

"Well, I have a work call . . ." Hugh began.

"And I have wedding stuff to do," Sydney added.

Andi was about to open her mouth when Cora picked up the cleaver she'd been using and whacked it down into the other half of the honeydew melon. "I'm packing food. You go get into your suits. We're going, and we're going to have fun, dammit."

All three of her kids stared speechlessly at her.

Only Molly spoke. "You heard Grandma. Let's go."

And miraculously, the four adults followed her upstairs.

The beach was giving them its all. Full sun. Quiet surf with just enough wave activity to play in. Plenty of room on the sand to choose your spot. Cora pushed her sunglasses up her nose and leaned back into her beach chair.

"How'd you pull it off?" Charley whispered to her.

She kept her eyes closed. "We had a little chat."

Hugh, never out of earshot, begged to differ. "She basically threatened us with physical harm."

Charley nodded. "Impressive."

They were all here. At the beach together. And talking. Cora smiled to herself. Mission accomplished.

"How did it go with your mother?" Cora asked softly. She did not want the others to overhear, but neither could she wait until they were back at the house to ask him.

Charley thought about it a moment. "She has her reasons. But I don't think you'll like them. And it doesn't change any-thing."

Cora sat up. "Do you like her reasons?" He could be like this sometimes, jostling between his mother and his wife with his empathies. Though he'd always been loyal to her and the kids. She suspected it was part of what drove Tish's thinly veiled disdain. She could not control her son anymore. And she didn't care for his life choices.

"No, honey. I don't agree with her reasons, assuming I can really understand them. It was a long lunch. She went back in time quite a bit."

Cora considered this. Tish was known for holding court at the family table. She loved an audience and she loved to steer the conversation. "What did she say?"

"Honestly? She told me about the first time my father took her home to the Sag Harbor house. My grandparents used to hold this big Memorial Day weekend shindig in the Hamptons. She was remembering that."

"What does that have to do with us? And giving away Riptide?"

Charley shrugged. "A lot, apparently. He paused. "When my father died suddenly, my mother had to make a lot of sacrifices. She was very young and very much alone. My grandparents didn't make it any easier on her. I knew there were tensions, growing up, of course. But I'm just starting to realize the extent of them." He turned to her. "It's pretty sad. They treated her terribly."

That was sad, Cora wouldn't disagree. Cora had long wondered what Tish was like before her husband died. She suspected she might have even liked her mother-in-law—that perhaps she was a different person before.

"Do you know, that weekend my father brought her home for the Memorial Day party, they were newly engaged. And what did my grandmother do? She invited my dad's old high school girlfriend and made a big deal about reuniting them. She tried to break my parents up."

Well. Cora settled back into her chair trying to picture another woman coming up against Tish. To her, Tish had always been the mother-in-law. Older, worldlier, and definitely the one with the upper hand when it came to Charley. She'd only ever known the overly protective and meddling woman. It occurred to her now that perhaps she hadn't always been that person. "How old was your mother then?"

"Twenty. Fresh out of college with a nursing degree. And from a family of much simpler means."

"Huh." Charley had mentioned that Tish grew up in the smaller city of Yonkers, the eldest daughter of a large Irish family. "I know her family was working class."

Charley rolled his shoulders back. "Through and through. First generation too. Can you imagine coming from that background and being thrust into my grandparent's blue blood world?"

She'd always thought of it as being transported, rather than thrust. More of the fairy-tale variety. "So it wasn't easy, I take it." Still, what did this have to do with them?

"Apparently, it was a lot harder than I thought. My grandparents were very controlling about where she could live with me and how she would raise me, once my father passed. They'd never really accepted her into the family. But then they were forcing her to live a certain way."

Cora could imagine that was a difficult time, but it had no doubt afforded Tish and Charley a certain lifestyle. "Yes, but I would think it came with some benefits. From what you said of her own family, it doesn't sound like they had the means to support a widow and her son. All of your mother's wealth, I assume, came from your dad's side. And let's be honest. There was a lot. She's lived quite the extravagant life."

"She has," Charley allowed, his shoulders sagging. "So have I."

His face clouded and she turned to him. "What's wrong?"

"You asked why my grandparents would do that," Charley said. "Why they'd impose expectations and rules about how my mother lived."

"So?"

"It was because of me." He let out a long breath. "I should have known."

"Oh, Charley." This was the heart of the matter, for him. And she could see it filled him with guilt. "How could you know? You were just a child. A child who'd just lost his father! What could you have done about any of it?"

"I don't know. Maybe I could've talked to my grandparents. Reasoned with them. Defended my mother."

Cora shook her head. Tish had really done a number on her poor husband at the tearoom. "Charley, you were five years old at the time. How the adults around you behaved is on them, not you. Don't you, for another instant, go down that path. Please." She grabbed his hand in hers. "Whatever sacrifices were made, that is part of a parents' job. It should in no way place you in a position of guilt." What she did not add was that whatever suffering Tish Darling apparently endured, it could not have been as terrible as Charley was fearing. His mother lived a life of luxury most could only dream of! A city apartment overlooking Central Park. Travel around the world. Car services. And always, a gilded roof over her head and the trappings of society in her closets. No, Cora's heart would not bleed for her.

As Charley looked glumly out onto the water, Cora thought about her own childhood. Working-class in the Midwest. Only child of two parents who were not college educated. And under a roof with a very controlling man of yesteryear notions about a woman's place in the world. Talk about enduring. Cora had escaped all of that by going away to Vassar and, later again, by agreeing to marry Charley. Becoming pregnant with the twins was nothing she'd planned or wanted as a student, but without any support from her family back in Ohio, she'd made sacrifices of her own. Sacrifices she could easily argue were just as great as Tish Darling's. And all without throwing ill will in the direction of any other person; without placing blame or pointing fingers. Or victimizing herself. The same could not be said of Tish. Her whole life since Cora knew her, she'd focused her laser-like ire in her direction. Blaming Cora for everything that ever went awry in Charley's life.

Hugh startled her, interrupting her thoughts with a sandy hand on her shoulder. "Mom? Did you hear me?"

"What?" she turned abruptly, shielding her eyes from the sun. Martin and Hugh stood beside her beach chair.

"We're going for a swim. Want to come?" She looked up at her tanned and trim son and his partner. At their warm expressions. Then at Molly, who joined them.

"It's going to be, like, freezing cold. But I'm dying of heat. So I'm going in."

Cora smiled. "Bracing! That's how it feels on a hot day, but once you sink in . . . oh! The heavenliness."

"So you're coming then?" Molly asked.

"No, dear. You go ahead. I'm having myself a little sunbath." She watched as the three of them trudged down to the water's edge. Martin went in first, brave soul. Then Hugh. Molly waded in one inch at a time. "Go on!" Cora shouted down to them, but they probably couldn't hear her over the ocean. The sun flickered off an incoming wave. The sea spray doused them all when it crashed at their feet.

This is the result of the sacrifices I've made, she thought, watching the two generations of her family playing in the water. She glanced at Sydney, who appeared to be sound asleep on her beach towel in her peach bikini. Already her hair was going golden in the sun. Then at Andi, who'd set her book down in her lap to watch the others. Everyone was having a good time. Finally.

She turned to Charley, who appeared to have momentarily settled down with all his motherly guilt, because his head rested against his beach chair, his mouth slightly agape. He snored quietly. Cora adjusted his fishing cap so that the shade it threw covered the pink tip of his nose. Charley was her rock. And she'd come to love him, dearly, if in her own quiet way.

The day she'd hung up the phone on her father in the dormitory common room was the same he'd punched out Robert Townsend, across campus in their own dorm. But she hadn't known that yet.

She was sitting on the edge of her bed, still crying when there came an urgent knocking on her door. *Robert!* had been her first thought. He'd come to his senses; he'd changed his mind.

Swiping tears from her cheeks, she checked her hair quickly in the mirror and hurried to the door. Her face fell when she opened it.

There, glistening with rain under the garish fluorescent lights of the hall, stood Charley Darling. His expression was desperate.

"What's wrong?" she asked. It was then she saw his hand, fist still clenched, red with blood. "Charley!" She grabbed it. The knuckles were grazed raw, the skin split beneath them. "What happened? Did Robert do this to you?"

Charley shook his head. "Marry me, Cora."

"Excuse me?" He must have gotten hit in the head. "You're talking nonsense. Come in. Let's get you cleaned up."

Wordlessly, he allowed her to pull him inside and close the door quickly behind him, hoping no one had seen. "I've got a small first aid kit. Sit down, there on the bed." She rifled through her drawers, searching for the kit. "Here!" She turned and held it up, but he was not sitting on the bed. He stood in the middle of the room dripping rainwater on her floor with that look on his face. "Charley, you're scaring me."

"Cora, I think we should get married."

"Stop that crazy talk and give me your hand."

Charley watched in silence as she cleaned his hand, applied first aid cream, and tried to affix Band-Aids, but they kept coming off. "Leave it," he said, finally. "I want to talk to you."

Cora did not want to talk, nor did she want to hear anything more that came out of Charley Darling's mouth. Clearly, he was befuddled. Maybe concussed. What she wanted was to bandage him up and get him out of her dorm room. Her head was already full of enough troubles. Frustrated, she tore gauze from a small roll. It was barely long enough to wrap his hand, but it worked. She secured it with medical tape, biting the edge with her teeth.

"You're a real Florence Nightingale," he said, examining his hand.

"And you're a comedian. There." She checked her work and let go of his hand. "You can go now. If you feel the need to get in any more fights today you should probably use your other hand."

For the first time since he'd arrived at her door the distraught look on his face lifted and he smiled. "Look who's the comedian." Then he did something Cora would never forget. He grasped both of her hands in his and pulled her gently to the bed. "Please, just hear me out. Then I'll go. I promise you."

It was the last thing she wanted, but his hands were gentle and his voice desperate. Besides, she was too drained to object.

"I am not marrying you," she said, withdrawing her hands.

He sat across from her. "Why not?"

Cora laughed out loud. This was insanity. "Because this is crazy! Because we barely know each other! Because, in case you haven't forgotten, I'm pregnant. With *someone else's* baby."

To her dismay, none of this bothered him. "Well, as Robert's roommate I've gotten to know you. I know you're smart and funny. And I know that you're a loyal person and that he treated you terribly."

"That happens in relationships, sometimes."

Charley went on. "I know you're a talented artist; I've seen your sketches when you've come by between studio classes. Beautiful."

Cora blinked. All these months Charley was just a person in the background when she visited Robert. A nice guy who held the door for her and asked about her studies, now and then. Had she ever asked him anything about himself?

"I also know you like chamomile tea. With honey. Robert always forgot the honey." His brows drew together. "I know that bastard never deserved a girl like you."

Cora listened, realizing with every word that Charley had been paying attention. Careful attention. That he cared.

Still. "Robert and I will figure this out," she said. "Or I will. Alone."

Charley appeared amused. "Is that so? Have you told your parents yet?"

Cora looked down at her lap. "Yes."

"So I take it they aren't exactly happy to hear the news."

"They haven't had time to think about it. But no," she allowed. "They are not happy at all. I've disappointed them."

Charley's voice softened. "You could never disappoint anyone."

She looked away. "I'll figure out a plan."

"Well, Robert has made it clear he's not sticking around. And your parents are not happy. What exactly is your plan, Cora?"

Who did this guy think he was? She'd had enough, from Robert and her family. And now this arrogant roommate of his who seemed to think he could swoop in and tell her what to do and rescue her from all of it. "That's none of your business," Cora said, standing. "I'm not a complete idiot. I'll think of something."

Charley watched her. "I'm sorry, Cora. I think you're one of the smartest people I know. I didn't mean to imply—"

She spun around, suddenly livid. "You think I'm smart? And funny? That I couldn't disappoint anyone?" She scoffed. "Tell me, since you seem to have all the answers about my life, how do you know these things, Charley?"

Charley looked at her as if deciding something. Then, slowly, he stood up and reached for his coat. Cora watched as he slipped it over his shoulders, preparing to go. "I'm sorry I bothered you. And made you upset." His eyes were soft with regret as he said it, but she was so angry she could feel her own burning holes into him. "Thank you for bandaging my hand. I'll leave you alone now."

He walked to the door, giving her a wide berth in the small room.

"No!" Cora cried. "Answer my question first."

Charley turned, looking pained.

"What makes you think you know me?" she barked.

"From listening. Your parents are from Ohio and your mother wanted to be an artist. Like you."

She bit her lip. "So you eavesdropped."

Charley shrugged. "Pretty hard not to, with three people in a two-person dorm room. I remember you said you felt like you were living her dream sometimes. But that after everything she'd done for you, it was a small burden."

"What about it?" This detail embarrassed her deeply and she felt her cheeks flush. She'd not even recalled Charley being in the room when she shared that with Robert.

"It told me how loyal you were to your mother. How grateful too."

"That was private. It doesn't mean anything to you."

He looked past her, to the window. "I remember the day Robert was going to a protest on the quad. He wanted to rally a lot of people, he was really pumped up. But up to the day before he hadn't even advertised it."

Robert was full of big ideas and told even bigger stories. Cora had been so attracted to that energy.

"He was tired from a frat party the night before, but you stayed up all night making those signs. Organizing people. I saw you working in our common room until midnight. That's dedication."

"I was only helping."

"Did he even thank you for that help?"

"I don't remember," she said, crossing her arms.

"Yes, you do."

Cora did not like all the things Charley was saying: personal things. About her. But she could not stop listening either. He understood so much.

"You saw me make signs. You listened to our private conversations." She threw up her hands. "That doesn't mean anything, Charley."

He looked down at his bandaged hand. "The essay you were both assigned for that Faulkner class you and Robert took together? You came over to help him, though I think you ended up writing the whole thing yourself."

She made a face.

"There was that one line, that you read aloud. 'A man like that in the desert, dying of thirst. He was more barren, more parched, than the landscape that consumed him.'"

Cora took a step back. "I wrote that."

"You did." He looked up at her. "It was the most beautiful and sad thing I think I'd ever heard."

"I can't believe you remember it." Outside, the rain picked up, pelting her windows. The gray skies turned her room to shadows. "What do you want from me, Charley?" Tears pressed at her eyes.

"I'm in love with you, Cora. From the moment Robert brought you to our room I fell in love. First, because of your smile. Then, because of your mind. And your heart. I tried not to be, believe me. But you were always there, and I guess I just gave in." He held up his hands. "Who can blame me?"

"I don't love you, Charley. I barely know you." The words came out like stone. But he had to know this.

"Let me help you, Cora. Let me help you and the baby. I can give you a good life. Everything you and your baby will need. I think we can make something out of that, together. And even if you never fall in love with me, I will love you enough for the two of us."

It was preposterous. Outrageous. And an offer so generous she was afraid of it.

When Charley graduated in May, Cora stood in the crowd clapping softly for him. With the baby already growing in her belly, they married that summer in a small civil service. Cora did not return to Vassar for her senior year, just as Charley did not attend Yale medical school. Instead, they moved into a small house outside of the city and Charley began working for the family foundation, to his grandparents' delight and his mother's despair. Any talk of medical school fell away as quietly as the leaves from the trees that fall semester.

Aside from Charley, Cora was very much alone. As she tried to busy herself setting up a nursery in the strange new house, her college friends packed their cars and returned to school without her. Cora's father would not speak to her. Though she suspected it was done in secret, her mother managed to call and write each week. Then, in late fall, a handsewn patchwork quilt arrived in a box from Ohio. "For my baby, for her first baby," the card read. Cora ran her hands over the soft cotton squares, tears spilling down her cheeks. Charley laid it in the tiny bassinet in the nursery. He was right by her side the day before Thanksgiving, letting her crush his hand as she gave birth to not just one baby—but to their shock and surprise—twins!

Charley Darling kept his word. Just as he'd promised, he loved her and both her babies like they were his own. In time, they made a life no different than most of the young couples they grew to know. A Volvo wagon. A house in the suburbs. The very picture of an all-American family. And eventually, after many failed attempts to have a baby that would be from them both, Sydney came along. They were a family of five. Pieced together like the squares of her mother's patchwork quilt.

It was not the life she'd planned, nor the life she'd dreamed of. Some things came more easily than others. From the beginning, Cora loved her children with a fierceness she was not prepared for. And, with time, she eventually grew to love their little house and the life they built. But, in spite of all that, no matter how hard she tried and wished and prayed, Cora did not fall in love with Charley Darling.

Andi

She couldn't help it. All this wedding talk dredged up the divorce.

It wasn't Sydney's fault. Andi was genuinely happy for her little sister and she was thrilled to be a part her big day. That was a fact. But there were other facts she could not escape: Andi was the only unmarried bridesmaid. A forty-four-year-old single mother who would be lined up in the (not terribly hideous but still rather unflattering) coral strapless dress with a bevy of childless, recently married, beautiful twenty- and thirty-somethings Sydney counted as her closest friends. The thought of it made Andi cringe. Plus, there was the fact that she was matron of honor. Which meant she had to plan a night out for the other bridesmaids when they arrived. Andi had not gone out in ages. The idea that she had to manage a rousing, all-in, big night for her little sister filled her with dread. She had no idea how to keep down more than one cocktail these days, let alone where to go to find a good one with a gaggle of girlfriends who were well-versed in the lifestyle of being young and carefree. Andi's idea of a big night was grading her students' English papers over Thai takeout and going to bed early to watch anything British on PBS. Plus, the biggest reminder of her divorce was on his way now. Her ex-husband, George, was due to arrive at Riptide at one o'clock that afternoon to take Molly away for a few days. And his not-so-lovely "true life partner," Camilla, was the final glaringly ugly fact.

"What time are we expecting them to make land?" Hugh quipped. Andi sat in the kitchen staring at her third cup of coffee with shaky hands, thinking that she probably shouldn't have had the second. But she needed to do something besides eat ice cream and it was just too early for a cocktail. She glanced at the clock on the kitchen wall. "Half an hour." Her stomach roiled.

"Well, well, well," Hugh said. "Do we roll out the carpet or batten down the hatches?"

Martin had a softer approach. "What can we do to help you steel yourself?"

Andi smiled at him gratefully. "Keep me away from the coffeepot and distract me. I am not looking forward to this."

"You're tougher than you think," Sydney offered.

Hugh slid onto the stool next to her. "And if you find that today's an off day, give me the signal. I'll hold Camilla down while you take your best swing."

In spite of her frayed nerves, Andi laughed. She had to find the positives. Molly was looking forward to this trip, she reminded herself. Since eight o'clock that morning (a practically predawn hour for a teenager!), Molly had already been packed and set to go. Andi had had to force herself to act like she was just as excited for her too. Instead, as she went through her duffel bag one last time checking to make sure she remembered sunscreen, a light jacket, and the frayed, pink stuffed elephant she still slept with, Andi found herself fighting silent tears. The thought of Molly going away on her first vacation without her was too much. As it was, she'd never spent more than a few nights away from her since the day she'd been born. And now Molly would be going on a trip—one ferry ride and sixteen nautical miles away (she'd looked it up, of course)—with two people Andi truly could not stand.

"You guys don't have kids, so no offense, but letting go of your daughter for a week is hard to do."

The look on Martin's face made her regret it the moment the words left her lips. "It's not like we don't want them," he mumbled.

Sydney winced and instantly Andi felt like an ass. God, was everything in this family a minefield?

"I'm sorry! What I meant is that I've always been the parent who organizes Molly's life. From making sure she does her algebra to reminding her to eat her broccoli to nagging her to apply sunscreen."

Hugh let out a low whistle. "You sound like a ton of fun to vacation with."

"Shut up, I'm serious. It's not a fun job, but someone has to be the parent."

"George isn't?" Sydney asked.

"Nope. George never says no to her. Never oversees homework or enforces curfew, let alone cooks a healthy meal. Forget sunscreen! She's going to fry under his watch this week."

Her voice had become shrill and she caught herself. The last thing she wanted was Molly to overhear this upstairs. But it just wasn't fair. When it came to parenting, George wanted to be Molly's pal, not her anchor. He left that hard work to Andi.

"That sucks," Sydney sympathized. "You get laundry and

soccer-mom duty while he gets takeout pizza. You should be allowed to have fun with her too."

"And I want to! I hate always feeling like the warden."

"So let's list the good stuff!" Sydney suggested, a little too enthusiastically. "There have to be some positives about this trip for Molly. And for you."

"I forgot you were a cheerleader in high school," Hugh pointed out dryly.

Sydney ignored this. "This week Molly will have a little independence away from you. Maybe she'll learn to take care of herself."

"My turn," Martin said. "The kid's not exactly going to suffer on the Vineyard. She's hitting one of the hottest vacation spots on the East Coast. Think of the selfies she can take for her Insta page."

Andi had to give him that. "When I bought her extra sunscreen yesterday, I also got her the cutest polka-dot bikini she'd been eyeing in town."

"Plus, *you* get a little vacation from parenting this week. Think about that." Martin squeezed her hand. "After a whole week away, I bet Molly misses you and comes home appreciating you even more."

Hugh, who'd remained silent, scoffed at them all. "No, she won't. Molly's going to stay up late and live off crappy takeout food and will forget to call you. And she'll likely skip all that expensive organic sunscreen you bought and will fry her derriere off in that cute little polka-dot bikini. But . . ." He looked Andi squarely in the eye. "You will survive this. And she will have a good time with her dad."

Andi pressed back tears. "I do want her to have a good time."

Hugh shrugged. "Well, it's not like you can do a damn thing about it. Camilla the Gorilla is on her way."

Andi beat Sydney to it and punched Hugh in the arm. It made her feel slightly better.

When Molly came downstairs with her bags, everyone made a big deal about her trip. But Andi couldn't hear what they were saying because she couldn't take her eyes off her. Molly looked older in a fitted green dress and a cropped denim jacket she didn't recognize. Her hair was blown out and for the first time since arriving at Riptide she had put on makeup. Andi forced a smile. "All set?"

"Dad texted. They're ahead of schedule."

Andi's chest ached. "But Grandma isn't back from the grocery store to say goodbye. And you didn't eat lunch yet. I was going to make you a sandwich!"

"Dad can buy me something on the ferry."

"But you get motion sickness, remember? I'll pack you a Dramamine and whip up a quick sandwich."

"Mom, I already packed some and I'm not hungry."

"But—"

"Please. I'm fine." Molly glared at her. This was not how Andi wanted their first goodbye to go.

Hugh wrapped an arm around Andi's shoulders. "She's *fine*."

It was happening already. Molly didn't need her and was distancing herself. Already at the bow of the ferry, arms open, shedding all of Andi's hard mothering work. She reached for the fruit bowl. "A plum?"

"Mom."

Hugh took the plum away from her and set it back in the bowl. "Family photo!"

"No . . ." they all groaned.

"Yes." He pointed at Molly. "It's, like, your favorite pastime."

"Yeah, when *I take them*. Not you guys." Molly groaned. "You guys are horrible at it."

Hugh handed Molly his phone. "Have at it."

They trudged out to the porch and squeezed together for what seemed like one hundred shots. After, Molly swiped through them with a sour look. "Hideous."

"Let us at least see them," Hugh said.

Molly passed his phone back. "I deleted them."

"All of them?"

Molly shrugged.

"No." Andi snatched the phone from her brother. "We are getting one picture before you go." And before Molly could object Andi threw her *the look*. It was the one she reserved for desperate public moments or near death. And it didn't always work.

But to her relief, it did. "Okay. One photo. But I get to approve it."

This time Andi squeezed in closest to Molly, her siblings around them. They were so close Andi could smell her shampoo and for the hundredth time she had to remind herself not to cry.

"Finally," Hugh said when they got the shot. "I just lost five years I can't get back."

By then their parents had rolled into the driveway, just in time, and it was a Darling family pileup of goodbyes and well wishes.

Andi stood back, as everyone had their turn.

"Find a cute boy and send me a photo," Sydney told her niece with a wink.

"Don't forget to call your mother," Martin said.

"Oh, honey, have fun!" Cora told her granddaughter as she slipped a twenty-dollar bill into her hand. "Buy yourself something cute."

Charley gave Molly a bear hug. "They have some great deep-water fishing around the island. See if your dad will take you."

Hugh was last. "No sex, drugs, or rock and roll." He looked at Andi. "Your mother said."

Molly turned five shades of scarlet but laughed.

Finally, it was Andi's turn, but with it came the sudden crunch of tires on the shell driveway. "They're here!" Molly cried, grabbing her duffel bag. Andi's stomach lurched.

"Wait, honey." She'd wanted to say something bright and cheerful. Meaningful but not mushy. As Molly swiveled with an impatient look, instead Andi said, "Remember your sunscreen."

Molly was already halfway down the steps toward the gleaming black Escalade as Andi chided herself.

"Whoa." Martin let out a whistle. "That thing's a beast."

"So." Hugh elbowed Andi. "That's why he can't pay more alimony?"

"Shut up," Andi hissed. But he was right. George's new car was ridiculous.

George exited the beast first and Molly rushed her dad like a linebacker. *This is good,* Andi told herself. *They need father-daughter time together. All good.*

Then the passenger door opened.

Camilla stepped out like she was arriving at the Academy

Awards, one open-toed heel (did she not know she was about to get on a windy, rocky ferry boat?) first. She was dressed in all black and she remained planted by the car as she took them all in, sliding her oversized sunglasses down the narrow bridge of her nose.

"Ferret-like," Hugh had once commented when Andi showed him her Instagram page.

Well. Andi would be the bigger person. "Hello, Camilla. Nice to see you."

Camilla didn't budge. "Andi." Her smile, if that's what it was, didn't quite reach her cheeks.

By then, George had come around to the front steps. "Hey, Andi." He waved sheepishly at the rest of her family, who Andi realized were lingering on the porch in one nosy, obvious huddle. "Hi, everyone."

Andi's dad rescued them all, heading down the porch steps and extending his hand. "Good to see you, George. Molly sure is excited for this trip." And everyone followed Charley's polite example. Andi appreciated all of it, her eyes on Molly. It was important for her to see that they could all behave themselves and get along.

"New wheels, huh?" Hugh asked, which delighted George.

Andi couldn't help but feel a little sorry for Camilla, standing in the driveway like a dark omen, at the edge of it all. She smiled at her. "You've had a long drive. Would you like a glass of water? Or maybe use the restroom before you go?"

Camilla's nose wrinkled. "I'm good."

As if suddenly remembering his "true life partner," George peeled himself away from the car tour to introduce her. "I'd like you to meet Camilla. She'll be traveling with Molly and me this week." He paused self-consciously. "She's my—"

"Life partner," Camilla interjected.

Andi resisted the urge to add "true."

This triggered a few obligatory nods and faint mumblings, followed by a long uncomfortable silence standing in the hot sun. Andi wondered how hot Camilla felt in her all-black attire.

"All right then, off you go." It was time. She handed George the little sandwich she'd secretly packed, despite Molly's protest. "Lunch. And extra Dramamine." She could feel Molly's eye roll across the driveway. "Remember, she gets seasick?"

"Oh right, yes, of course," George said, accepting the bag, but Andi could tell he did not remember at all.

Andi ticked through the packing list. "I wasn't sure what you've got planned, but she packed a variety of clothes, both dressy and casual, and sweaters for cold nights . . . but wait— I forgot a raincoat!"

"She needs a raincoat," Cora echoed from the porch. *Solidarity!* "It often rains on-island."

Molly was glaring again. "Mom, stop. It's going to be sunny."

Andi shot a look of her own. "Honey, there's rain predicted. I'll just be a minute."

She was about to run back inside, but George shook his head. "We'll buy one if she needs it."

"But . . ."

"She can use mine. I came prepared." Camilla crossed her arms as she said it and Andi wasn't sure whether to thank her or sneer. Before Andi could reply, Camilla flicked her wrist impatiently. Her oversized gold Rolex gleamed in the sunlight. "We should go," she said flatly.

George hopped to it. He grabbed the bag from Andi and

turned for the car. But not before pausing to open Camilla's door with a flourish. "There you go, darling."

Camilla slipped into the dark enclave of the SUV and fluttered her hand to no one in particular. The door slammed shut.

To her consternation, Andi realized Molly had already gotten in the car too. But she hadn't had a chance to hug her goodbye!

Before she could say so, George's driver's-side door slammed shut. The engine started.

"Okay, show's over," Charley said. The family traipsed inside. Except for Andi, who could not.

"Wait!" she called as the reverse lights went on.

As the car backed up Andi hurried around to its passenger side, waving her arms. But the tinted windows were too dark to see inside.

"George, hang on!" she shouted. How could they not see her? Or hear her? She bet Camilla could. "Molly!" she called again as they rolled down the driveway, Andi trotting alongside. But George didn't stop.

Andi threw up her arms in disbelief. She was not about to chase the car down the street like an unhinged person. As her daughter sped away in her ex-husband's new SUV with his ferret-faced girlfriend.

Or was she? She broke into a run.

The car turned onto the street, Andi right behind it. Stress sweat broke out under her arms. "You guys!" she shouted after it. But no one seemed to notice and the car surged ahead. It was too late.

Deflated and out of breath, Andi halted in the middle of the road, bent over, hands on her knees. She'd missed her goodbye with Molly.

"Andi!" someone shouted.

It was Hugh, standing at the end of their driveway. "What the hell are you doing?"

She started to cry.

"Come back," Hugh called. "Let her go."

"I can't," she cried. She was divorced and alone and about to be in a wedding. And Molly was gone.

But then there was the sound of tires halting abruptly. Andi looked up. The car had stopped halfway up the street. The reverse taillights flickered. And the Cadillac rolled backward.

Andi choked back a sob. Then a laugh.

About ten feet away the car stopped and the back passenger door flew open. Molly leapt out.

"Mom!" she cried.

She ran into Andi's arms, nearly knocking the wind out of her. "I forgot to say goodbye."

Andi choked back a sob. "No, you didn't."

The hug ended too fast, but there was one more thing Andi had to say. "I hope you have fun with Dad."

"I will." Molly smiled at her mother, a very grown-up look in her eye. "Don't worry so much, okay?" Andi couldn't help but feel that their roles had flipped, if only in that moment.

Andi laughed. "I'm trying, kiddo."

And then Molly was off. Enveloped in the big black car once more. Disappearing around the turn.

Andi was still standing in the street staring after them when Hugh pulled up alongside her. "That was quite a stunt. Not every day you see a barefoot, middle-aged woman keeping up with a Cadillac SUV."

Andi looked down at her dirty bare feet. "God. I didn't even notice."

"It's okay. The rest of the neighborhood did." Hugh threw his arm around her. "C'mon, Mama. Let's get you a drink."

Back inside, everyone was loitering in the living room, pretending to busy themselves.

Cora looked up from her unopened book. "You okay, honey?"

"She chased the car down the street," Hugh announced. "Never saw her run that fast in high school track!"

Charley came around the kitchen island and held out his arms. There was still such confusion in her head about her parents and there was so much tension in the house, but none of that mattered in the moment. Andi stepped into his hug like she was a little girl. "It's hard, Dad. This whole post-divorce co-parenting thing is so goddamn hard."

That was the thing about her father. He didn't say anything to the contrary. Nor would he try to fix it. His unshaven chin was comfortingly familiar against her cheek as he nodded and listened. "I know, kiddo. It's hard for us too. But we're all here."

Andi stepped back, wiping her cheeks. She looked around at all their faces. How she loathed pity. "You know what we should do?"

"Open a bottle of wine?" Martin offered.

"We need to get out of the house." She turned to Sydney. "We haven't been to the Beach House Grill yet. What do you say we toast the wedding and have a shark attack?" It was their long-standing favorite Cape Cod frozen drink named after Chatham's Great White influx. Dubiously named. But delicious!

"I'm in!" Sydney said. "Hugh, Martin, you coming?"

They nodded in unison.

Andi turned to her parents. They'd been listening at the edge of the conversation, trying to look as if they weren't. "Mom? Dad?" It was a small olive branch. But they had to start somewhere.

Cora looked uncomfortable. "Oh, I don't know. That place is for young people. You kids go ahead."

But Charley disagreed. "No, Cora. I think you should go. I think we should both go."

Andi watched as they shared a silent exchange. "All right," Cora said finally.

"All right, then," Andi said, her spirits rising a little.

As the rest of them headed upstairs to get ready, Andi felt something inside her shift. "Good call," Hugh whispered when it was just the two of them left in the living room couch.

Andi shrugged. "I guess we'll find out." She lowered herself onto the couch. "I know you're still upset with them and I am too. But we need them. At least I do."

"I know," Hugh said, flopping down beside her. "But manage your expectations, okay? Baby steps."

That worked for her. It was a concession. "Look, I'm also sorry for what I said earlier. About you and Martin not understanding because you don't have kids."

Hugh waved his hand. "Don't give it another thought."

It was already a sensitive topic, probably made even more so by all the recent family upset. She should've realized that sooner. "How are you guys doing with all of that?"

He glanced at the staircase, lowering his voice. "It's made us talk, at least. And listen to each other."

Andi let out her breath, her marriage therapist's waiting room flashing in her mind. How many hours could they have saved themselves if they'd just listened more? "That's good," she said. "The listening is harder than the talking."

Hugh laughed sadly. "No kidding. When I really think about what Martin is saying, and why he wants to have a family, I realize that I'm not against the idea of having kids. I just don't want to race into it. It's a big deal."

Hearing Hugh admit that made Andi smile. "It is." She'd been careful to keep her mouth shut, but she could see he and Martin with a child. In fact, it was easy to picture. "Sounds like you guys are making progress."

Hugh shrugged. "I thought so too. But then this damn family secret came out." His voice fell away. "It makes me doubt everything again."

"How so?"

"About parenting. About what your responsibilities to your children really are." He shook his head. "I don't even know my biological father. How can I think of being a father myself when everything I thought I knew about my dad was a lie?"

Andi leaned against her twin. It had made her wonder too. About loyalty. And honesty. And blood.

About how doing something you thought was protecting your child might actually have the opposite effect. "Well, I'll tell you what Tish once told me, before I got pregnant with Molly. 'There's never a good time. And it's never easy.'"

Hugh looked at her incredulously. "Tish? The least maternal person on the planet gave you parenting advice?"

Andi laughed out loud. "I couldn't believe it either. But she sure loves Dad, even if the way she shows it is screwed up."

"So you're still going to call him that?"

It took Andi a moment to realize what he was getting at. "Why wouldn't I? It's who he is."

Hugh nodded, leaving it at that. And she let him.

"For what it means, I see the love you and Martin have. I envy it, even. And I think you two would make great fathers, if that's what you both decide."

Her twin looked away, but she could see the faintest smile on his face before he did. "All right," he said, "you're being too nice and you need to shut up, or I may have a turn crying." He hopped to his feet. "Let's get out of here."

Andi looked down. "First, I should probably wash the pavement off my feet." She lifted one foot so he could see its tar-colored sole.

"God help the first guy who drives off with your daughter on a date."

Andi cocked her head. "Speaking of guys."

It had been an emotional day. Saying goodbye to Molly. Seeing her ex. Now a family dinner with all of the tensions still rippling. "I was thinking about what you said earlier. Why should George and Camilla have all the fun?"

Hugh raised one eyebrow. She didn't need to tell her twin what she was thinking.

"I'll call him right now," he said.

She was halfway up the stairs when the call went through. "Nate, it's Hugh. Say, what're you doing tonight?"

Tish

She has no choice; Tish *must* extend her stay at Chatham Bars Inn. It's not easy, being back on the Cape surrounded by memories of Morty. It's also not easy during high summer season. That sweet young receptionist in the main lobby tells her that her cottage is already reserved for the coming week by another guest, but not to worry—they can find her a vacant room in the main inn! This is not what she wants to hear. Tish has grown fond of her cottage by the sea. It has the harbor view. It is oh-so-private. And the longer she stays, the longer the unrest and unease in her bones seems to dissipate. Is it the ocean air? Or the Cape Cod memories of her dear Morty? She suspects a bit of both. Whatever it is, for the first time in decades Tish feels a lightening of some invisible burden across her shoulders. She does not possess the usual pressing urge to flee from the family. No, it is certainly not easy being back on the Cape surrounded by ghosts and old hauntings. But something about it feels necessary. She wants to see it through. And besides, Charley still needs her, even if he does not know it.

As such, Tish needs to keep the Mooncusser Cottage. If not, they will have to drag her out by her ankles. Inexplicable as it may be, since she's arrived, something has happened within the walls of this cottage. She sleeps through the night. She has a voracious appetite. Most of all, she can think of Morty for the first time without the searing pain that filled her limbs whenever he crossed her mind. Her whole life as a widow, she has steered hard away from memories, lest she come undone by the suffering they brought. Now she climbs into bed, slips beneath the crisp hotel sheets, and waits for the dreams to come. With moonlight glinting off the bay outside, she lies ready and willing. Her old heart is finally opening again, like the petals of a flower unfolding.

If she were to uproot herself now, she fears the connection she feels to her past may be lost. She tries to explain this to the young receptionist without sounding like a crazy old bat or getting personal—two things she will not do. But alas, it does no good. The cottage is already spoken for. As a last resort, Tish asks to speak to the hotel manager. An impeccably mannered gentleman named Ross with a soothing lilt to his voice. Ross wears a linen suit sporting a bright lavender pocket square. *Dapper,* she thinks when he strolls across the lobby to greet her. Men today are such slobs; they could learn a thing or two from Ross.

Tish has a *situation* on her hands. But there are two things on her side: born a first-generation American with little means, that fighting spirit still flickers within. As does the influence of the family name she married into. Both possess the power to assuage a situation, though the balance is delicate. Tish smiles as she takes Ross's hand in her own and employs both. A quick sweep of the reservation board later, and voilà! The Mooncusser Cottage is available, after all. She thanks him and takes him up

bone structure for that. Classic beauty cannot be eroded by time, her hairdresser once told her. Though she was pretty sure he was not hitting on her; he was gay. Like Hugh. Oh, Hugh . . . and the rest of the grandchildren.

Tish had not come to the Cape to stir up trouble. It's no secret to the whole family that she and Cora are not fans of each other and, though she regrets the tension it may have caused the children and Charley, the fault is not hers. Cora had swept into Charley's carefully orchestrated world and dismantled it. A world that Tish herself had spent years cultivating and fostering, all the while protecting Charley from the expectations and pressure from his side of the family. It was a high-wire act she'd perfected out of necessity, but it never got easier. Morty's parents, while he was alive, were cold people. And after his death, they never warmed as she'd foolishly hoped they might, but rather set up a fortress of rules they saw as opportunities for young, fatherless Charley, but that Tish knew were a strategic set of controls.

Like her, who'd loved medicine and longed to use her Columbia nursing degree, Charley took an interest in medicine. Tish saw a light. If she could just withstand his grandparents long enough, the education he had and the circles they lived in could certainly help secure a future in medical school. Charley was a bright student, but soft and sweet. Easily distracted by others. Tish needed to make him tougher if he were to grow into the man who could free himself from the Darlings and forge his own path. Then, and only then, would she be free of them herself. Her work as a mother would be done, her child raised and poised on the precipice of a bright future, and she could escape the talons of her mother-in-law and live however and wherever she wished. Vassar was a good enough school, yes, but the fall of his senior year when they learned he got into Yale medical school? Aside from marrying Morty, it was the best day of Tish Darling's life. She would tell Matilda Darling the good news: Charley would not be working for the family foundation, after all. No, he'd gotten into an Ivy League school! His future was wholly his own.

But then Cora came along. With her glowing skin and swollen breasts, an undeniable beauty, even with that round belly peeking from beneath her cardigan sweater. Charley was besotted and Tish realized that the maternal push and pull she'd cultivated so carefully no longer held the same power. Now Cora did. And she saw it, in her own time of need, and seized upon Charley Darling. He was an opportunity. A family name of means who could support her and get her out of the hole she'd dug herself into. Seeing as her own family wouldn't take her back, who else would help her? A loyal, loving, gentle man who looked with kindness on those less fortunate. Unable to feel the claws that were sinking into his hide as he looked into her cornflower-blue gaze and promised away his future.

Tish would never forgive Cora that selfishness. Robbing poor Charley of his talents and dreams. And Tish too, if she were sentimental; which she was not. But oh, the salt air was doing something to her.

Morty, she says. *I need your help with Charley.*

Outside the restaurant window, the boats rock quietly on the bay. The sun glints off the harbor. "Mrs. Darling? Your chowder."

Ha! It's not Morty. But her appetizer looks sumptuous. She thanks her server. As she savors each spoonful of the creamy chowder, her mind drifts.

The same year she and Morty were married, her youngest

brother, Kieran, married his high school girlfriend just after New Year's. She and Morty were living in the city and they drove the short distance north to Yonkers. The wedding was to be held at St. Mary's and the reception afterward was at the Irish Community Center, just as all their siblings and schoolmates did. Tish was the only one in her family to marry anywhere else outside the neighborhood. "What do you mean, you're not getting married in the church?" her mother had sputtered when she'd first broken the news to her.

"Mom, it's not a big deal. You know Morty's family is Protestant."

"My God!" her mother had clapped both hands over her ears. "But that doesn't mean you are." Then, "Wait, Patricia Jean O'Malley, so help us, Lord. Tell me you're not converting?"

"No, Morty's family isn't religious, like we are, Mom. Morty even said as long as I'm happy, he doesn't care what faith I practice, if any."

"If *any*?" Her mother had spun on her heels and out of the kitchen. Probably to pray for her.

To her mother's horror, Tish and Morty were married at Central Presbyterian on the Upper East Side. It had been a silent but piercing thorn in their relationship since.

Kieran's winter nuptials were the first time the family had celebrated a wedding in six months, which was saying something for her large extended clan. It seemed like forever since she'd seen her sisters and brothers. "You live so far away now," her little sister, Imogen, had complained when she'd moved out.

"So far? I'm in Manhattan, Imogen. Not Minnesota." But it sometimes felt she may as well have been in Minnesota. Her siblings rarely made the trip into the city to see her, despite many invitations to dinner or to come see the apartment, complaining of the slow trains and stops along the route. Since she'd married and moved, Tish missed her sisters and brothers. Now as they snaked their way along the Saw Mill River Parkway, it was her hope that Kieran's wedding that evening would help make up for some of that.

She glanced at her husband in the driver's seat, dressed in a brown wool suit. Earlier that day, when Morty had pulled his tux from the closet, Tish had shaken her head. "Honey, I told you it's not formal like that. Weddings in my family are more like . . . parties."

Morty had nodded. "I like a good party!" But Tish was a little nervous. Morty was gracious and down to earth with everyone, but her family was still so formal around him and it lent an air of discomfort on the rare occasions they gathered.

"Wear the brown suit," she'd suggested. It was the most casual suit he owned.

Outside, the day was as gray as the cold Hudson River, but as they neared her old neighborhood her anticipation warmed her. Tish hadn't seen her cousins, so many of whom she'd grown up with no different than siblings, in months. Her closest cousin, Nora, was expecting her third baby. Tish couldn't believe it. They'd always talked about marrying and having kids at the same time, but while Tish went to Columbia Nora headed for the altar. Already it felt like Nora was a decade older and away, but still—they'd been like sisters their whole lives and Tish was eager to see her.

They had to circle the block three times to get a parking spot, but they somehow arrived on time. The ceremony was lovely, Kieran and Heather so young and excited, and the pews packed with familiar faces.

"Your brother sure has a lot of friends," Morty remarked as the service let out and people streamed down the front steps of the Catholic church.

"Oh, most of the people here are family," Tish said.

Morty's eyes widened in disbelief. "You're related to all these people?"

Tish laughed. "Wait until you get to the reception."

The Irish Community Center was the hub of activity for the neighborhood and weddings were no different. The Irish folk band her father played in on weekends would be heading up the entertainment. "Harmonica," Tish told Morty when he asked to be reminded. "My uncle plays banjo and my cousin Rowan the fiddle. They're really quite good."

They could hear the band as they walked up the sidewalk. Tish paused at the doorway.

"What is it?" Morty asked.

She reached for the button of his suit jacket and slid his coat from his shoulders. "You won't be needing this anymore."

Morty looked worried. "I won't?"

Tish winked at him. "I hope you like dancing. I know you like beer." The moment they swung open the door they were met with the sound of celebration.

Everything was as she'd hoped, at first. The feast was abundant: a buffet dinner of roasted pork with colcannon and a traditional beef stew. Meat pies. Soda breads and assorted jams. Boxty, miniature potato cakes. The elderly relatives lined up first, followed by the youngest. As Tish and Morty waited their turn in line, she pointed out the wedding cake: a three-layered fruitcake Tish knew to be laced with cherries, spices, and almonds, all soaked in whiskey, ordered specially from the neighborhood bakery. How disappointed her mother had been when Tish ordered from a bakery in Manhattan, that Morty's mother recruited. "They make the best buttercream frosting," she'd said. It was delicious. But it was not the traditional cake Tish had dreamed of.

The community center was packed to the gills and the insides of the windows filled with steam. After several rousing toasts and rounds of drinks, the folk band started up again and Kieran and his bride took to the dance floor. Tish grabbed Morty's hand. "Come on!"

Morty was not familiar with the traditional jigs her family was so fond of, but that did not stop him; as her brothers grabbed his arm and pulled him into the center, everyone clapped. "He's god-awful!" one of her uncles clamored, throwing his arm around Tish's waist. Tish laughed. Morty was not a convincing dancer, but it pleased her so to see him out there with her brothers and family. For the moment, it all felt right.

Tish was standing in a cluster of cousins talking to Nora, who looked full-bellied and tired, when another cousin, Fran, tapped her roughly on the shoulder.

"And when will it be your turn, missy?" she asked with a mischievous wink. "You better get to cracking."

Tish smiled. It was the polite thing to do for an impolite question, but it was how things went in her family. "I'm working first," she told her cousin. "Remember, I got my nursing degree this past year?"

Fran scoffed. "Working? With all the gobs of money you just married? Now, why would you wanna do that?"

There was a collective pause, but then Fran's vulgar laugh pierced the silence and the rest joined. All except for Nora.

"Ignore them," she whispered. But Tish could not. Here was Nora, the same age as she, never having gone to school or worked outside the home and already strapped with two toddlers and another on the way. The embodiment of success in her O'Malley family's eyes. "You look so pretty," Nora added. "I love your pearl earrings." Tish put a hand to her ears. She'd thought them so beautiful when Morty gave them to her for her birthday. "South Seas pearls," he'd told her and she didn't know what he meant until she later asked the jeweler. Looking now at her cousins' unadorned ears and simple dresses, Tish felt utterly ridiculous. Like a circus horse with one of those pink plumes on its head.

Luckily, an aunt rescued her. "Honey, I think your mom could use some help in the kitchen."

Grateful, Tish veered away from her cousins' inquisitive stares and to the rear of the community center. There, she found her mother, aunt, and sisters crowded in the kitchen spooning ice cream into silver bowls and filling carafes of coffee for the dessert hour. The women were laughing and talking, and barely noticed her peeking in the door.

"Well, at least she looks happy," her aunt Mary was saying to her mother. "Maybe she'll bless you with a grandchild soon."

Tish's mother was bent over a carton of chocolate ice cream, her back to her. "Happy. What a fleeting, foolish thing." Tish froze in the doorway.

Tish's sister Imogen saw her first and cleared her throat loudly. The chatter ceased.

Her mother straightened and turned, cheeks flushed. "What do ya need, Tish?"

Tish wondered how long she'd been working in the kitchen

that night. A world away from her own white glove affair at the Carlyle for her wedding.

Abashed, she reached for a stray apron. "I came to help."

Her mother's eyes traveled up and down her green velvet dress. "You'll ruin your frock, dear. Go enjoy yourself."

She was being dismissed. "Mother, let me give you a hand. You deserve a break."

"Deserve?" There was an exchange of looks among the women.

"Oh, honey. You look so pretty tonight!" her aunt Mary chimed in finally. "Go dance with that handsome new husband of yours." Her warm smile was tinged with pity.

"Thank you, but I want to help," Tish insisted. She tied her apron tightly about her waist.

"Have it your way." Her mother passed her the ice cream scoop and wiped her hands matter-of-factly on her own. The chocolate ice cream was melting, running down the sides of the tub. "I'll go have myself a drink."

"That's a girl!" Mary said. "Yes. Have yourself a drink."

In her mother's wake the kitchen fell silent. Tish rolled up her sleeves as best she could and began scooping ice cream. She made quick work of it in her frustration, filling the trays of silver dessert bowls faster than Imogen could carry them out.

"Slow down," her sister complained.

"Keep up," Tish snipped.

Aunt Mary came over and lay a hand on her arm. "Honey, we're all very proud of you. She is too."

Tish knew who Mary meant. She swiped at a stray tear. "Then why doesn't it ever feel like it?" She was sure her cousin Nora didn't feel that way. All the aunts and cousins coming up to her, touching her pregnant belly, gushing about her glowing cheeks. They kept a polite distance from Tish, in her fancy attire and patent heels, suddenly unsure how to talk to her. It was nonsense.

Aunt Mary shrugged. "Dunno, darling. Different generations, I guess. She'll come around."

By then Tish had filled another tray of dishes with ice cream. Impatient for Imogen's return, Tish grabbed the tray from the counter.

"What're you doin'?" Mary asked. "You'll ruin your dress!"

"I wish everyone would stop worrying about the dress." She whisked the tray from the counter and carried it to the doors. "I'm married. Not frivolous."

At that moment Imogen returned to the kitchen, pushing through the double doors in her haste. The doors swung ajar, catching the lip of Tish's ice cream tray and sending it upward.

Imogen shrieked and Tish hopped back. The serving dishes flipped against her chest, before clattering to the floor, spraying their feet in a melted milky mess. "Tish!" Imogen cried. "Oh God, Tish, I'm sorry!"

Even with the band in full swing, guests nearest the kitchen spun around to see what was the commotion, Tish's mother among them. She shook her head.

Tish swallowed her tears. As Mary and her mother dabbed and swabbed the bodice of her dress, Tish stood obediently at the sink. She stared at the rush of hot water from the faucet, the noxious smell of dish soap and soiled sponge rising on the steam between them.

"There, there," Mary soothed her, thinking she was upset about her outfit.

Her mother said nothing, scrubbing up and down across Tish's chest. With each sweep of the rough sponge, another cluck of her tongue. When Tish looked down the velvet was crushed and stained. She did not care.

On the drive home, Morty recounted an evening so different than the one she'd had, she had to wonder if they'd been at the same reception. "Everyone was so friendly, so celebratory!" he remarked. "I have to say, honey, I was beginning to wonder if your family liked me. But I think tonight was a good night, don't you?" He looked across the seat at her sympathetically. "Aside from your dress, of course. Don't worry, we can get you another."

Tish stared out the window; she did not want another dress like it. She never wanted to wear velvet again. "Yes, Morty. It was a good night."

Cora

When she was restless at heart, she painted. Her medium was oil. Her implement was despair. It had always been that way.

Creative process was a specific thing, as individual to an artist as personality is, Cora had learned. Over the years she'd met many painters. Those who worked professionally and hobbyists like herself who painted at home and kept their work largely among friends and family. There was a common thread among them: they painted when inspired. How she wished the same could be said for her! But for Cora, painting had always been more of a release valve. A way to process and sort through the layers of some personal discomfort, something that kept her awake at night. It began as an adolescent in Ohio, when her mother snuck home a beginner's set of paints from a craft store for her. Cora had long shown an interest in art as a child, but it had been diminished by her father—considered worthless at best, a sign of arrogance at worst. "Fancy notions," he called them. "Don't get to thinkin' you're any better than the rest of us."

The night her mother slipped the paint set into her backpack of a single peach. She still remembered how she came to paint it: Sydney had just been born the fall before and it was her first summer at Riptide. She was teething and unable to be soothed, crying all through the night. As such, so was Cora. And the twins were so much older—wanting to have all their friends over and go swimming at the beach all day, things Cora simply could not do when Sydney was napping all day. Nobody was happy. After a particularly rough night Cora had stumbled into the kitchen to make coffee, her head throbbing and breasts raw from another ceaseless night of nursing. She'd collapsed at the kitchen counter. The peach was the first thing she saw. A bright, blonde-tinged beauty. Ripe and fragrant. Even in her state, it gave Cora hope, and she sent Charley and the kids straight to the beach as soon as they woke and painted right at the kitchen counter until they returned. It was an innocuous piece and yet also her favorite. So different than the large portrait hanging over the fieldstone fireplace in the living room, her most ambitious effort to date. That was painted the year the twins graduated from high school and Cora, fearing an almost-empty nest right down to her bones, had found herself compelled to paint the entire family. Something she never deigned to attempt. She'd seen enough of her colleagues' work to know how risky it was to paint someone you knew, let alone loved. No matter how skilled your eye or hand, it was daunting to capture their essence. Be it the characteristic turn of mouth or the knowing look in an eye, when it came to replicating life on canvas, family members posed the most risk for disappointment. (There it was again—art imitating life!) But that one summer Cora had had enough of tossing and turning in her upstairs bed, worrying about the twins going off to college and counting down the days until they did, so she'd risen in the dark and gone downstairs. Straight to the old pine hutch in the living room she went and pulled out all the drawers in search of what she was looking for: a family photo of the five of them. In the photo, they were down at the beach for a sunset walk. It was such a stunning event that night, Charley had pulled a beachgoer aside and asked them to please take the picture, just as the setting sun was threatening to tumble into the jetty. The person had captured the whole family right before the pink orb dipped. There they were—her brood—cast in the hopeful glow of one summer Cora wished she could make eternal. Everyone looking at the camera! Everyone smiling! Miracle of miracles. As soon as she found it, she raced to her easel, grabbed a fresh canvas, and set out her oils and turpentine and brushes. By the time Charley and the kids stumbled still half-asleep downstairs the next morning, two of the five family members had made appearances on canvas. It took her all summer to finish, but it was hanging over the fireplace before they left to take the twins to college. And it wasn't half bad.

Now in the front hall, she stopped at another small oil. An oceanic image, all frothy wave and churning sea, threatening to spill outside the borders of its frame. Andi has always claimed it as her own and each summer as they closed up the house for the season and packed to go home, Cora had to check to make sure it was still on the wall before leaving. That's how much Andi liked it.

This summer, there'd been plenty of angst to paint with. It made her think back to childhood, and her mother. How she missed her since she'd passed away many years ago. Her mother had only gotten to know her grandchildren through a few short visits during their early years, always without her father. And then she'd fallen ill with cancer and died just a year after. It still felt unfair to Cora, losing her so young. Painting was one way she still felt close to her. But Cora was not liking what she'd produced so far this summer. As she sat in the small sunroom off the kitchen, tapping her dry brush to her lips, she contemplated the raw canvas in front of her. It was another beach scene with two penciled-in people walking by the water. In the foreground was a tumble of beach grass and rosa rugosa. A sea-battered dune fence listing to one side. And an unfinished beach path with no clear direction. The path felt important to the scene. *But where did it go?* she wondered. She could not paint the rest until she knew.

Maybe she should start a big breakfast, the kind they used to have. But no, Molly was gone for the rest of the week with her father and that curious woman, and the rest of the house was still asleep. The kids had sure had a late night. She could only imagine what they all talked about once she and Charley left the Beach House Grill where they'd all had dinner. The last she knew, they'd headed out to a pub together with Nate Becker. How funny it was seeing them together again. All these years later and sometimes it still felt like they were little kids. She wondered if she'd ever stop worrying about them.

The old saying was so true: you were only as happy as your least happy child. Right now who was most unhappy? Hard to say. Andi was still going through so much with her own family, trying to start a new future, and now she'd been slammed with the news that her past was not what she'd thought. And Hugh. She knew Hugh and Martin were struggling with next steps in their marriage. Martin was ready for a family. Hugh was not quite there yet. And now—with the shock that Charley was not his biological father—well, she could not imagine what damage that had done to any thoughts of fatherhood for himself. Sydney, the baby of the family who had always been so easygoing, should have been happy: a wedding around the corner to a lovely young man they all liked. And now—a wedding gift of the family beach house.

Cora rubbed her temples. Riptide brought such joy to the family. How dare Tish step in and rip it from all of them, regifting it in such an ugly way? Cora knew the old bag was still in town. She had a mind to drive over to the Chatham Bars Inn and unburden herself of some of her more pointed thoughts. But so far she'd restrained herself. For Charley. Sweet, loyal Charley. He'd asked so little of her in their long marriage. She couldn't very well turn down this one request.

With painting not an option for the moment, Cora turned to her desk in the corner of the living room by the front window. The list of wedding things to do was endless. Resigned, she ticked through it. Sydney had finalized the flowers with Molly and Andi. The dresses were tailored. The band was contracted. The catering menu had yet to be finalized, but that was really up to Sydney and James. She examined the menu selections thus far: roasted corn and tomato salad, lobster bisque, oysters Rockefeller, poached cod in tarragon butter sauce, honey-lavender chicken. Such a simple yet elegant menu and so Sydney. Cora's mouth watered. Maybe she would make that big breakfast, after all. She'd been trying so hard to be good, to watch her weight so that she could fit into the lilac dress she'd chosen for Sydney's wedding. But the thought of bacon frying in a skillet was enticing . . .

The stair treads creaked and she looked up. Charley stood on the bottom step, looking around.

"Kids still asleep?"

"Still asleep."

He glanced around the kitchen. "Shall I start a pan of bacon?"

Cora smiled. The man was a saint.

She watched as he took the old cast-iron skillet from the cupboard and pulled ingredients out of the refrigerator. They had their routines in their marriage and in this house. How strange to think it was now Sydney's. "How is the painting going?" he asked.

She sighed. "It's not, really."

Charley knew what this meant. "Still stalled?"

"I started feeling so sure of myself and I began sketching right away. But now I look at the canvas and I have no idea what direction it's going in."

Charley nodded. "Sort of like this summer."

Cora wandered back out to the sunroom. She stared at her raw canvas. At the pencil lines of her faceless people. At the beach path with no end. There was something she needed to do. And suddenly, it hit her.

She took the narrow stairs down to the basement. In the darkness she fumbled about for the lightbulb chain and pulled it impatiently. There, in the dimly lit corner, was the storage shelf where she'd hidden it.

Over the years, Charley and Cora had brought many things from their Connecticut house to Riptide. Things they needed at the cottage: tools, an old vacuum cleaner, runoff belongings that they didn't have the heart to toss but never ended up using at the cottage. Even a few Christmas decorations for the one year they celebrated it here. But there was a particular thing Cora had purposely brought up one summer, something that she never even told Charley about. It was because she couldn't stand the thought of keeping it in their family home. But she couldn't get rid of it either. Cora exhaled with relief when she found it on the bottom shelf, shoved behind a few cans of old paint.

The shoebox was a bit crumpled, the cardboard soft from basement air. But to her relief, the photos inside were still fine. Sitting cross-legged on the concrete floor, Cora pulled out a stack and flipped through. There she was, a college girl at Vassar, smiling at the camera with her freshman-year roommate. Her hair was so golden, her complexion so bright. Ah, youth! One was of her and a boy whose name she couldn't recall, all dressed up for a dance. Another was her friend, Audrey, at a soccer game one fall. Cora traced her old friend's face lovingly. How long had it been since she'd talked to Audrey? But none of that was what she was looking for.

She set them aside and grabbed another handful. A few photos in, there he was: Robert. Cora studied him. Thick, brown hair, like Hugh's. Those dark, almond-shaped eyes that both twins had inherited. He sat at his dorm desk, glancing over his shoulder at the camera. Cora wondered if it were she who'd taken the picture. The next photo was of the two of them. Robert had his arm thrown around her shoulders and she was looking sideways at him. Cora saw it now; the casual ease of that arm. His intense gaze, only for the lens. While hers was fixed on him. What a naïve girl she'd been.

She set it down and riffled through the rest. Finally, she settled on one of Robert alone. He was sitting on a stone wall in the campus arboretum. It was fall, the leaves dense with color. Robert looked benign in this photo, she decided; a safe choice. Not too full of himself, not too comedic. No doubt very handsome and oh-so-young. This was the right one. She tucked it carefully in her back pocket.

Back upstairs, she found the bacon had gone and done its job, rousing everyone from their beds. As they finished breakfast and scraped plates and poured more coffee, Cora studied her adult children. Hugh still made that face whenever someone said something he didn't like. "You guys have an appointment today to get your wedding suits fitted," Sydney announced. "Remember?"

There it was again: Hugh's furrowed brow.

"How was last night?" Charley ventured. After dinner at the Grill, the kids had gone out for drinks while she and Charley had begged off. They were treading carefully. The kids were allowing them to share the same space and some conversation, which was a start. But the hard stuff hadn't been dealt with yet.

"Andi has a crush," Hugh exclaimed.

Cora looked to her daughter, whose fierce red cheeks gave her away.

"Don't be ridiculous," Andi insisted.

Martin was gentler. "Well, let's just say an invitation to dinner was issued. And neither Hugh nor I was invited."

"Nor me." Sydney chuckled.

"Is that so?" Cora asked. She pressed her hand to the photo tucked safely in her back pocket. It could wait.

"So I'm having dinner with Nate," Andi allowed. "But that's it. Dinner. You can all go back to your regularly scheduled programs now." And with that, she swept her phone and book from the counter and slipped upstairs before anyone could ask for more details.

"Where is Nate taking her? And when?" Suddenly, Cora was hungry for details. She would like to see Andi allow herself to have a little fun. And besides, Nate was a known commodity. A safe start for a first venture into dating.

Martin shrugged.

"No clue," Hugh said.

"Impudent Oyster, seven o'clock, tonight," Sydney told them all. You could always count on Syd. As the youngest, she'd spent enough years in the background listening in and taking notes. "Back to suit fittings. Hugh, I really need to check this off my wedding list," Sydney pleaded.

Hugh groaned. "I was planning to go to the beach."

"Just go now and you'll have the whole day for the beach."

"All right, all right." He looked to Martin. "Come with? We can hit some shops while we're in town."

As chairs scraped the hardwood floors and dishes clattered into the sink, Cora felt the photo burning a hole in her pocket. *Now,* she thought to herself. But Andi was upstairs. And she didn't know if Sydney and Martin should be a part of it.

Charley looked at her. "Breakfast dishes are washed. Should I go get changed for the beach, or did you want to paint instead?"

Neither, Cora thought. She stood up, but Hugh was already heading for the door, looking for his keys. "Wait!"

Her voice gave her away.

Hugh halted at the screen door, a look of concern on his face. "You okay, Mom?"

She had no choice now. "Hugh, do you have a minute?" She looked at the others. "I'd like to talk to Hugh, in private."

Charley locked eyes with her. She'd not discussed this with

him. She could see him lean in, trying to gauge whether he was needed. "If you could please call Andi down?" she asked him.

Outside, Cora sat on the front porch swing, the photo pressed between her fingers. The day was bright, the sun bright. She patted the seat beside her and Hugh sat down obediently. A moment later, the door opened, then closed. Andi looked between them. "Dad called me down. What's going on?"

"Come sit," Cora said.

With one child seated on either side of her, the swing felt snug and sun-warmed, like an embrace. *As it should be*, she thought. "I have something to show you both." Cora held up the photo of Robert on the stone wall.

Andi gasped. "It's him."

Hugh said nothing.

"Yes. This is Robert," Cora explained. "I thought you might want to see what he looked like."

"God," Andi said, studying the photograph. "Hugh looks just like him."

Hugh scowled. "No, I don't."

He did, but Cora would not press him. "I found this down in the basement. There are more, if you're interested."

"What're they doing, here? At Riptide?" Hugh asked.

She'd prepared herself for questions, but not that one. It gave away too much.

"Well, some things have a way of making themselves between the two houses."

But she could tell they did not believe this. The truth was she didn't want remnants of Robert in their family home back in Connecticut. It felt like a betrayal to Charley. It felt like a betrayal to herself, after what Robert had done to her, leaving her like that. But she'd known she needed to keep them for the twins. For that "someday" when she decided to tell them. Riptide had always been their safe haven, their escape. It made sense to store them there.

"I kept it here for both of you." She looked between them. "Do you have any questions?"

"Well, yeah. What does he do? And where does he live, if you know?"

Cora shrugged. "I honestly don't know. Like I said, we haven't spoken since college."

Andi bit her lip. "Not even a letter? Or a call?"

"Nothing."

"But he knew about us." It wasn't a question, but Cora heard the inquiry in it. And it broke her heart.

"Yes, honey. He knew I was pregnant. And that I planned to have you. But that was all."

"Were you surprised he never reached out?"

"In theory, yes. Robert was young and also a bit arrogant, I'm sorry to say. But I figured maybe when he grew up he'd wonder. Maybe he'd reach out." It was true, but it was also something she'd feared. "But that kind of thinking can be dangerous. You don't know what you're inviting and so I left it alone. He did not reach out and neither did I. Maybe that was a mistake. But—you two had a father. A wonderful father."

Andi was quick to reply. "We still do."

"Yes." Cora smiled with relief. "You still do."

All this while, Hugh remained quiet. He wasn't ready yet. "What about you?" she asked him.

"I'd like to show Martin."

"Of course." Cora held out the photo. She wanted Robert out of her hand. "This belongs to you now."

"Oh, I don't want it. Not to keep, I just meant . . ."

"I do." Andi reached for the photo, and Cora relinquished it. "I'd like to keep it. And I'd like to see the rest."

Her brown eyes were intent with what Cora recognized as both worry and determination. But this was good. "They're all yours," Cora told her. "Why don't you come down to the basement with me. I'll show you where they are."

They rose and went to the door, but Hugh remained. "You coming?" Andi asked.

"Not yet."

Cora let Andi go ahead. She rested her hand on Hugh's shoulder and it tightened beneath her fingers. "I'm sorry, honey," she said. "I thought you'd like to see what he looked like. Maybe it would help make this feel real."

Hugh's tone was sharp. "Oh, it feels real."

A fresh sadness rose up in her throat. Cora walked into the house alone.

Down in the basement, she showed Andi where the box was. "Would you rather bring that upstairs? It's so dark down here, so damp."

"I'm fine," Andi murmured, and Cora knew to leave her alone. As she climbed the stairs, she looked back once. Andi had stopped sifting through photos, her attention grabbed by one in her hand. Cora couldn't help but wonder which. Was it the one of her gazing at Robert?

Upstairs she went to her sunroom. Hugh was out on the porch with Martin. She would leave them alone too.

As she stared at her canvas, she felt as uncertain as the sketch in front of her, but also somehow lighter. It reminded her of how uncertain she'd felt leaving Vassar. Of accepting Charley's crazy marriage proposal. Of holding the twins for the first time, that day in the hospital. She'd never felt so uncertain as she had then, one baby in each arm. Wondering how she'd breastfeed two. How she'd raise them. How on earth had she gotten to that place?

And then along came Tish, to meet them. Cora would never forget it. After the briefest of hellos, Charley had swept his mother down the hall to the nursery, leaving her in her private room to rest. But Cora could not. She pictured Tish staring at them through the plate-glass window and what Tish would think about her babies. If she'd come around. If their little faces—her only grandchildren—would make her heart turn. For what felt like forever, Cora waited in her hospital room for them to return. Finally, Charley poked his head around the door. "She loves them!" he said.

It was more than she'd hoped for. Cora's breath caught. "She does?"

Charley was elated. "She says their names are great. And that they look big and healthy for twins. I think she's happy to be a grandmother." The look on his face made her almost believe it all.

"Where is she?" Cora asked. "Isn't she coming back in?" She pulled the covers up about her.

Charley shook his head. "No, darling. She knows you're exhausted. She said to give you her love and let you rest."

Her *love*. This she could not believe. But then again, who knew? She'd heard that babies had that magical effect on people, especially grandparents.

"Why don't you have a nap," Charley suggested. "I'm going down to the cafeteria to get some coffee. Want anything?"

Cora shook her head, sinking gratefully into the pillows of the hospital bed. She was sated enough.

It had finally happened. In the innocent faces of her twins, Tish had softened. Now maybe Charley would have some peace of mind, free from his mother's guilt. Maybe now they could try to be a real family. Something Cora so longed for, since childhood. Especially with her mother far away in Ohio, and now somewhat estranged, thanks to her father. She lay down, the smallest smile on her face. She was so sore, so tired, but now she could rest.

She'd just started to doze when she heard the door open. "Charley?"

She opened her eyes and rolled over. The afternoon light slanted through her window and her mother-in-law stepped into it.

Cora pulled herself up. "Oh, hello. I thought you'd left." She was a mess, her hair unwashed and rumpled.

Tish strode right up to the edge of Cora's bed and placed both hands on the railing. Her gold rings clanked against the metal. "If you think for one second that this changes anything, you are dead wrong."

Cora blinked in confusion. Charley had just said . . .

"Right this moment, my son is supposed to be at medical school. At Yale." Tish leaned in so close her Chanel perfume wafted over the bed. "But instead he is stuck here, with you. Taking care of your fatherless children."

Cora recoiled. "You need to leave."

Tish was not done. "You have ruined Charley's life. You have bewitched him and derailed him from the dreams we worked to build! But worst of all, you don't even love him."

Cora fell back against her pillows. "Get out!" she begged. How could this be happening? Where was Charley?

"Do you hear me?" Tish hissed. "You will never be part of the Darling family. *Never.*"

Cora hauled herself upright. "I said get out!" she screamed. Her ears rang as she did.

There was the click of heels and the whoosh of the door and, just as quickly, Cora was alone in the room, the rattling of her heart the only sound in her ears.

Fearing she would be sick, Cora searched left and right for the pink plastic bin the nurse had left. It was nowhere.

Instead, she sank into her bedding. Tish was gone. The babies were tucked away in their nursery. And she was safe from her mother-in-law's rage. *Breathe,* she told herself.

Her pulse had finally slowed when the door opened again. Cora startled, ready for her. Ready to fight.

But it was Charley. He smiled softly. "You're still awake?"

Cora opened her mouth, but her lips were like sand, the words too hard to choke out.

"Here, let me pull the shades," he said. Charley crossed the floor and the room fell into darkness. "That's better now, isn't it?" He turned to her and rested a hand atop her sweaty brow. His face fell. "Darling, you feel hot. Should I call a nurse?"

Cora shook her head, unable to tell Charley what just happened. "No, just some water."

Charley hurried out to the hall and came back with water.

And a nurse. He was so nervous, so doting. As the nurse went over her vitals, Charley fretted by her bedside.

"I'm fine. Really," Cora insisted.

When the nurse left, Cora sipped her ice water under her husband's watchful gaze. She realized then she could not tell Charley. Not then. Maybe not ever.

What Tish said had lodged in her heart and she braced herself against it. But she could not deliver the same blow to him; not after everything he'd done for her and the babies.

"Are you sure you're feeling all right?" he asked, taking her hand in his.

Cora looked into his hazel-gray eyes. "I'm sure."

No, she would not speak of the dark things his mother had unleashed on her. What Tish had hissed in her ear that day was odious. But far more odious was the thought that had stayed with her ever since: *What if all of it were true?*

Andi

It was almost a gibbous moon, and gentle light spilled through her bedroom window. Her walls were splashed with it. Across the wooden floorboards was more. Andi sat in bed, knees tucked to her chin, staring at the amber glow surrounding her. It was otherworldly, like something out of a fairy tale. As was the thing she was about to do.

It was after midnight, and she was sneaking out of the house. If such a thing could be said of a forty-four-year-old single mother on vacation with her family. But it was true. Her parents were asleep and none the wiser, down the hall. As were Martin and Hugh, who'd turned in early that night. Sydney's doorway had glowed with lamplight as she talked late into the evening with James, their bedtime ritual, but now her doorway was dim too. And it signaled to Andi that it was almost time. As would the *clink* of a pebble against her window, any moment now.

Andi pulled her knees tighter to her chest and tried to will her heart to slow while she waited for it. It was the most exhilarating thing she'd done in decades. Seconds later, there was a sound outside. Then silence. Andi strained to hear. And just when she'd dismissed it as a nocturnal animal, there was the stony *plink* of pebble against siding. She leaned forward and slid her window open as high as it would go. Below, in the shadows, something moved. Nate Becker stepped forward and he too was cast in moonlight. Andi laughed out loud. "This is crazy!" she half shouted and half whispered.

"Yes, it is. Now get down here."

They laughed the whole way down the beach path, side by side, the sand cool beneath their bare feet. The leaves of the rosa rugosa glowed like silver and when the path ended they tumbled out onto the beach below. Andi halted.

"What is it?" Nate asked.

She was almost out of breath, but that wasn't the reason. "Look," she said, pointing to the silvery ocean ahead. Then turning slowly, to the dunes they'd just run through. And finally, up overhead. A few stars on the edge of the moon still twinkled. "I want to take it all in."

Nate stepped closer and took her hand in his. "That's nice."

Andi looked up at him. "You're pretty nice yourself, Nate Becker."

For a beat they locked eyes. Andi laughed, nervously. "Where'd you hide that beer?"

Nate slipped a small canvas cooler off his shoulder. "Want one?"

"Maybe two?" she joked.

They sat at the high-tide mark, just beyond the stretch of seaweed and shells. "Tide's coming in fast tonight," Nate observed, cracking open two bottles and handing her one.

"It used to scare me." She clinked her bottle against his.

"The waves?"

"No," Andi said. "The thought of the tide coming in, like it was coming to get us. Especially during storms. I used to worry it might come in right up over the dunes, swallow up the house." She looked at him. "When I was little."

"And now?"

"Now I find it comforting. Like it's something coming to meet me halfway. Something that washes away the day and sweeps the beach clean. Kind of like a fresh start."

Nate stared out at the water, listening quietly. Only the sound of the surf rose in the air between them. "How do you feel about starting over, Andi Darling?"

It was a question Andi had been asked a lot that year. "It's daunting, for sure," she said. "But it's also an opportunity, you know? A second chance."

Nate leaned her way and bumped against her shoulder. "I hear those are hard to come by."

Andi turned to him. He was staring right at her. Before she could reply, he pressed his lips against hers.

If anyone had told Andi as a teenager that someday she'd kiss Nate Becker, she would probably have laughed. Not now.

Nate's lips were warm and full and certain, tinged with the spicy citrus taste of summer ale, and she found herself kissing him back intently. There was no awkwardness. No fumbling. Their lips and tongues moved together, a buzzing give and take, and Andi felt herself brimming with desire.

She pulled away, her breath short.

"Andi . . . I'm sorry."

"No," she said, touching his face. "I'm not." Nate's gaze was so earnest. But she needed to go slowly. Dancing, always, at the edge of her own needs and wants was the constant thought of Molly. It was all for naught, probably; Molly was fine, away with her father and having a wonderful time, according to the few quick texts she'd sent. But now, here on the beach, making out with a new man for the first time since she'd said her marriage vows fifteen years ago, Andi felt off kilter. As wonderful as it was.

Nate must've sensed it. "C'mon," he said, standing up. He reached for her hand and pulled her up.

"Where are we going?"

"You'll see."

They walked down to the water's edge and turned right. "You seem to have a plan."

"I do, but it's a bit of a walk. You up for one?"

Between the moonlit beach and the kissing and the sudden sense of freedom swirling up in her, Andi didn't want the night to end yet. "Lead the way."

They followed the shoreline, skirting the frothy edge of the incoming tide. The air was balmy, despite the late hour, the smell of salt heavy. It lent the night an eerily beautiful feel, as if anything was possible, and as Andi walked beside Nate she felt heady with anticipation.

They talked about their work, his in New York and hers in Connecticut. How much she loved teaching middle school students, but often struggled relating to her own teenage daughter. "I remember parents telling me I'd make such a good mom, because of how I taught." She shook her head at the memory. "Turns out there's little correlation there."

"Oh, come on," Nate said. "I've only seen you and Molly together a few times, but I can tell you're tight. She seems like a great kid."

"Thanks. Though her mother is still a work in progress."

Nate chuckled. "Aren't we all?"

"You look like you're doing pretty darn well for yourself," Andi said, glancing up at him. From what he'd shared, he had a nice place in the city. A good job. And here he was, back on the Cape in his parents' renovated summer home.

"I'm not sure you always thought that," Nate said. "I think I was just this goofy friend of Hugh's to you. God, I was so skinny and awkward in middle school."

Andi laughed. "I remember!"

"Yeah, well, that's not how I remember you." He reached over and squeezed her hand. "And all these years later, here you are. Even better, if that's possible."

Andi didn't know what to say. It meant something to hear that someone from a happy past thought you were doing okay, even in the troubled present.

For a while they walked the remote stretch of Lighthouse Beach, the waves the only sound. Andi imagined it must be really late, but for once she didn't feel tired at all. "So where exactly are you taking me?"

Nate laughed. "Yeah, it's farther out than I remembered. Sorry about that."

"No!" Andi insisted. "I'm enjoying the hike. Just making sure you aren't abducting me or leaving me out here in the wilds. This would be the place to do it."

"Not tonight," Nate teased. "Have you heard of the dune shack?"

Andi shook her head.

"No?" Nate was surprised. "Wow, I know something in Chatham that the Darling family doesn't? This is too good."

"What's that supposed to mean?"

"Nothing. It's just that your family has such ties to this place. To Chatham and Riptide. Growing up here in the summers I always felt like a newcomer by comparison. But in a good way. You guys showed me around, taught me all the cool spots." He grinned at her. "Now it's my turn."

It made her think of Riptide. And all that had happened. "Did Hugh tell you about the beach house?"

"About your grandmother giving it to Sydney?" He looked empathetic and guilty all at once. "I didn't want to say anything unless you did."

"It's not like it's a secret." Then she laughed at the absurdity of what she'd just said. "Did Hugh tell you about the thing that *was* a secret?"

Nate cocked his head. "I don't think so . . ."

"Well, good thing it's a long walk." As they worked their way along the water's edge, Andi filled Nate in. Not just on Tish's "wedding gift" to Sydney, that had shocked them all, but to the real shocker—the revelation of the family secret surrounding their biological father. By the time they stopped near the point of South Beach, Nate was still struggling to wrap his mind around it. "So let me get this straight. Your dad isn't your biological dad? And you guys are just finding out about that now?"

Andi stared at her bare feet, which she could almost make out in the moonlight. "Pretty much. Crazy, isn't it?" Talking about it to someone outside the family made it real. "You're the first person I've told this to."

Nate grabbed both her hands. "Andi, I'm so sorry you're going through all of this. But I'm touched. That you told me."

"Well, you're a family friend. And kind of like a brother, so . . ."

"Like a brother?" Nate cringed. "Yikes. I didn't see that coming."

Andi could've kicked herself. "No! Not like a brother, at all. I meant that you're someone I grew up with and you were one of Hugh's best summer friends, that's all. Back *then* I thought of you like that."

"And now?" Nate's voice was soft, his tone more serious.

"Nothing like a brother." This time Andi leaned in and kissed him. There it was again, that soft, sweet pull each time their lips met.

After a moment Nate stepped back, and for a second she feared she'd blown it. He looked at her intently. "Still not a brother, right?"

This time they both laughed and she swatted his arm. "C'mere," he said, leading her up toward the sand dunes. "This is what I wanted to show you."

At first Andi was confused. As they climbed there was nothing to see beyond the dune grass. But then, in the dimly lit distance, a small, rambling structure came into focus against the horizon. Andi squinted. This section of Lighthouse Beach was notably remote and wild, protected by the Cape National Seashore; beyond the sand and surf there was nothing else around. "What is that? A clubhouse?"

Nate quickened their pace. "Come and see."

Sure enough, as they got closer, the low-lying structure took shape. It was a ramshackle wooden outbuilding of sorts. But raw and wild and open, like the land surrounding it. They halted in its sandy front yard, if you could call it that. The shack was flanked on either side by a crooked fence constructed of driftwood and salvaged sections of beach fencing. A tangle of old buoys hung from it like haphazard Christmas ornaments. In the center there was erected a tall pole from which flew a small American flag. "This is crazy. How did this get here?"

"Flotsam and jetsam," he said appreciatively. "The ocean built it." Nate watched her walk around it, inspecting each nook and cranny. "Everything here was washed ashore by storms and sort of cobbled together."

"By whom?"

Nate shrugged. "Unofficial caretakers, I guess you could say. Locals. Wash-a-shores, like us. People who love Chatham and wanted to preserve it as a little sanctuary of sorts."

"And yet I've never even heard of it."

"It first showed up about six years ago and has turned into quite the local legend. Pretty iconic, isn't it?"

Andi was too consumed by the magic of the little shack to speak. She walked carefully around the outside of it, running her hands over its treasures: a rusted anchor leaning against a post, a broken lobster trap, a plastic statue of a bird nailed to the fence. "No Vacancy" said a tattered sign, painted in red lettering, affixed to the doorframe. She peered inside. People had carved their names into the wooden boards. "It's like a little driftwood clubhouse. A shrine to the ocean."

"Yeah, there's something spiritual about it," Nate agreed. "People come out here to meditate. Others to take a selfie. Some folks leave a little talisman after they visit. If you come back during the day, there's usually a guestbook inside you can sign."

Andi climbed inside the small interior and sat. The three

exterior walls were loosely fashioned sections of wood and the breeze whistled through the slats. Sure enough, there was a small guestbook resting on a piece of wood. Looking up, she could see the stars through sections of the tattered roof. "It's magical." She had to show Molly! And Hugh, and the rest of them. How had she not heard of this little shack before this summer?

After a while, Nate poked his head in. "May I?"

It was cozy inside, but Andi happily scooted over. They sat in silence, listening to the ocean and staring out at the sky.

"It feels like we're the only two people on Earth," she whispered. "Like we're in some kind of quirky fairy tale."

Even in the dim light, she could see him smile. "That's why I wanted to show it to you. I knew you'd get it."

Andi was touched by his admission. But then a terrible thought occurred to her. "What if this place gets washed away? It's so close to the water."

"Part of the fairy tale, right? Nothing lasts forever."

The thought of that made her suddenly feel very small. Nate reached around and pulled her closer and Andi let her head rest on his shoulder. It felt surreal and yet so natural.

"The ocean always gives back," he reminded her. "The dune shack has made it six years already. But I guess if it gets washed away, then something new will wash up. And people can start again."

She liked the sound of that. Rebuilding. It was what she had tried to do all year. With Molly and their new house. With her sense of self, as a newly single woman in the world. At times it consumed and exhausted her. At others, she was overcome by the sense of possibility. "I can relate to that," she whispered.

"Andi," he whispered back. "I'm glad you like it out here."

She looked up at him. "I like you, Nate Becker."

And then they were kissing. Softly, at first, and then more urgently. Elbows and knees bumping the wooden walls, they maneuvered in the tight space so that they could face each other. Suddenly, Nate pulled away. "This is crazy." He laughed.

It was a relief to hear him echo her thoughts. "I know. We're acting like two teenagers."

"No." Nate shook his head, smiling shyly. "It's more than that. Andi, I've always felt something for you."

"You have?" She'd had no idea. Not even once in all their summers together.

"Yes! From that ruffled orange bikini you wore in high school, to the woman you are today."

Andi laughed out loud, and clapped her hand over her mouth. "My orange bikini!" She'd nearly forgotten all about that old bathing suit. "Nate, you have to be kidding."

"I'm serious. I've tried to get that thing out of my head for years." He was laughing now too. "You were so beautiful. So sure of yourself, and I was just this skinny friend of your twin brother's."

It was quite possibly the sweetest thing anyone had ever said to her. This tender admission carried all these years by a kid she'd always liked and now this beautiful man sitting beside her. Andi reached up and traced the edge of Nate's jaw, her fingers moving down his shoulders, across the breadth of his chest. Gone was any trace of that skinny kid. He watched her as she did, his breath coming in short puffs. He was letting her lead, taking her cue. And it emboldened her.

She reached for the hem of his shirt and tugged it up, over his head. Obediently, Nate raised his arms as she slipped it off.

His chest was warm and strong and she pressed the palms of her hands against it. A tear slipped down her cheek.

Nate pressed his thumb gently against it, swept it away. "What is it?"

She shook her head. "I don't know. You. Me. All of it."

He kissed her cheek where the tear had been. "Breathe, Andi Darling. Just breathe."

And she did. Andi let her mind wander with her hands, taking her time. Savoring the way this man made her feel. The sensations he elicited. Without hesitation, she pulled her own shirt over her head, let it fall to the floor of the shack. When she pressed her chest against his they fit like two pieces of a puzzle.

Andi exhaled as Nate ran his hands across her back, down her spine. She sucked in her breath. Beneath his touch she came alive in ways she had not imagined she ever would again. Maybe taking things slowly wasn't so important, after all.

"Look at you, Andi Darling. You've no idea how exquisite you are."

She'd tried to imagine being with another man. Someone new, whose heart and mind she did not know, any more than she knew the curves or angles of his body. The thought had terrified her. Shedding her clothes was about shedding so much more. She was no longer twenty years old. Her body had served her well, carried and birthed her daughter. But in doing so it carried the stretch marks and lines and all the rest that came with all that living.

But now here she was with Nate. On a deserted stretch of beach. Nestled into a magical little shack that felt like they were the last two people on earth. As they peeled away the remains of their clothes there was no sense of hesitation. Nate was wholly new to her, and yet so familiar. Andi felt safe. And desirable. And so damn good.

As Nate lay her gently down against the sand, he cupped her face in his hands.

"I can't believe this. My whole life, I couldn't get you to even look at me."

Andi pressed the naked length of her body against him and wrapped her arms around his neck. "I'm looking at you now."

Tish

The sea air has restored in her an energy she has not felt for a long time. Probably not for the last decade. Certainly, not since her recent cardiac diagnosis. She has kept that to herself, mixed as she feels about this. Telling Charley was part of the plan when she decided to come back here. At her advanced age, it really should not come as a shock to him; not everyone lived to be ninety. Her lifestyle and good health, until now, have kept her trotting the globe years beyond anyone's expectations; her own included! Each time she looks in the mirror Tish is momentarily startled: *who* is that old woman staring back at her? She supposes she should be grateful for all the time she's had, and not mourn how little her doctor says she has left. Telling Charley will complicate that; she loathes pity. She won't stand for it. But most of all, she loves her son, and she does not want her aging heart to place any burden on his own.

The last time Tish visited the Cape she was twenty-nine. Now, when she smells the salt air and hears the roar of the surf, she is transported right back. When Morty was alive and well and they were young and happy. And Charley—well, Charley was just a little boy. When she wakes up and sees the sparkling bay waters outside her window at Mooncusser Cottage, Tish believes for a fleeting glorious moment that they are just the way they were then. That it is the summer of 1961 again and her life is a book barely begun, the pages of which she is certain hold a happy ending.

Oh, she has tried to avoid thinking of that summer since she's returned. Morty has filled her dreams and the family has riddled her thoughts since she's returned. But she always skirts the memory of that fateful day, the way she used to skirt the incoming tide: dancing about its frothy edges, but never letting it pull her in. But today is a beautiful day for walking and though she is slow and must focus, she is going to walk down to that beach, so help her God. Charley would not like it, so she does not call him. There is a reason she has a cane, despicable as she finds it. Today, she takes it in hand and rings the front desk. "I would like to arrange the same driver I had the other day: Jonathan," she tells the girl at reception. "Tell him to put on his walking shoes."

"Walking shoes?" the girl asks.

"Yes. Tell him it's me—Tish Darling. He'll understand."

Tish has made friends with Jonathan, and she likes to think they have an understanding. What she requires of his services is simple enough; he is middle-aged and strong. He is patient. She has no doubt he will be up for her special request today.

An hour later, when Jonathan knocks at Mooncusser Cottage, she is ready. Tish dons a cashmere shawl, wide-leg white pants, and her Kate Spade leopard print lace-up sneakers. She hopes they will hold up for a walk on the beach.

"Good morning, Mrs. Darling," Jonathan says, holding the door ajar for her. "Where to?"

As she hoped, Jonathan is game for anything. And she knows just where to go.

"I need to see the beach," she tells him from the backseat.

Jonathan adjusts his rearview mirror. "Any one in particular? I am guessing we are looking to walk, not swim, today?"

"You are guessing correctly. But it needs to be private, Jonathan. I have something I need to think about."

Jonathan considers this. "Lighthouse is less crowded, but there are many stairs."

She knows that beach well. Morty used to love to beach-cast there. No, there is no heaven or earthly way she can manage the staircase there.

"Forest?"

"Nothing on the bay. It must be ocean-facing." There is a reason for this and Jonathan does not ask. This is why she chose him.

"Very well," he says, and puts the car in drive. He does not say where they are going, but Tish doesn't worry. It will be the right one.

At the end of Ridgevale Road, the car turns right into a private neighborhood. In the 1950s, when Riptide was just their cozy, two-room beach shack, this neighborhood was just one expanse of beach grass and a smattering of small, rustic cottages like their own. Now the homes are valued in the tens of millions, tucked tight together, their American flags whipping audibly on their Atlantic-facing poles. "This is a private community," Tish says.

But Jonathan already knows this. "Don't you worry about that, Mrs. Darling," he tells her. "I know someone."

Sure enough, he does. Jonathan parks the town car in a vacant driveway of a sprawling two-story house perched at the edge of the barrier wall. It is quintessential Cape Cod, with weathered, gray shingles, a gabled roof, and porthole windows on both sides. When he opens the door, the smell of low tide fills her nostrils. "Will they mind?" Tish asks, nodding toward the house.

Jonathan shakes his head and takes her hand. "You have all the time you need."

The house is right on the beach and, to her utter relief, the steps are manageable and few. With one hand in Jonathan's and the other holding tight to her cane, Tish takes them one at a time until they reach sand. It shifts beneath her feet and she tilts to one side. "Ma'am?" Jonathan asks.

"This way," Tish says, leading him one diminutive step at a time toward the water.

As they approach, the sand beneath her feet firms up and the going is more even and less worrying. Tish stops about five yards from the surf. There is a large piece of driftwood washed ashore, a makeshift bench. She stares out at the horizon line, where water meets sky. The sun is high and hot, the breeze still. Here, she thinks, closing her eyes to the bright warmth. Here is where she needs to do it.

"This is the spot," she tells Jonathan.

As such, he helps her as she lowers herself gingerly onto the driftwood. Jonathan seems reluctant to let go of her hand, so she gives him a look she knows he can interpret even behind her oversized sunglasses. After all, it's what they agreed to.

"Very well, then, Mrs. Darling." He points to the opening in the seagrass by the steps they just came down. "I will be right over there, should you need anything." He pauses. "Anything at all."

"Jonathan?" she says.

"Yes, ma'am?"

"Go away."

He smiles and turns for the stairs.

This stretch of private beach is perfect. The narrow strip of sand is empty, save for a few small dinghies, overturned. Tish stares at the metal hull of the one closest. It reminds her of the underbelly of a whale. She wonders how a man could cling to it if his boat overturned in a storm. There seems nothing to hang on to. Nothing to save you. "I'm here, Morty," she whispers aloud.

The ache starts at the base of her skull and Tish steels herself against it. It's what happens every time she thinks of that day, as the gates of memory open. She turns to the sea, so calm today. The undulating surface glassy, the waves so timid they barely ripple onto the shore.

It had started out just like this, that summer day. Tish will never forget it. They'd awakened early, the sunrise dancing at the edges of their bedroom curtains. Tish wanted to roll over and sleep some more, but she sensed her husband awake beside her. It was how Morty got on mornings he planned to take the Whaler out to fish. By sunrise she could feel him practically humming next to her with childlike anticipation. As if sensing the energy, young Charley trotted into their room and leapt atop their covers. Morty sprang up and caught him, tucking Charley's sprawling limbs together and pulling him in, a little wild animal. Their little animal, hair sun-bleached and skin bronzed from a whole Cape Cod summer. Tish laughed as she watched them wrestle in the covers. In one week they would close up the cottage for the season and head back to the city. Their summer had been so idyllic, Tish didn't want to go.

She'd made an early breakfast of waffles and bacon and, as she stood at the stove, she watched through the screen door where Morty and Charley stood on the patio. The tackle box was open on the picnic table, a congregation of bobbers gathered on the wooden surface. Morty was showing their son how to string a fishing rod.

"The water is calm today," Morty remarked when they came in to eat. "Like glass." Tish would never forget those words. She knew he'd already been down to the beach to check it out. Mornings he fished, her husband headed down to check the tide before he even poured a cup of coffee, so excited was he to climb into the new Whaler they'd bought the summer before. With custom wooden seats. And the name *Charley* painted across its stern. "Unsinkable!" Morty liked to tell everyone he could. The thirteen-foot boat was Morty's pride and joy. Fishing was his diversion on the Cape and recently he'd started to bring Charley along with him. Tish loved that Morty was teaching Charley. But that morning was the weekly children's story hour at Eldridge Library and Tish was bringing Charley. After, when story time was over and Morty had returned with his daily catch, they'd meet back at Riptide for lunch before heading to the beach for a family swim. It was as busy as their summer days got. It was perfect.

After breakfast, she packed Morty a snack. A joke between them, as Tish liked to remind him he did little more than sit and float for a few hours. But she never sent him off empty-handed, and so that morning she wrapped three dill pickles in wax paper, along with a small wedge of cheese and a handful of crackers. When Morty kissed her goodbye in the kitchen, he stopped in the doorway and came back for one more; she would always remember that fact too.

Story hour was entertaining. The children's librarian sang a song using teddy bear puppets. Afterward, Tish and Charley lingered in the children's section and checked out two picture books that they would never return. When they came outside, to her surprise the day had completely turned. Tish glanced skyward. Dark gray clouds tumbled past the First Congregational Church steeple. Wind whipped the hem of her dress. "I'm cold," Charley said, pressing against her knees.

"Let's get you home." For a beat, Tish thought of Morty out in the boat. But he was a skilled fisherman and he knew to keep his eye on the horizon when on open water. By the time they got home he'd probably be waiting for them.

It was hard to keep her eyes on the road as she drove home to Riptide. Overhead, it seemed as if the sky was skating past. Main Street emptied quickly as shoppers hurried to their cars, and as they neared the Orpheum Theater, the first pelts of rain hit the windshield. By the time Tish pulled up to their cottage the rain was coming down in silver sheets.

"Morty?" she shouted as she raced through the front door with Charley in her arms. To her surprise, there was no sign of his return.

She set Charley down and hurried to the rear bedrooms—but both were empty.

At the kitchen window she peered out through the storm, certain he'd come running up the beach path at any moment, but it was empty. He was probably still tying up the Whaler down at the cove. Morty could be fussy about his new boat and gear, especially with a storm coming in. No matter. She put the kettle on the stove for tea.

An hour later, however, there was still no sign of him. The storm had not slowed, as she'd hoped, but picked up. Wind gusts whipped against the windows, shaking the walls of the cottage with each blast. Rain thundered against the panes.

"Mommy," Charley whimpered, following her from room to room. Tish picked him up and held him close. Even within the small confines of the cottage, she could not stop pacing.

"It's okay, sweet boy," she murmured. "Daddy will be home soon."

Over the course of the hour the sky had turned from charcoal to an eerie green hue. Tish had spent enough time by the coast to know this was not a good sign. She kept checking the back window for signs of Morty: a flash of yellow slicker running up from the beach. But there was nothing but beach grass blown sideways and rain. Endless sheets of rain. A slow panic began to pulse through her.

There was no phone in their cottage. She thought of the Nickersons, up the street. They were year-rounders and she knew they had one. But what to do with little Charley?

"Charley, I need you to stay here," she said firmly, kneeling to look straight into his eyes. She did not want to leave him alone, but neither could she imagine running up the street through the storm with him.

To her relief, he did not howl in protest, but sucked his thumb worriedly. She tucked him on the couch with one of his new library books and his stuffed ducky. "I will be right back in two shakes of a lamb's tail!" she promised. "No matter what, you stay inside."

Geared up in raincoat and galoshes, she went to the front door. "Be a good boy," she reminded Charley one last time. But no sooner had she opened the door than it blew back on its hinges. Tish stumbled backward. Water blasted inside the cottage. Her umbrella collapsed inward.

It took all her force to close the door, shutting out the storm once more. Once done, she stood dripping, staring in disbelief at the puddle of water around her feet. There was no way she could get to the Nickersons'. Charley started to cry. Tish felt she might too.

For what felt like hours, they waited. When the lights flickered and then went out, Tish lit the kerosene camping lamps Morty kept hanging on the kitchen wall. She pulled Charley onto her lap and they read the library books, over and over again. By dinnertime, when Morty had still not returned, she dumped milk and cereal into two bowls with shaking hands.

"For dinner?" Charley asked.

"Just eat," she snipped. Then, more gently, "It's a treat. When the power goes out we get breakfast for dinner."

The waiting was agony. All the while the winds whistled and the rain battered Riptide. Unable to eat or think, Tish stood at the kitchen window willing Morty to come back up from the beach. He had to have found cover. He loved that damn boat too much. Surely, he'd have brought it to shore somewhere down the beach and was riding out the storm in some Good Samaritan's house. They would laugh about this later.

By eight o'clock, when it should have been getting dark and Charley should have been getting ready for bed, the sky lightened. The rain slowed and the winds died down. Without warning, the sun peeked out from behind a cloud. Tish hurried to the door and pulled it open. Outside, the world glittered. Water was everywhere: pooled in the front yard, flooding the driveway, streaming down the street in angry little makeshift rivers. Tree limbs littered the ground wherever she turned. Tish raked her hand through her hair. "Put on your boots, Charley. We have to go look for Daddy."

They went out the back and down the beach path holding hands. Charley's little legs could not keep up, but Tish could not wait any longer. Despite his protests, she broke ahead into a run. At the base of the path, where the dune turned to beach, Tish halted. Before her was a sea she had never witnessed. A sea she'd only read about in *Moby Dick*. Or seen in old black-and-white photos at the diner in town. The storm may have left the sky, but it was not yet done with the ocean.

Tish looked up and down the beach in both directions, searching for a sign of Morty. But the beach was empty. Charley caught up and she took his hand again. "Let's go to the cove!" she said, but he did not want to. He stared at the water, a primal look of fear working across his face. "We're going to find Daddy!" Tish cried over the roar of the surf. "Come, darling. Let's go."

Their beach was foreign to her. Sun slanted off the dunes, which were water-soaked and a curious shade of coffee. Driftwood and dense seaweed tumbled in on waves. The inlet, where Charley liked to play in tidal pools, was washed away and filled with sand. Buoys littered the high-tide mark and they hurried around them. Tish caught her shoe in the long rope of a washed-up lobster trap and stumbled. The cove where Morty kept the Whaler was just ahead, around the jetty, and they scrambled up the highest dune for a better look.

The cove was protected, a shallow inlet. Surely the boats would still be there and, she prayed, the Whaler too. But when she crested the dune, she saw only a few still tethered by their moorings, bobbing on the high, angry water. The Whaler was not among them. She swung her gaze to the spot where neighbors stored their smaller boats along the shoreline: kayaks, dinghies, Sunfish. She and Morty kept a small white dinghy there that he used to get out to where the Whaler was moored. But the area was swept bare. Beyond, in the distance, she spied a few of the boats, scattered and tumbled in various locations along the dunes, their hulls gazing skyward. She gasped.

Tish raced down the dune and toward them, ahead of Charley. Heart in her throat, she ran up to each dinghy, as one might soldiers on a battlefield. The neighbors' blue-and-white Sunfish was tossed up in the dunes on its side, its mast bent and sail torn to pieces. There was the little red rowboat she'd often seen a grandfather take his grandkids out in, half buried in sand. The watercraft were strewn like someone had lifted them skyward and thrown them back to earth, a boat graveyard. As Charley stood crying on the beach, Tish ran from boat to boat. Touching each hull. Searching the names on the sides. Crying out for Morty. Until she collapsed on the sand, her voice raw and broken.

Charley came and pressed himself against her. "Where's Daddy?"

But Tish could not comfort him. The sun turned pink, then orange, until a blazing red filled the sky and cast them in a fiery glow. Still, Tish sat in the wet sand, unable to move.

Eventually there was a voice. A man's voice. Tish's heart knocked to life against her ribs. She raised herself up, spinning around to see.

"Hello!" An older man in a dark raincoat crested the dunes. Waving. Hollering. It was not Morty.

It was not Morty who came and helped her up from the sand and walked her home with her son. Nor was it Morty who brought her dinner and held her hand on the couch that night, as neighbors stopped by and poked their heads inside the cottage door with pieces of news. The jetty at Ridgevale Road had washed out. Two fishing boats were lost at sea. Part of the Chatham Pier had ripped away from its pilings. But there was no news of Morty.

The next day, as the ocean gave back some of what it had taken, there were some answers. The Coast Guard trolled the shoreline and waterways. Search and rescue units made up of local fishermen and good neighbors were dispensed. Both of the missing fishing boats from the Chatham fleet were accounted for, all men aboard miraculously alive. A boathouse that had been washed away from one person's Harding's Beach house had washed up fully intact on Monomoy Island, perched on the sand just as if it had always been there. But there were losses; beach houses were washed off their stilts. Boats that had been sucked into the tide were chewed up and spit back onto land. Among them, a thirteen-foot Boston Whaler with wooden seats washed up on Cockle Cove Beach the next day. Named: *Charley*. Just as Morty always said, unsinkable.

Wordlessly, Tish packed bags. Left food in the fridge. Sheets on the beds. And her still-wet raincoat hanging on the back of the door. When Mrs. Nickerson returned with a batch of warm blueberry muffins, Tish was already filling up the car with gas off Route 28. When the police chief pulled into her driveway to check in, she had pointed the car south toward the Sagamore Bridge. By the time the ocean had slowed its tidal pull and a new day's sun was spilling over Riptide, Tish Darling's battered heart was already off-Cape.

Cora

The painting was a stubborn one. But so was she. Cora picked up her brush, swirled it in the mix of titanium white and Naples yellow oil she'd chosen for sand, and set brush to canvas. There was no going back now.

All morning she painted. The kids came and went in the background, just as they used to in the old days, and just like those days she could still tell what they were doing by sound. Refrigerator door and knife on cutting board: beach picnic being made. Front door slamming: Hugh returning from his run. Shower going on late afternoon: Andi getting ready for her "nondate" with Nate. Pacing footsteps: Charley, puttering around the house, unwilling to interrupt her work but not yet comfortable enough to follow the kids down to the beach or invite them to go fishing, without her. By late afternoon, she set her brush down and sat back to consider her work.

The background was complete. The two figures walking the beach had identities. And the beach path had a destination. Cora was momentarily content.

She'd escaped to her art all day; it was time to face the family. "Charley?"

She found her husband on the patio, not reading *The New York Times* in his hand. He was staring pensively out the back, toward the beach path, where she'd not long ago heard Sydney and Martin and Hugh head out to.

"What're you doing?" she asked.

Charley shrugged. "Honestly? I'm taking up space." He set the paper down. "I don't know, Cora. The blowup with the kids may have settled, but it's not the same." He looked at her. "That's my biggest fear. That it will never be the same again."

"They still call you Dad," she said as reassurance. "You will always be that to them, Charley."

He shook his head. "Things are different. It's not just my imagination."

She took a seat next to his and contemplated the view. Down there on that beach, their kids were basking in the sun. Together, even with all the upset. But Charley was right. The roles in their family were no longer defined. "Hugh doesn't know if he wants to be a father. I think he was on the fence, but ready to swing his leg over the side. And now this."

Charley nodded. "It's what I talked to my mother about the other day. She doesn't understand the upset. She only sees the upside."

"What upside?" This was what steamed Cora the most. There was none she could find.

"You have to understand, my mother had a complicated past. Her family had very little. And then she was whisked up in this life my father afforded her, because he loved her and his family had plenty." Charley stared out at the ocean. "She doesn't think I knew any of that, but I did. It was all over her face growing up. How torn she was between both worlds. And when my father died, well . . . she made sacrifices to make sure I didn't grow up without."

Cora had heard this before and the story still got her, but it was not an excuse. "But what does that have to do with dividing up the family like she did? Drawing bloodlines? Because that's what she did."

"I know. And I can't say it's any justification for what she did, Cora, but this is what she told me. Her parents felt uncomfortable about her marrying up; they didn't understand the world she lived in. They didn't trust it. On some level, they thought she was ashamed of where she came from and that offended them."

"Doesn't every parent want more for their child?"

Charley shrugged sadly. "I don't think they thought of it as more. They were strict Irish Catholic from a tight immigrant neighborhood. Everything they needed in life was within a handful of miles, from the Irish Community Center, to the church, to the grocer. No one left. They just married someone from the neighborhood and started over with the next generation. They saw it as her turning her back on everything they'd worked so hard to give her."

In that context, Cora admitted it made some sense. Tish's marriage had left her feeling both estranged from her past and struggling to fit in to her new life.

"My dad's family was Presbyterian." Charley laughed. "Not the most desirable arrangement for the daughter of a conservative Catholic family. But she and my father were so in love, she didn't let it sway her. Together, they had everything they needed. But when he died, so suddenly and so young, I think it left her in complete isolation. She didn't have the same support and ties from her own family and she'd never felt accepted or a part of his."

It was unimaginable, to lose your spouse at such a young age. And to then raise a child without a family's support. "At least she had the means," Cora pointed out. "You were both taken care of."

"Maybe. My family may have given materially. But they denied her everything emotionally." Charley's expression dimmed. "I was already fatherless. And my father's family owned everything. Our apartment. Our car. The schools I went to were all paid for by them. To keep me in that lifestyle, she had to give up a lot. She couldn't move away and start over. She couldn't marry again. Not as long as I was in their care.

"So she sacrificed. And once I was old enough she wanted me to have an escape. To be free of their control, as she saw it. Which is why she pushed me so hard in school as a kid. Why she tutored me and studied with me and enrolled me in every extracurricular she could: chess, golf, French, violin. You name it."

"That's a lot to expect of any child," Cora said. "We never did that to our kids."

"We didn't have to. My mother was preparing me for my future. It was a carefully charted path she gave years of her life to keep me on. And then, I didn't follow that path. I didn't go to Yale. I didn't become a doctor. I think it broke her heart a second time."

Cora sat back. "Because of me. And the twins."

"No," Charley said. "Because I went my own way. I didn't choose what she'd laid out for me."

"But didn't she want you to be happy?"

"Of course. But remember, she'd grown up with nothing, then married into everything. Both came with ties. Her idea of happiness was freedom from all of that."

Cora laughed, not unkindly. "Yale medical school. God, I wish one of our kids had gone. Then at least we could say it skipped a generation."

"Yale was my ticket, for her. So I didn't have to rely on the family name or money. So I wasn't sucked into the foundation, like my father had been. Like she was, after he died. *That's* how she saw things, as strange as it may sound. It was a different generation and she'd lost so much."

Cora heard the words, but they did not entirely reach her heart. "Charley, you sacrificed too. Not just your mother. Why can't she see that what you did was for love?" As she said the last part, Cora felt that old rush of shame. Charley had loved her wholly from the beginning. But the same could not be said for her, at least in the beginning. She'd decided to try, out of love for her unborn children. Out of fear of returning to Ohio and living in her father's shadow. "We all sacrificed," she said, rising from the table.

"Cora. Don't walk away in the middle of this, please."

She had to walk away because she could not look Charley in the eye. Cora had also given up love, just as his mother had. But she could not say that out loud. She never could.

"Cora!"

Charley never raised his voice with her. She halted at the screen door.

"I want to ask my mother back here. I want our family to sit down together."

It was the worst idea. The kids were just settling. The wedding was around the corner. James would be arriving and the dresses were not done being fitted and there was a rehearsal dinner to throw. "Charley, no. The one thing we all agreed to was to batten down this hatch until the wedding. We promised Sydney."

"Sometimes promises need to be broken. I think a call is in order. And I want to make it." His voice trembled with effort to contain himself. She regarded his flushed cheeks, his drawn expression. Charley did not push back on much.

"We're all together here," he reminded her. "Who knows when that will happen again. And my mother is not getting any younger. You didn't see her the other day at the tearoom, but she's fading, Cora. She's slowing down, all of a sudden. This trip back has done something to her."

It was true. Cora had noticed that Tish looked smaller than usual, that first day she swept into Riptide. The fire was still in her eye, but there had been a vulnerability in her gait. A frailness she'd never thought possible. What if Charley was right? Could she really deny them a chance to air their grievances at this stage? "All right," she relented. "But do you really think you can change her mind?"

Charley held out his hands. "She's already given the house to Sydney. She's already spilled our secret."

Cora couldn't help but note how Charley called it *their* secret. It was hers, really, but he'd been the faithful guardian of it all these years.

"Then what?" Cora asked gently. "What good will come of this meeting?"

Charley looked away, across the backyard and over the dunes below. To where the ocean glimmered, just beyond. "My father drowned somewhere out there. On a summer day, while my mother and I were right here. I can't rationalize what she did, but somewhere, in her bones, she believes this is the right thing to do. Somehow she thinks this honors my father's legacy. The Darling family name, which meant so much to him. Even if I don't understand it—or agree with it—this is her wish. Maybe her last. And I think it falls on me to somehow try to respect it."

Cora followed his gaze, out over the tawny spill of dunes and down to the sea. It was the golden hour and even the hard words between them were softened by it. She did not want to forgive Tish for what she'd done; she would never understand it.

But Riptide had started with Charley, Tish, and Morty. And Tish had done so much for her only son over the years. Maybe that was why Charley was able to do so much for *her* over the years. Maybe it's where his generosity was rooted. Maybe she shouldn't fault him for it.

She went to where Charley sat and drew out the chair beside him. When she sat, she was level with his sad gaze, and that did something to her too. "Were you happy?" she asked.

"Happy?" Charley sat up straighter. "Aw, Cora. What's this all about?"

She placed her hand on his. How small hers looked against his; those kind capable hands. "I need to know, so please tell me, Charley. Were you happy with your decision to leave medical school? To marry me?"

Charley's eyes watered. He blinked. "Terribly happy. Every day since."

She closed her eyes. How afraid she'd been to ask this question, all of their lives. But the need had never left her.

"What about you?" he asked, taking her hand in his. "I know I'm not the man you thought you'd marry."

"Charley."

"No, it's true. We don't speak of it. Ever. But let's speak our truths. Can we, please?" His eyes were so full of love. And sadness. And something else: forgiveness, Cora decided.

He wanted them to forgive his mother. Just as he had forgiven Cora for not loving him back the way he loved her.

"The truth," she said, feeling the swell of emotion rise up within her. Oh, the truth was complicated. Especially with the people you loved. Because Cora *did* love Charley. But in the beginning it had been different; in the beginning, her love was one tinged with relief and gratitude. With admiration and loyalty; but he knew, as did she, it may not have been the kind of love he'd held for her. The kind of love he deserved.

Cora loved his giant heart. The fact that he saw in her all the things her father had never seen and her mother was often too afraid to. Charley made her feel smart and capable and good. And worthy of the immense love he had to give. And somehow, over the course of a marriage, with all the ups and downs and triumphs and losses, Cora had come to love him. Not out of gratitude, as she had at first. But as a man. A strong, loyal, big-hearted man who had so much to give to their kids; all three of them. "The truth is, you have always made me happy, Charley Darling. More than you can possibly believe. I may not have been good at showing it or saying so, but it's true. From the first day you held the twins in the hospital and cried like a baby. I saw it: they became yours too that day. And every day since, that you've stayed by my side. Raising our kids. Supporting me. Encouraging my art, even though it didn't pay the bills. Hell, sticking up for me to your own mother, to whom I know you feel so beholden. All while encouraging me to tolerate her, which I hated to hear but needed to; even that made me love and respect you *more*."

Charley laughed softly. "She's not easy, I know."

"Neither am I." Cora held her hand to Charley's soft cheek. "We have made a life. This marriage, these kids, this house even . . . we have made a happy life together. And I will never stop loving you for that."

Charley Darling, even for his big heart, was not known to her to cry. Outside of the days the twins and Sydney were born, he had not shed any tears in her presence. But now they spilled down his cheeks, both, and down his shirt in big, shameless drops. "Cora."

He reached for her and she for him. And held each other tight.

Charley was asking her to do something that went against every fiber of her being; against a fairness she felt all three of their children were owed.

As he held her on the patio, Cora made a decision. She would do it, for him. It was the golden hour.

Andi

She couldn't help it; Nate Becker was all she could think about. For the first time in years, Andi was thinking about someone outside her family. Outside of work and Molly's school and what to make for dinner. She was thinking a lot about herself too, and if that made her selfish for the moment, so be it.

Since their night on the beach, all Andi wanted to do was be with Nate. At breakfast, she wondered how long until they'd meet up on the beach trail to go for a swim. When he went back to his place to shower, it was too long. When they went into town together to hit the bookstore or grab coffee, and he dropped her off to find a parking spot she held her breath until he rounded the corner. It was consuming and immature and absolutely teenage-like behavior. And she was going to wallow in it every sexy, summery second she could.

Molly was away for five days on the Vineyard and Andi missed her terribly. She worried how she was faring with George and Camilla. If George was taking good care of her; if she felt like second fiddle around his "true life partner." She'd hoped for a distraction to help her through the first time Molly was away from her, and boy was she getting it.

But it wasn't without its complications. If feeling like a teenager with a summer crush was the utmost summer escape, having to behave like one around her family was a buzzkill. "I don't understand why you don't want your family to know about us," Nate said as they strolled down Main Street. "We're not kids. We don't need to sneak around."

"Sneaking around is fun," Andi countered. And it was. But not always. Lately, she'd found herself fibbing to her parents like she was a kid caught after curfew.

They stopped at Chatham Perk and Andi ordered two of her favorite: iced mocha lattes with fresh whipped cream.

"I feel like you're trying to hide me," Nate said, taking a deep sip of his latte. "And fatten me up! God, these things are good."

Andi smiled. It had taken her exactly one visit to Chatham Perk to turn Nate on to the decadent iced drinks and already it was part of their routine.

"I'm not trying to do either," she said. "But I am sorry. It feels weird having Molly away and now it feels weird dating—for the first time in almost twenty years—around my parents. It's like they're watching us."

Nate laughed. "They are watching us. You live with them." He took her hand as they walked up the sidewalk. "But there is a solution."

"Oh?"

"Come stay with me."

"Oh." Andi didn't know what to say. Staying with Nate was exactly what she wanted to do. And exactly what she could not possibly do.

"Until Molly gets back, of course," he added quickly. "I get that whole thing, believe me."

"Right." There was no way Andi was introducing Molly to anyone she was dating until it was serious. That part she'd been clear about. But Nate lived on the other side of the backyard fence and he knew Molly already. Hiding it would be even harder when she got back. "God, this is complicated."

"But why? Your parents know you're an adult. Who does adult things. Do you think they think Molly was divine conception?" He was joking, but it was just too close to home.

"Let's keep Molly out of it for now. It's my parents, yes. The thought of doing the walk of shame home while my father is having breakfast at the kitchen table feels sleazy. And the timing . . . the whole family is in a bad place right now. It feels insensitive."

Nate didn't say anything.

Andi could tell he was upset. "What?"

"Sleazy and insensitive. That's how you basically described us." He stopped in the middle of the sidewalk, a look of genuine hurt on his face.

"I didn't mean that about us!"

"Then what did you mean? Andi, the last few days I feel like we've been lying to everyone. You wait until late at night and sneak over to my place. And then you sneak back before sunrise. You want me to come over to your place, but you keep ten feet of distance between us when your family walks in the room. Are you embarrassed by me?"

It was the *last* thing she wanted Nate to feel. She was completely mismanaging this. "No! Look, this is all new to me."

Andi threw up her hands. "I don't know how to date at my age. I don't know how to date with a kid and my parents under the same roof. And a wedding on the way and a family crisis! I'm trying to balance all that while also trying to hang on to a shred of privacy. And here I was thinking I was doing a good job, but it turns out I'm screwing it all up!" People were turning to look at them and she realized she was making a small scene.

"Okay, okay." Gently, Nate pulled her over to a shaded bench in front of an antiques store. "C'mere. Catch your breath. I'm sorry."

"Why are you sorry?" She was suddenly so angry—with herself more than anyone. Why was she making this complicated? Nate was right, they were two adults. But she couldn't help it—it all just felt . . . weird.

"It's not you, Nate. It's my own baggage. My crazy family and my sad, single life. I'm a mess."

Nate put an arm around her. "You're not a mess. And you're right, I forget that this is new to you." They watched a young family walk by and Andi's heart ached. They looked happy and together; a nuclear family. Andi nodded in their direction. "That. That's what I'm grieving this summer."

Nate followed her gaze. The couple was passing an ice cream cone back and forth between them as the dad pushed the baby stroller and the toddler held the mom's hand. "Did you have that married to George?"

"No. Not even close."

"Okay. So let's talk about *grieving* that. Ten bucks says that baby in the stroller starts screaming bloody murder any second. And when he does, that ice cream cone is going to get dumped down the mom's white pants when the dad scrambles to get his screaming kid out of that contraption. Then the toddler won't be able to go to the toy store because her kid brother is melting down. And the whole happy family portrait will go up in flames right here on Main Street." He turned to look at Andi, a satisfied smile playing at the corners of his mouth. "Am I right?"

Andi had to give it to him. "Not bad for a single guy with no kids."

Nate laughed. "I've spent plenty of time with my sister and hers. Believe me." Nate paused. "Look, I've been single for a while. I don't have kids. And my parents are in Florida, not living with me in my house. Thank God."

Which made Andi laugh. "Can you imagine if both sets of our parents were in the beach cottages with us? Just like old times!"

"Maybe they'd entertain each other while we snuck out." Nate turned and planted a kiss on her head. "So we've got some things to figure out. So what? We will."

Andi looked up at him. How did she end up with a guy like this right in her backyard this summer? "You're pretty great."

"You're okay. I guess." Nate ducked, fully expecting the punch to the arm she delivered.

When they pulled into his driveway later, Nate turned to her. "Want to come in for a bit?"

She did. More than anything. But there was something else she needed to do. "I have a better idea." Andi nodded toward Riptide. "Want to come for dinner?"

Nate threw her a look of mock horror. "Will your family be there?"

262 • Hannah McKinnon

"Sadly, yes."

"Well, I don't know . . ."

"Shut up." Andi leaned across the seat and kissed him. "You were right. There's no reason we should be hiding this."

Whatever it was they were doing, it was at that fresh new stage of sweet perfection where all she wanted to do was sleep, eat, breathe it in . . . with no overanalyzing. *This is a summer romance,* she told herself. A superb first foray into dating, with a guy she knew and trusted, who just happened to be—well, let's face it— pretty fantastic. As Hugh had said, "Let yourself have some fun."

Andi knew women her age who got swept up in remaking themselves when they found themselves starting over. Brunettes who went bleached blonde overnight. Attractive, middle-aged women who felt pressed to drop three dress sizes and shove themselves into their teenage daughter's skinny jeans. One of the teachers she worked with, and had always liked, divorced the year before Andi had. "The first thing I did after I sold the house was get my boobs done," she confided in the teachers' lounge.

Andi had been so surprised she almost dropped her coffee mug. "Oh. Was that something you had always wanted to do?" she'd asked, trying not to stare at her friend's chest.

Her friend laughed. "We're not twenty anymore. At our age, if you want a second chance, you've got to look your best."

Andi had been shocked that this attractive, intelligent colleague felt it necessary to undergo all that to make herself desirable to some imaginary pool of available men. She couldn't help but wonder how hard these men were trying, and if they felt half the pressure.

And now here she was, sitting in Nate's car. A guy who seemed to appreciate everything about her, just as it was, all these years later. And who felt like she was hiding him.

"Come back to my place," she said, tugging his hand. "Everyone would love to see you."

At the foot of the porch stairs, Andi halted. "Can I ask you something?" She was doing that thing Hugh hated; asking a question about asking a question.

"Shoot."

"What exactly are we telling them about us? If they ask." She was fooling herself, she knew. Her family would never ask, at least not in front of Nate. Even Hugh would behave. The question was for her.

Nate looked bemused. "I don't know—maybe we let them know that we're hanging out."

"Hanging out." She swallowed. What had she expected him to say? "Okay." She started up the steps, then stopped again. It was not okay. "Is that what we're doing?"

"Hey." Nate touched her chin. "To be clear, I didn't mean we're hanging out, like it doesn't mean anything. Maybe we should talk more about this." He nodded toward the door. "After dinner."

It was the nicest thing he could have said. Yes, she would take him up on that. After dinner. And after a glass of wine, which she suddenly craved.

"Deal." She trotted up the porch steps and opened the door. Hugh was right. She was going to be herself and enjoy it. "Hey, everyone," she called out. "I've brought company."

She knew her family would be happy to see Nate. Everyone always was. But when the door swung open, nobody looked happy.

There at the kitchen island stood Hugh, holding a glass of wine. The rest were in the living room: her parents seated on one couch. Sydney and Martin on the other. And in the wingback chair between them, in a crisp white pantsuit adorned with a ruby silk neckerchief, sat Tish. The only member of the family without a strained look on her face.

Tish looked directly at Andi. "Good, she's here. Now let's get started."

Tish

It's the second time she's been back at Riptide since Morty left this world. It's taken her the better part of fifty-plus years. She never could let the cottage go, but neither could she bring herself to stay in it. The memories were just too painful.

She can't believe it's been almost ten days since her first visit when, as Charley claims, she "divided the family" with her wedding gift to Sydney. That part has bothered her and she is uncertain about how she will find them today. But when she returns this time, what she sees is a family intact. (Perhaps united against her? The visit will tell.) In a house that Morty provided all of them; a haven for not just summer vacations, or a July wedding, but also for the hard stuff. A haven from the disappointments and hurts that come with living. Tish knows this, at her age, and even if they don't realize it now, someday they will. Keeping Riptide in the family is important. She will try to explain this.

Charley asked her to come back. As such, she is now a guest in a house that is no longer hers and she will try to behave, as Charley has implored her to do. But there are things that need to be said.

When Hugh lets her in, she finds herself without words. She has always thought him a clever, funny young man, even if he was Cora's. The look in his brown eyes—even if they are not Darling blue—is one she recognizes. Hurt.

"Hello, Tish." Hugh holds the door open for her and as soon as she's inside, she surprises herself as much as she surprises him: she gives him a hug. Tish does not like excessive or public displays of emotion and she's pretty sure this qualifies as both. But she is as old as dirt, she knows, and her heart is no longer keeping up with her head, as she feels more and more each day. So when the urge strikes, she looks up at Hugh and opens her arms.

Hugh is a gracious man. Despite his surprise, he bows, because he is much taller, and he not only lets her throw her arms around his neck, but he hugs her back. It's not terrible.

When they separate, Tish looks deeply at him. No, his is not the face of a Darling. Nor an O'Malley. But it is an earnest face and, as Charley has reminded her, he is family—if not blood. Tish is working on that concept. These modern families; all disjointed and messy. But they are a sign of the times—times that are passing her by—and so she will try. She will start now. "Hugh, you are a good boy. I have always thought so. This situation, it's not personal. I hope someday you can come to understand that."

Once more, she can tell she has surprised him. Tish has always maintained a formality with the family. It's best that way. Feelings are one's own, not to be aired out and strung up on the clothesline for all to see. But now she wonders if she should've made more exceptions. Today, at least, she owes him this much.

"Thank you for saying that, Tish," he says. "I won't lie; it felt personal. But it's nice to hear you say otherwise."

She regards his pained expression with more regret. "Well, I am sorry to hear that."

He ushers her inside. "Would you like some wine?"

She considers the afternoon that lies ahead of them. "Bourbon," she says. "Neat."

Sydney is waiting her turn, and with Hugh dispatched to the liquor cabinet she takes it. Tish can feel her about to bubble over; there seems to be a lot she wants to convey. But first, Tish takes her hands and gives her a once-over. There it is—the Darling nose, straight and upturned at the tip. And those steel blue eyes. An O'Malley mouth, just like Tish's mother's, heart-shaped and full. Unlike Tish, whose lips are customarily zipped with discretion, Sydney's are garrulously put to use. Like now, as she begins spilling everything on her mind right there on the threshold. "Grandma, I'm so glad you're here. Before the family meets, I would like to talk with you in private. About the house. It's so wonderful, it really is. And I've been thinking a lot about it. And talking to James, of course—but I don't know. It's so much. And I want to be sure you're sure. So I was thinking—"

"Grandchild." Tish holds up her hand. Oh, to have all that youthful energy again! "Take a breath, dear. I am here to talk. And that is just what we'll do. But may I come in first?"

Goodness, Charley was not exaggerating. Everyone in this house is on edge. She was right to come.

"Oh gosh, I'm sorry! Yes. Come in, Grandma!" Sydney is the only one who has ever called her that and, if she's honest, the only one for whom Tish would probably suffer the title. Realizing that now she feels a dab more of regret. She's held them all at such a distance all these years. It seemed so necessary then. But now . . .

"You're looking well," Martin says, approaching her next. Apparently, she has entered some kind of receiving line. Tish has barely taken two steps into the house. Ah, well. It's better than the greeting she'd feared. Tish allows him to give her a peck on the cheek. "May I take your purse?" he asks politely.

Tish smiles at him appreciatively. But she does not hand over the purse. She never surrenders her purse; she likes to hang on to it. But this time there is another reason for that. "Thank you, Martin. But I'll keep it with me." She looks him up and down. So handsome. And polite. If Hugh had to end up with a man, she is glad Hugh ended up with a man like him. Martin appears to be quite wonderful.

And then there is Charley. Her beautiful boy. "Hello, Mother. Good to see you." The furrow in his brow has not gone, but there is new color in his cheeks. This is good.

Tish is invited to sit in an armchair. The moment she sees it her breath catches. It's upholstered in a blue-and-white seashell toile, but Tish instantly recognizes its Chippendale legs. "This chair." She turns to Charley. "You kept it?"

"Of course," he says. "Cora reupholstered it. It was her idea."

Tish looks at the young adults who are watching curiously. "This was your grandfather's chair," she tells them. And then, carefully, she lowers herself into. It is as deep and encircling as she recalls; the one piece Morty brought from the city to the rustic cottage when they first got it.

"It's such a spartan little place," Tish had protested when he had it delivered. It was too formal for the space.

"Trust me," Morty had said. "One needs a good chair with a view of the sea."

Now she lets its cushioned depths engulf her. *Morty,* she

thinks again. The cottage is so changed and yet she feels its bones in her own.

"Cora will be right down," Charley says. "Any minute, I'm sure." But Tish knows her son. He's not sure, at all.

"Until then." Hugh brings a bourbon.

She glances around at their faces. "Am I to drink alone?"

There is a flurry and everyone dispatches to the kitchen. It gives her time to look around more closely without feeling rude.

The main part of the cottage—the hull, as Morty used to call it—remains. The front door leads right into the living room— no formality there. The living room in which she sits is the old living room of before. Though behind her the kitchen has been expanded and additions added on either side and overhead. She glances about. There is a bump-out dining room, informal with a rustic table and white chairs. In keeping with the white Shaker kitchen cabinetry and butcher block island. Minimalist coastal design, she will give Cora that. It honors the cozy cottage feel. The walls, once untreated pine, are painted a cloud white. The two-foot, square-shaped sash windows had been replaced with large picture windows, to better let the light in. And the beach view, with it. It's pleasing, she has to admit.

There are bookshelves with worn paperbacks. Seashells scattered across the mantel, which she is pleased to see is the original stone face Morty had commissioned for her. Beneath her feet are the original floorboards, resurfaced and stained. She taps a toe to them now. These very floors she paced on the last day she awoke with her husband. Her heart flutters in her rib cage and Tish closes her eyes, willing it to slow.

As ice clinks against glasses in the kitchen behind her and a cork is popped, she rises carefully from Morty's chair. There is a painting over the fireplace that has captured her attention. In fact, she realizes, looking around, all of the walls are adorned with paintings. Seemingly done by the same hand. She moves in for a better look.

The painting is an oil. And as soon as she is close enough, she recognizes the faces. Sydney at the center, Hugh and Andi flanking her. And behind them, Charley. And Cora. They are splashed in pink sunset hues, smiles beaming. Tish squints at the artist's name and gasps. *Cora Darling*. She moves on to another, hanging on the opposite wall. It's a much smaller ocean scene. Dark and stormy. She can almost hear the crashing waves. Again, in the bottom right corner: *Cora Darling*. Tish cannot believe this. She'd known Cora was studying some kind of fine art at Vassar, but it had been lost in all the excitement when Cora and her situation were introduced at Charley's graduation. Tish assumed she'd given up her art, along with her hopes of a degree, when she married Charley and had the twins. "I stand corrected," she whispers now to herself.

"What's that?"

Tish turns, startled at the voice behind her. It's Cora.

Tish feels caught in the act and is about to pivot right back to Morty's armchair where her glass of bourbon awaits, but stops herself. She meets Cora's gaze. "I'm admiring your work," she admits.

If Cora appreciates this, she does not show it or say so. Tish is reminded why she has stayed away from Riptide, besides the obvious reason. But she is game. She will try once more. "I did not know that you still painted."

"I never stopped."

Tish knows what this means. She would have known if

she'd asked. If she'd stayed in touch and connected with her daughter-in-law, or with any of them, for that matter. There were invitations issued—to Christmas, to birthdays. She attended infrequently. And left early regularly. She supposes the Connecticut house is also full of Cora's art, but she can't say. She never stopped long enough to look at the walls or spend time in the home where her son has lived with his family. Her heart bangs in her chest, again, and she puts a hand to it.

And then Cora does something shocking. "Would you like to see more? I'd be happy to show you."

Whatever the others are doing, Tish cannot say, because at this moment she is engaged. Warily, but willing, she follows her daughter-in-law from room to room. Cora explains each piece matter-of-factly, but as they go, Tish hears the lilt in her voice and notes the ease in her demeanor. Cora loves her art and loves sharing it; this she cannot hide. There is a painting of a peach, Cora claims as her favorite. And the ocean scene, Tish already saw. But the way Cora describes her work, hands and face animated in a way Tish has never witnessed, only deepens the artistry. Tish is given quite the tour. Through the living room and kitchen, into the dining area, and then into the rear bedroom she once shared with Morty that is now a den.

Here Tish is momentarily unable to follow what Cora is saying. The footprint of her old bedroom is the same. As is the golden view of the dunes through the window. This is the bedroom she shared with her husband for the last time that fateful morning. Where they awoke early, limbs entwined. Where Charley scrambled across the covers and squealed in delight as his father snatched him up playfully. Cora stops in the doorway, puts her hand to the frame to steady herself. Her heart is rapping now, off course, and out of kilter. She feels suddenly dizzy.

"Tish? Are you feeling all right?" Cora is very close to her, but blurred. She puts a hand to Tish's arm and Tish's instinct is to pull it away, but she can't.

"Shall we sit?" she asks, and it is not a question. Tish allows herself to be helped to the desk chair.

Once seated, Cora comes back into focus and Tish's heart rattles back to its normal beat. "Forgive me," she says. "This was my old room."

Her daughter-in-law looks at her with what can only be described as empathy. "Would you like a water? Some tea?"

What she wants is her glass of bourbon, but she declines politely. Her heart is not good, but this is not her heart. At least not in a wellness sense. She is overcome and she needs a minute. Already she is starting to feel better. She can feel Morty with her.

"Thank you for letting me come today," she tells Cora. It's just the two of them and though this moment alone would never have occurred to her as desirable, she is suddenly grateful to have it. "I am sure it wasn't easy."

Cora doesn't answer right away. "You're family," she says finally.

"Yes," Tish has to agree. "That is true."

But there is more. Cora's voice is soft but her message sharp. "It's what I wish you felt for all of us under this roof. It's how Charley feels. And has always behaved toward all the children."

Touché. Cora has gone straight for the elephant and Tish gives her credit for that. She is no shrinking violet.

There is much she wants to say to all of them, on this matter, and she plans to save it for the family sit-down. But she will say one thing, in private, now. "I am not sorry I gave the house to Sydney. As unpopular a sentiment as that might be."

Cora inhales. "Then why did you come?"

"I want there to be peace." She rests a hand on her heart and Cora's eyes follow it there.

"All right," she says finally. "I want that too. For Charley. For all of us."

Tish looks past Cora, at the waving dune grass outside. "There are things a mother must do to protect her family."

"I am no stranger to that instinct," Cora replies.

"As much as the Darling family has constrained my life, so too has it broadened it. And yours as well." Here she raises her eyebrows and she can see Cora follows.

"Fair enough," Cora says.

"When Morty died, I was left with a responsibility to the foundation. Everything we owned was tied to it, including Charley and myself."

Cora looks away. "Responsibilities can sometimes feel like burdens."

"You understand then." Tish is sorry to have to say this, but she is of a different generation, with different obligations. "It's not personal, Cora. Riptide was Morty's and Sydney is blood."

Cora looks away and Tish feels their differences settle in the space between them like a light fog. She didn't expect to change Cora's way of seeing things and she isn't about to let Cora's perspective change hers. But this airing out, however uncomfortable, is a relief of sorts.

"I'm afraid that is where we differ. Family is family," Cora tells her. "However it is made up and whomever it's comprised of."

"You may all still enjoy Riptide," Tish reminds her. "Sydney is a good girl. She's part of you and part of me. I like to think that between us she will figure it out."

Cora does not reply, but neither does she argue further. There is no hugging, no sentimental promise made.

The two women have spoken their piece, even if they do not see eye to eye. Tish knows they will not. And that is all right.

Charley appears in the doorway. "Andi just drove in, next door. She's coming."

"Well, then." It is time for the family talk.

Before Charley can offer his assistance, Cora rises. She holds out a hand. "Let me help you."

Tish accepts it. Charley scoots aside and allows his wife to help his mother out to the living room.

As Tish passes by, she locks eyes with her son. The look on his face is why she has come. No matter how this family meeting goes, she has done right.

Cora

This summer vacation had not gone as planned. If anything, she could call it a disaster. Certainly no one would argue that. But there was a wedding to be performed. And a family to hold together. And, most pressing, a rehearsal dinner that Cora was responsible for. Good Lord, what had she been thinking when she agreed to that?

All morning the doorbell rang. First, the event rental company. Their tall, white box truck backed unceremoniously into the seashell driveway and began unloading tables, chairs, and tenting supplies. Cora and Charley stood aside, watching as their backyard patio was magically transformed. A sailcloth tent went up, its pennant flag flapping smartly in the ocean breeze. If that weren't enough, round wooden tables were rolled in and dressed in creamy linens. Followed by gold Chiavari chairs. Silver pitchers of blue hydrangeas. Strings of globe lights. Cora stood beneath the tent in awe as her backyard was turned into a coastal wonderland. She was just about to run inside to fetch them when Sydney and James wandered out, both sleepy-eyed but smiling.

"Good morning, James! Did you get any sleep?" He'd arrived

late the night before to much fanfare. Despite his late arrival and long week at work, she couldn't believe the two had slept through the hubbub of the backyard setup.

"I sleep like a baby every time I'm here. Must be that salt air." He planted a kiss on Cora's cheek.

"Oh, Mom. Can you believe it?" Sydney stepped under the tent mouth ajar, taking it all in.

Cora could not believe it. Her baby was getting married. The weekend weather looked perfect. And everyone was speaking. "You're going to be a beautiful bride," she said, wrapping an arm around her youngest. To James, "You're a lucky young man."

James swept a boyish flop of hair out of his eyes and grinned. "Don't I know it." James was a full foot taller than Sydney and sandy-haired and blue-eyed, just like her. They looked like two peas from the same pod, in their matching pinstriped pajama pants Sydney had bought earlier that week for the honeymoon. Even with all that was going on, James only had eyes for Sydney. The way he looked at her as she fluttered about the tent gave Cora heart. The two were so natural together, so give and take; in all the ways Cora had wished she could have been with Charley when they were that age.

Still, James's arrival had been a bit of a worry, to Cora. After all, he was to be the new co-owner of Riptide. A transaction Cora still had so many questions and concerns about. *Would Sydney keep the house in only her name once married? Wasn't that the sensible thing to do, to protect a family treasure?* Riptide had already been transferred unhappily within the family and, although Cora wanted to believe James's and Sydney's love would last forever (as much as she could tell it would), she was too seasoned to make suppositions. Anything could happen.

And then there were the other two: Andi and Hugh. Sydney being singled out as Riptide's sole proprietor was hard enough for the siblings to stomach. And now, here was handsome James, striding through the front door with his gregarious smile and collared shirt looking ready to take on the world. Would they also see him as taking over Riptide? The thought of an outsider laying claim to the family cottage was another blow altogether. Cora feared it might stir the pot that had only recently been reduced from full boil to simmer. And if anyone was going to make a stink, it would be Hugh.

Sure enough, last night when James put his bags down in the doorway just in time to catch Sydney as she launched herself into his arms, Hugh couldn't help himself. "Welcome!" he'd said, offering James his usual fist bump. Then, "Though I suppose that sounds silly, as the place is now yours."

The whole living room had fallen silent, Andi throwing a stern look that her twin blatantly ignored. But to James's credit, he did not take the bait. With an arm around his bride, he addressed them all with a smile. "It's good to be here. I can't tell you all how sorry I am that I got stuck at work this week and couldn't come sooner to help out." Then, he'd turned to Cora. "But I'm here now. What can I do to help?" And the subject had been changed as swiftly as the table linens Sydney would later realize were the wrong shade of ivory. Thankfully, there was simply too much to do to argue.

"So what *is* the plan?" Charley had asked, later that night in bed. After a quick toast to welcome James, they'd slipped away upstairs, leaving the younger set to round out the celebrations.

Cora was exhausted, and so relieved when Charley joined her beneath the covers, wrapping his arm around her soft middle. "If we're going to say anything at all, the window is closing. Before we know it, they'll be off on their honeymoon."

Cora knew what he meant. The ownership of Riptide was not going to change. All they could do now was inquire with Sydney about keeping the title in her name. The fact was, marriage changed things when it came to material things and, as Cora knew only too well, material things changed people. Oh, she did not want to talk business with Sydney the weekend of her wedding. But what choice did they have?

She turned over to face Charley. "We can only ask. We may not like the answer, but at least we'll have asked."

"Want to do it together or want me to?"

Cora had another idea. "May I?" It was a big ask. Riptide's history was Charley's, not hers. "I know Sydney is our daughter, but I can't help but feel it was my situation that led us all here."

Charley shook his head. "Cora. Stop, please."

"No, Charley. You've taken care of me and the kids, all these years. Let me try to take care of this one thing. Please?"

Charley stared at her in the dim light, then pressed his lips to hers. It was decided.

The morning of the rehearsal dinner, Cora had paced the kitchen floor. There was a quiet pause, after the rental trucks had gone and before the caterers arrived. Andi, Hugh, and Martin had driven down to Hyannis to pick up Molly, who was just returning on the ferry from her Vineyard trip. James and Sydney had taken a leisurely breakfast and gone for a walk on the beach after. Cora tried to busy herself as she awaited their return. She fretted about the kitchen, tidying things that were already tidy and checking to-do lists that were either already done or it was too late to do anything about now. Finally, the screen door squeaked open.

"How was your walk?" she asked.

"Really nice," Sydney said. She was beaming. "I just pray this weather holds."

"It will." James went to the coffeepot and Cora hopped out of his way a little too abruptly. "Would you like a cup?" he asked her.

Her nerves were frayed. "Oh, gosh, I'm plenty caffeinated already." She turned to Sydney. "Honey, I was hoping we could talk a minute."

Sydney's nose wrinkled. "Sure, but I've got to check in with the bridesmaids. Everyone's arriving at different times and I just learned that the hotel made a mistake on one of the bookings." She pulled out her phone. "And I haven't heard from the caterer about the rehearsal dinner gazpacho. Have you?"

Cora's heart fluttered. This was their only window, as Charley had said, and she could feel it closing down on them. "It'll just take a minute, Syd. I can help you with all that after . . ."

But Sydney was staring at the screen of her phone, already lost in texts. "That's okay, James can help me. It shouldn't take long."

Cora glanced helplessly at James.

To her immense relief, James took the hint. "You know, it was hot down on the beach. I think I'll grab a quick shower. Syd, give your mom a minute and we can make those calls after."

.   .   .

Cora led her youngest outside, to one of the tables. They sat, looking out at the dunes and ocean below.

"So what's up?" Sydney asked her.

Cora studied her daughter carefully. Her nose was already freckled by the sun, her skin tinged with peach. What a beautiful summer bride she'd make. "I wanted a minute with you, before things get too crazy. How're you doing?"

Sydney smiled and shook her head. "It's surreal, Mom. I can't believe I'm getting married tomorrow. And everyone is on their way." She glanced at her watch. "This is the calm before the storm."

"Are you nervous?" Cora ventured.

Sydney lifted one shoulder. "A little. Suzy was supposed to be here two hours ago." Suzy, her college roommate and maid of honor, was known for being a lot of fun. But not exactly punctual. "And from what I heard, the groomsmen who arrived late last night are already hungover at their rental cottage on Ridgevale." She made a face.

Cora laughed. "Sounds about right to me."

"And the weather forecast is calling for high humidity tomorrow. I don't want people to sweat to death at my reception." She made another face. "*I* don't want to sweat to death at my reception."

All understandable things to worry about, Cora reasoned. "Well, you can't change all that, I'm afraid. I'm sure it will all work out beautifully. Try not to worry."

Sydney turned to her. "I guess the one thing I'm not worried about is James."

This made Cora happy. Unlike her wedding day to Charley in the county courthouse. A shotgun affair his own mother refused to attend. Attended only by all of Cora's fears for what she was about to give up in the name of her growing belly. Now she reached over and squeezed Sydney's hand. "That's all that matters. You and James are already way ahead of where your father and I were." Cora had never spoken this way with her youngest, but now, sitting under the white tent with so much ahead of them, it felt right. "We love each other, very much. But it has not always been easy."

She could feel Sydney's curious gaze. "Mom, I never had any sense of that. For what it's worth."

Cora smiled ruefully. "I guess we pulled it off then. Just know that there will be good times and difficult ones. Neither last. The one thing that helped is this place." She looked around, at the dunes, the decorated patio, the cottage behind them. "Over the years, this place has always brought us back together. Given the family a place to come to." Sydney's brow furrowed and Cora wondered if she'd said too much. She didn't want to cause doubt, but she did want to be truthful.

"I know that, Mom. Riptide is special to all of us."

Cora looked at her. "That's what I want to talk to you about. Your grandmother has given you both a gift and a burden and I don't know if I should congratulate or console you. Just remember all the good things that have happened here. Like tonight's dinner for your wedding. There's a history of great love in this place. Good times and bad. Kind of like a marriage."

"We've been lucky," Sydney agreed.

There was so much Cora wanted to say. About marriage. About family. And the obligations and mistakes that come with both. And the forgiveness they required.

But she couldn't, without first being honest with Sydney about her own. "Honey, I want to apologize to you for all the messy family stuff that erupted right before your big day. Here, I've been so mad at your grandmother for spilling a secret. But there never should have been a secret between us to begin with. That's on me."

"Oh, Mom." Sydney shook her head. "It's been ugly, yes. But there's stuff that probably needed to be aired out for a while now."

"Oh?"

"Yeah. Not just with you and Dad. Things between us kids too."

Cora wondered what that meant exactly, but she wasn't done with everything she needed to get off her chest. "We should have told you kids, when you were old enough. About the twins' biological father, about our mixed family. All of it." She paused. "That's my biggest regret."

Sydney grew quiet. "Mom. Can I tell you something?" Her voice wavered and Cora worried she'd struck some fresh nerve.

"What is it, honey?"

"I always knew." Sydney stared into her lap.

"Knew what?"

"I always felt different from them. At first I used to think it was the twin thing. That Hugh and Andi had this special bond I wasn't a part of and that they didn't want to share with me. Later I thought maybe it was because of our age difference—they were teenagers while I was this nosy, little kid always following them around. Either way, they left me out." She blinked at the memory. "I always felt lonely."

"Honey. That must have been awful." It was certainly awful to hear it, as their mother. Cora knew there'd been challenges with the kids, but she'd had no idea about this.

Sydney shrugged. "It did, for a while. But then I realized it wasn't just the twin thing or the age difference. Andi and Hugh used to complain about it and I realized they were right. I *was* treated differently."

Cora's heart began to sink. She didn't want to hear more. It was one thing to realize you were screwing up as a parent while on the job, while the kids were still growing up. At least then you could try to fix it; there was still time. But to hear this now—well, it was too late. It was like being told the only job you'd ever had and ever loved, you'd failed at. "Sydney, your dad and I tried really hard to raise you kids the same—"

"No, Mom." Sydney put a hand on hers. "I don't mean it like that. You guys did great. I meant Tish."

"Tish." For a woman they didn't see a lot of, she'd left quite a mark on the family fabric.

"I knew she felt differently about me. That she saw something in me she didn't in them, for whatever reason. And I *loved* it. I was so jealous of the twins, of their whole weird twin bond. And I was desperate for attention. So when Tish sent me bigger gifts or lauded me with praise in front of them, I sucked it all in. I basked in it. I wanted to feel more special." Tears spilled down her cheeks. "And when she gave me Riptide, for a second I went right back to being that insecure ten-year-old kid. Only this time I had the upper hand. I was given something they prized. And it was all mine." She burst into tears.

Cora pulled her chair closer and pulled Sydney in tight. "Oh, honey. We are all human. Messy, complicated humans." She laughed, sadly. "Don't beat yourself up."

"All week they've tried to talk to me about Riptide. And each time I wouldn't. I said I needed to wait until James came up. Until we talked it over. But none of that was true."

"What is the truth?" Cora was almost afraid to ask.

Sydney swallowed hard. "I thought about what I could do. And what I *should* do."

"And?"

"I've decided to keep it. It's selfish, I know. But you heard Tish when she came here the other day. Riptide was hers to do with as she pleased. And it pleased her to pass it down to me." Sydney sniffed and dabbed her eyes. "But that doesn't mean I want to keep it all for myself. I want it to stay in the family and for everyone to use it, just as we always have." She looked around the yard. "This place is too special. I would never sell it."

Cora sat back in her chair. So that was where the chips fell.

"Are you disappointed?" Sydney asked, voice wavering.

It was a hard question. "No, honey. I'm just relieved you aren't going to sell it. It's a complicated situation and it's going to take some getting used to. But the choice is yours."

It was the one thing Cora struggled with most about her kids growing up. They were their own people. Try as she might to steer them or guide them or offer her own two cents, they were autonomous human beings she had raised and she did not have any right to sway or push. Though maybe a nudge, now and then . . . oh, it was hard, this letting go.

"Have you told the others?"

Sydney shook her head. "James and I talked about it. We want to wait until after the wedding."

"Very well." Cora would do her best to honor Sydney's wishes. "And as far as James goes?"

"Mom." She frowned. "I know what you're getting at."

Cora would make a terrible poker player, but she didn't care. There were things she understood at her age that her children didn't yet. "Honey, life throws you surprises. I'm glad you're keeping Riptide. But I want you to think about protecting it too. The deed is in your name now. I'm sure James would understand if you kept it that way."

"Mom."

Cora stared at her hands. She'd said her piece. Sydney had listened. To press further would be to drive Sydney away. "Yes?"

"You're going to have to trust me."

The window Charley had mentioned was closed. There were still questions, but Cora bit her tongue. "I do trust you," she said instead.

That night, as everyone gathered under the big white tent for the rehearsal dinner, Cora found herself watching from the sidelines as if watching reels from an old family movie. Amidst the groomsmen (who were hungover) and the bridesmaids (who showed up late but ready to celebrate) and the caterers (who served up the most divine lobster rolls and corn on the cob and gazpacho) were the faces most important to Cora Darling's life. Charley at the head of the table, raising a glass in a toast to their youngest. Hugh, bending to whisper something in Martin's ear and Martin, who gazed back at him so lovingly; they would make excellent parents, she was sure of it. Andi, who was so happy to have her daughter back she kept wrapping an arm around suntanned Molly, who kept shrugging it off, good-naturedly. Nate, who couldn't take his eyes off Andi the whole time. Even her mother-in-law, who arrived in usual fashion, in a silk emerald pantsuit, looking every bit as dazzling and aristocratic as ever, but also something else—tired, Cora decided, worriedly. But they were there, all of them, and that's what mattered.

As glasses clinked and laughter echoed and music spilled into the night, Cora Darling excused herself. She walked across the patio in her open-toed heels and, when she got to the edge, she slipped them off. The head of the beach trail was cool, a salt-tinged ocean breeze wafting up over the dunes. Overhead stars twinkled. Cora stepped onto the trail, her toes sinking gratefully into cool sand. *This*, she thought. *This is where I belong, right now.*

She glanced back at the patio, glimmering in candlelight and lanterns, shimmering with friends and family. Tomorrow would not be a perfect day, just as the summer had not been. Someone would stumble over a vow or the hem of their dress. Someone would break a wineglass. The weather would be balmy and the guests were always a wild card. But that was life. Messy and imperfect and full of possibility. And hope.

She was midway down the path when there was the reverberation of footsteps in the sand behind her. Cora spun around.

"Trying to escape without me?"

Charley looked so handsome in his sports jacket and striped tie as he swept up alongside her. Cora pressed her hands against his chest and looked up at him.

"I never could shake you," she said.

He winked at her. "You're getting too old to outrun me."

Cora slipped her hand in his and pulled him down the path with her.

Andi

Good Lord, it was a relief to have Molly back. All week Andi had worried and fretted. And missed her. But she'd done other things too. Things she would not have done had Molly been there. Things she was glad she'd realized she needed to do. This was all still new to her and it was going to take some getting used to. And balance. Balance was important, she was learning. Just as important as parenting.

As soon as she picked Molly up at the ferry, the questions spilled from her lips. "Did you have fun? What did you do? Where did you go?"

Despite how happy she was to see her mom, Molly was having none of it. "Mom. Please chill. It was fun and I'm home." Then, "What's for lunch?"

Andi did not ask the things she wanted to: did you miss me? And worse, how was *she*? All week, Camilla had loomed large in her thoughts when they turned to Molly.

"Of course she missed you," Hugh reassured her when they got home and Molly had gone straight up to her room. "She just can't show you. She's a teenager."

He was probably right. But she also wondered about Camilla.

If she'd been kind to Molly, if she'd been fun to be around. And worse—what if she had been?

"That woman will never replace you," Hugh had added. "You're Molly's only mother. Even if you do suck, she's stuck with you."

Andi kicked him. But he was right. Camilla had made it clear she was not going anywhere. Of course Andi wanted Molly to feel comfortable around this new person in her life. And of course she wanted Molly to have fun. Just not too much.

But now that Molly was home there was another matter of *new* people. The matter of Nate.

The past week had been the stuff of a summer rom-com. It was a total cliché and it was wonderful. For the first time in years, Andi had let her guard down. And the results spoke for themselves.

"Did you go to a spa?" Molly asked. They were getting ready together, standing in front of the mirror in Andi's bedroom. Molly swiped some of Andi's lip gloss.

"Go easy on that," Andi warned. "And no, why?"

"I dunno." Molly regarded her curiously. "You look pretty. And kind of . . . happy."

It almost broke her heart as much as it buoyed her. "Do I look unhappy to you, most of the time?"

She could tell Molly didn't want to answer. "Not really. Maybe a little."

Maybe a little. Which in teen speak meant "yes."

Andi sat down on her bed. "C'mere," she said, patting the blankets.

Molly groaned. "Not another talk. Please."

"Oh, please yourself. We haven't had one in ages."

. . .

The whole week, as Andi let herself take a little vacation from worrying, there had been one new worry she could not escape: what to do about Nate.

"What do we tell her?" Andi had asked him the day before Molly returned. She couldn't wait to throw her arms around her daughter, but she also knew it spelled the end of their alone time together, whatever that had meant.

"Why do we have to tell her anything?" Nate had replied.

It had led to their first fight.

"You don't get it," Andi had argued. "Kids smell things. They see things. She will know as soon as she sees us together."

"I do get it. But it doesn't mean you have to share your personal life with your child. Don't you think you're entitled to some privacy?"

"So I should lie to her?"

"What?" Nate sputtered. "Who said anything about lying?"

"First of all, you need to realize that is exactly what her dad did to her when he jumped into dating Camilla. Molly had a feeling and, when she asked him, he lied. It hurt her. Don't ask me to do that."

"I didn't!"

"And another thing, my personal life is personal. I don't plan to share the details with her, unless they have an impact on her. Only then would I tell Molly about someone."

"Andi, slow down. I respect that. I agree with everything you're saying."

But Andi was already too worked up. The mama bear in her had been poked and there was no going back.

"You don't have kids, Nate."

"I know that."

"This is exactly what worried me. I need someone who understands the responsibilities I have as a parent."

Nate threw up his hands. "I'm trying to understand. If you'd let me get a word in edgewise."

Andi had turned on her heels and stormed through the screen door into the house. And just as quickly she came back out. "You need to know this: my kid will always come first. *No matter who I date.*"

"Wait." Nate had looked more delighted than he should have for being in the midst of a fight. "So we're dating?"

She could feel herself grow flustered. This was not what she wanted to focus on. "No, what I meant was—"

"Yes." He crossed his arms. "You said we were dating."

Andi bit her lip. God, he could be so infuriating. And also so charming. "We are not dating."

Nate's face fell. "No?"

"Well, unless you want to. I hadn't really thought about it." A big, fat lie. "But I guess we should think about it, now that I'll be going back to Connecticut and you'll be going back to New York." It was what they'd tiptoed around all week. And what had kept her awake some nights. She liked Nate. A whole lot. But Nate was a bachelor. She a single mother. Connecticut and New York City were not exactly close by, though she supposed it was better than him being in LA. Still. "We live almost an hour and a half apart."

Nate looked at her a long time, letting things simmer, and Andi could feel herself growing impatient. "That's just geography."

"Geography isn't a small thing."

Her whole life Andi had known what she wanted. To go to a good college. Fall in love. Be a teacher. Live in New England. Raise a family. All things that seemed so simple, yet proved to be so hard.

She'd fallen in love, married, and lost it. She'd started a family and now it was split. And here was Nate, looking at her in earnest. Asking a simple question: were they dating?

Andi stared at her feet. Was it possible to let her guard down, go back to her life in Connecticut, and give this a chance? She considered her pedicure, already faded from the sun. That's what happened: things faded.

Andi swallowed. "Do you want to keep seeing each other, after this summer?"

When she got up the nerve to look back at Nate, his eyes were still on hers. "Yes, I do. But I also know you've got a full life at home with Molly. And long distance isn't easy."

Her heart beat a little faster. So, Nate had given this some thought. "I like this. I like you," she told him, feeling her cheeks flush. "A lot."

Nate grabbed her hands. Unlike hers, his palms were not sweaty. Unlike her voice, his was steady. "Andi, you and I have a history." He nodded toward the house. "We grew up together, each summer here on the Cape. Those summers shaped me. Didn't they shape you?"

"Of course they did," she said. "I loved every one of them."

"And here we are. This summer." He paused. "You. Me. Back on the Cape again. With years between us, yes. But also years behind us."

"Some of the best," Andi allowed, her voice catching.

Nate smiled softly. "If you're willing to give it a shot, I want more of this."

Andi had to look away. His words meant too much. "Nate . . ." she began.

"What?"

There was so much to say. Things that worried her, things that stood against them. Most of all, how much this meant to her and how much she'd hoped to hear those very words he'd just said. "Okay."

"Okay?" Nate sat back, a smile playing at the corners of his mouth.

It was her turn to smile. "Okay. Yes. Let's give it a shot."

Nate tipped his head back and started to laugh.

"What?" She didn't understand. "What's so funny?"

"After all that, all you can say is 'okay'?"

Andi made a face. "You asked. I said okay." She narrowed her eyes at him. "Would you like me to reconsider?"

"What I'd like to do is kiss that smart mouth of yours."

Now two nights later and sitting on the edge of her bed with Molly, Andi wanted to share a small piece of that decision with Molly. To be honest with her teenager.

"What is it you wanted to talk about?" Molly asked, plopping reluctantly on the bed beside her.

Andi looked at Molly. Already she looked more grown-up that summer. Soon, they'd be home in Connecticut and she'd be starting her freshman year of high school. She had so much ahead of her. And that night was supposed to be special. Andi changed her mind; she wouldn't tell her yet.

"Nothing," she said. "I just wanted to say how proud I am of you. Going off to the Vineyard with your dad. Hanging out here with me and the crazy family, despite all the hoopla. You're a great kid, Molly. I'm lucky to be your mom."

Molly screwed up her nose. "*That's* what you wanted to tell me?"

"Want me to think of something else?"

"Nope! All good." She jumped up and reached out to her mother. "Now can we stop being sappy and go? We're going to be late and Grandma will kill you."

Down at the rehearsal dinner party, Andi found her twin standing by the bar with Martin. "So how're we doing? Preparing a sarcastic toast? Plotting to burn down Riptide before you go?"

Hugh handed her a drink from a tray of champagne being passed. "Very funny and no. I've decided to make peace."

Andi and Martin exchanged looks of mock horror. "With yourself? Your choices in life?"

"Shut up." He took a sip of champagne and made a face. "This weekend is too important to Mom and Dad. And Sydney."

Andi put a congenial arm around him. "Good brother. Was it what Tish said?"

"No, not really. It was more about this place. I never wanted to inherit it for financial reasons—Martin and I are grown-ups. We can take care of ourselves."

It was exactly how Andi wanted to feel, though, to be honest, it was worth a lot. And she was a single parent with a decent but underwhelming teacher's salary. "I'm still working on that part," she admitted.

"No doubt," Hugh allowed. "We are too."

Martin nodded. Clearly, the two had had quite a talk.

"But we've had a lot of good years, here at Riptide. I've got to hope Sydney will keep those going, no matter who owns the place." He looked at Martin and winked.

Andi wasn't sure what the wink meant, but from the look on his face Martin seemed to. Maybe they'd reconnected that week, amidst all the family chaos. Chaos did that sometimes; if it didn't break you, sometimes it pushed you together. Maybe it was something else. Whatever it was, they looked happy and Andi wasn't about to pry. Despite the heartache of their vacation, there was a wedding to celebrate. Somehow, by some stroke of luck or love, each member of the Darling family had had something good that had come of those two weeks together and Andi would leave it at that.

She found Nate ordering a drink at the small bar on the edge of the patio. "Look at you," he said, holding out a hand.

Andi did a slow twirl, then impulsively pecked him on the lips. "You look quite handsome yourself."

At that moment, she felt eyes on the two of them. It was Molly. Staring across the crowd with a look Andi could not read.

Panic coursed through her. Dammit—she should've said something to her upstairs, when they had a moment alone. "Molly!" she called, waving her over. "Come here, honey."

Slowly, Molly made her way to them, her eyes locked on her mother the whole way. Andi's heart rattled in her chest. "You remember Nate?"

To her relief, Nate rescued them. "Good to see you, Molly. You look lovely tonight. How was your trip to the Vineyard?"

Molly looked between them for an eternal moment. Then, "It was nice. We went to the beach mostly. There's this cool spot to hike, the Brickyard trail. Oh . . ." She turned to her mother, "You'll never believe it: I tried lobster! Camilla gave me a bite of hers. It was kind of gross, but not completely disgusting."

Andi felt her jaw fall open like a cartoon character. "After all these years on the Cape, you finally tried lobster? Without me?" She did not add, "With *her*?"

Nate nudged her, trying unsuccessfully to hide his smile.

Andi breathed a sigh of relief as Molly swiftly switched gears from sullen teen to impassioned oversharer, regaling them with every minute detail of her trip, in true teenage-girl form. She was especially grateful to Nate, who listened in earnest and didn't look away once, even when Molly whipped out her phone and scrolled through an endless Instagram feed of selfies and sunsets. "I have more photos, but I have to edit them first."

"Well," Nate said when Molly finally finished. "Sounds like a great trip to me. Maybe your mom and I can take you out to dinner one night and you can show us the rest?"

Molly beamed at him, then turned to Andi. "Can I have my own glass of champagne tonight?" She was pushing it.

"Here, you may have a sip of mine."

When Molly walked away, Andi turned back to Nate in shock. "You got more out of her just now than I have since she returned."

Nate smiled. "Did I do okay?" He looked genuinely concerned that he had, and Andi found herself leaning in, not caring who saw now.

"Better than okay."

Dinner under the white tent overlooking the dunes was enchanting. Cora had wonderful taste and, as hoped, everything went off without a hitch. Even Tish's presence. Andi found her grandmother at the family table and took the empty seat next to her.

"Hello, dear. You look lovely. Still speaking to me after our family meeting?"

"I am." Andi set her champagne glass down between them. It had been just a few days since the family meeting, where Tish had said her piece and the others had had a chance to air theirs. Tish's decision still stung, but after hearing about her grandmother's past, Andi was able to look at it from a different perspective: the loss of Charley and Tish's own independence, the estrangement from her own family . . . these were things Andi was not familiar with, but just imagining them allowed a sense of empathy to root itself in her gut. They were two generations apart and things had certainly changed since Tish was a young woman. Andi liked to imagine she would've made different decisions had she been in her shoes, but then, who knew? People weren't just shaped by the family that surrounded them. They were shaped by the times they lived in.

"I know it hasn't been easy. But I want to thank you for respecting my choice." Tish regarded her, a slight tremor to her chin that Andi had not noticed before. "I have always held great affection for all three of you kids. Even if I was not very good at showing it."

The sentimentality caught Andi by surprise. "Thank you, Tish. It went both ways." And as she said it, despite everything, Andi knew it was true. She lifted her glass of champagne. "Can I get you one?"

"No, thank you. I've had my bourbon, which is about all the celebration I can have for one evening." She glanced around the patio. "There are younger people who can pick up the slack for me."

Andi followed her gaze. The bridesmaids were on their third or fourth prosecco toast to Sydney, who looked stunning in a creamy white sheath dress with her hair pulled up in a loose chignon. The groomsmen flanked them, raising their beers noisily, James and Sydney at the center. "They make a sweet couple," Andi allowed.

"As do you." Tish nodded across the way where Nate stood talking with Martin.

"You really don't miss a thing."

"You don't get to be my age without paying attention." She turned to Andi. "It's nice to see you happy. I never liked that man."

"My ex, George?"

"That one." Tish wrinkled her nose. "He wasn't sharp enough for you. You deserve more." Andi found herself looking at her grandmother more closely. She was dressed to the nines. But there was something different—her cheeks had less color. Her eyes looked a little less mischievous.

"Are you enjoying yourself? Feeling all right?" Andi asked.

"Goodness, you're the third person to ask that tonight." Tish swatted the air between them. "Affirmative to both, though if one more person asks . . ."

Andi smiled. There was still plenty of cantankerousness within and that was a good sign.

"Though I could use a hand with my purse."

"You're going already?" Andi rose with her. It was Tish's standard exit, swift and early. But still, something about her seemed a little bit off.

Tish nodded toward the caterers. "Dessert coming out is my cue. How do you think I keep this svelte figure?"

When they found him, Charley took his mother's arm. "I'm going to drive her back to the Inn," he told Andi. "But look for me when I return?"

Dessert was simple and summer perfection: tiny shortcakes with fresh strawberries and whipped cream. Andi was just finishing dessert with Sydney and some of the bridesmaids when Molly returned to the table with seconds. "I think I'll get married here too," Molly said, licking the edge of her fork.

Andi looked up in time to see Sydney glance between them.

"You absolutely should," Sydney said. "I think that would be wonderful." She winked at Andi over her niece's head.

Andi found herself exhaling. So there was a future at Riptide for all of them, after all. Time would tell and she'd need to be patient. But it was a hopeful sign.

The evening began to wind down; it would be a big day tomorrow for the wedding. Andi looked for Nate in the thinning crowd. Instead, she spied her father; she'd almost forgotten he'd wanted to talk. She followed him over to the two Adirondack chairs on the side lawn.

"Everything okay?" she asked. The night was balmy and the breeze ruffled the edge of her dress. It was nice to get a quiet moment away from the party, but she sensed something heavier.

"I wanted to check in with you," he said, lowering himself into one of the chairs. "How're you doing with all this wedding fuss?"

Andi glanced back at Molly, seated among the bridesmaids. And Nate, who was now talking with James. "Actually, Dad, I'm doing okay. How about you?"

"Now that I hear that, better." He patted the seat of the chair next to him and she sat. "Tomorrow looks like it will be a beautiful day for your sister. I'm glad. But there is something I discussed with Hugh earlier today, that I also want to say to you."

"Oh?" Andi hadn't known they'd talked privately. For once her twin had not told her everything. Perhaps that had had something to do with the improvement in Hugh's outlook.

"There have been a lot of changes these last few weeks. But one thing has not changed." Her father leaned forward and gripped the arms of her chair, pulling it in close to his, just as he used to when she was really little. She was surprised at his strength, that he could still do it all these years later. "From the first breath you took, you were my daughter. I have never felt otherwise."

Charley Darling's kind eyes were an exquisite hazel gray, the most unique thing about his otherwise ordinary face. They were almond-shaped and almost always crinkled at the corners with happiness. But now they were wide and sad, and even in the sunset the hazel was as gray as she'd ever seen it. She took his hand. "I know that, Dad."

His eyebrows raised with hope. "You do?"

"Yes. I've always felt it."

When her father began to cry, Andi felt the uneasy rumble of their roles reversing. She had never seen her father cry before, not once. But now he heaved quietly in his chair, overcome as the sorrow escaped his body. *Such a strange, sad gift,* she thought.

Charley Darling had always been a gentle soul. A family man who took care of them all. Whose love she never questioned and whose heart was always open. Her whole life Andi had come to him, often before her mother, to hold out her hurts. Her first broken heart in high school. The dented fender in the family car. A failing grade in college. Recently, the bone-deep sorrow of her divorce. He had borne it all.

But now it was her turn. As he cried, Andi slipped her arms around her father, just as she did for Molly. Even when the soft heaves of his back stilled, Andi did not let go.

Or the salt air? She was lighter than she'd ever felt. As the stars began to dot the darkening sky, Charley invited her for a slow waltz on the edge of the ballroom floor. Tish followed his gentle lead; just like his father, light on his feet.

Afterward, when her driver finally pulls up to Mooncusser Cottage back at Chatham Bars Inn, she is almost sorry. The night has been more than tolerable. It has been magnificent.

The clock tells her it is almost midnight and Tish cannot believe it. Where have the hours gone? But she is strangely untired. She changes into her silk pajamas, pours a glass of water, and takes it to the bay window. Outside, the moon is half full; waxing or waning, she wonders? As for herself, she is waning. Her days are winding down, she knows. She can feel it when she puts a hand on her chest, the hum of her heart uncertain. But Tish knows one thing for sure; her life has been full.

Charley, her second great love in this life, is going to be all right. He has done her proud, raising all three kids, even if she had not considered all three his to raise. She was wrong about that, she understands now. Charley did not go to Yale or to medical school. He did not escape the Darling family ties as she'd so desperately wanted, but rather embraced them. For, she realizes now, he had never seen them as ties. His life was robust, full of opportunity she had not considered. And in the end, happiness. Which, if she is honest, is all she ever wanted for him to begin with. Oh, she was mistaken and for that she is glad. His definition of that storybook ending was different than hers, but no less valuable. And Cora? Well, if she robbed him of a future as a doctor, she bestowed on him the gift of being a family man. Tish wonders about that. Family: it is something she held in the palm of her own hand, once upon a time. It is no small thing, she knows.

Outside, the water is calm, the air still. It is not enough to look. Suddenly, Tish needs to feel the night outside. She lifts her cashmere shawl from the back of the chair and unlocks the patio door. Charley had made her promise that she would not come and go from her cottage, without first requesting assistance from the front desk, the driver, any of her many choices at this lavish spot on the ocean. But Charley is a worrywart and the summer sky is not to be missed. Tonight is the first time she has broken that promise. *Just a little visit with the ocean air,* she tells herself.

Barefoot, she pads across the flagstones, leaving the door ajar. She giggles to herself. She is a kid again, a teenage girl, sneaking out of the house. Out into the night! Well, not too far into the night, just across the small patio is a lovely chaise lounge. Tish moves gingerly toward it and eases herself down onto its cushions. Wrapped in her shawl, she draws her knees up against her chest and reclines. It is heaven.

It is quite dark at this edge of the resort. Mooncusser Cottage is perched along a grassy bluff, its fenced white border gleaming in moonlight, the water dancing through the slats of the pickets. Below, on the sandy beach, Tish hears the water lap. Fishing boats rock gently on the bay. So too does her mind.

Morty brought her here. Not just to the Cape, but to life. A city girl who was afraid of the wild dunes and ocean expanse. A stubborn, first-generation Irish-American girl, first among her nursing class at Columbia to graduate before marrying into a white-collar Protestant family. Always striving for more. To straddle the two worlds she lived in, both past and present. To fit in among the Darlings. His little Riptide, Morty called her.

A breeze stirs off the water and Tish lifts her nose to it. The brackish scent fills her senses. Her heart thumps against her ribs. She is back in 1958, and young Charley is wiggling in her arms. Towheaded and suntanned, she can barely contain all his boyishness, but she does.

"Over here!" Morty calls to her. She turns. There he is, her husband. Her beloved. Standing at the end of the beach path that rolls down the dune behind their happy, shabby little cottage. Unfurling itself through salt grass and sand, right to the water's edge. Where Morty stands now, waving to her. "Come," he calls to her again. "Come, my love!"

Tish's eyelids flutter. A buoy's bell clangs somewhere out on the bay. A stray star streaks across the sky.

Her heart thumps once, twice. No more. "I'm coming."

ACKNOWLEDGMENTS

I always save my acknowledgments for the end, eager as I am to thank all of those who go into the pages of my books. As with most things, indeed, it takes a village.

Always to my incredible editor, Emily Bestler at Emily Bestler Books, thank you for staying the course through this, our seventh novel together! *The Darlings* would not be what it is without your guidance, support, and encouragement. I look forward to our next projects already underway. As you say, cheers to vows renewed!

To my agent, Susan Ginsburg, agent extraordinaire. From the moment we joined forces, I knew I was in the best hands. I cannot aptly express my gratitude for your generosity, your steadfastness, and your humor as we navigate this wild world of writing and publishing. And I can't think of a better partner to guide me!

Thanks must also be given to the entire team at EBB: to Lara, editor and the woman who can always answer any question (and patiently!), I am thrilled for your new title and thankful for the pleasure of working together all these years. To Sonja Singleton, production editor, I'm grateful for your guidance and keen eye from copy edits to final passes. To the design team, and specifically art director, Jimmy Iacobelli, thank you for letting me throw my two cents (and more) into the cover design of each title. I'm ever grateful for Holly Rice, publicity, and Zakiya Jamal, marketer, and the whole publicity and marketing team. To Libby McGuire, Publisher, and Dana Trocker, Associate Publisher, and Paige Lytle, Managing Editor, thank you!

In this digital day, there is still nothing like a book in hand. And a cozy bookstore corner where you can find your next one! I remain in awe of the many fairy godmothers who inhabit, lead, curate, connect, and wave their wands in the Indie bookstores we authors are so fortunate to know. They are the ones who connect readers to titles and authors to readers, and their role in the publishing industry cannot be sung loudly enough. There are too many to name, but to some of my beloved who have supported me along the way: Savoy Bookshop & Café, Bethany Beach Books, Bank Square Books, RJ Julia, Fairfield University Bookstore, Byrd's Books . . . thank you, thank you, thank you. In that vein, thank you, too, to all the Bookstagrammers, reviewers, bloggers, and hosts of book events: you are the colorful ribbons that bind us all together! And to my author friends, who cheer on, commiserate, and laugh with me; I have found such generosity in your friendships!

Finally, to my friends and family, I maintain deep gratitude for all the years and all the love. For reading my books, supporting my work, and understanding when I go underground to draft. For showing up at events and for spreading the good word. You know who you are. To my parents, Marlene and Barry Roberts, who raised a family of readers and encouraged me to do the same with the next generation. To John, for being my loyal and loving partner, as quick with the wit as you are with the humor. Life is so much richer with you in it. Finally, to Grace and Finley, to whom this book is dedicated. From this past year of college searches, drivers licenses, and high school field hockey games, you keep me ever mindful of sweet time and the blessings of family. My cup runneth over.